City of the
Plague God

City of the Plague God

SARWAT CHADDA

RICK RIORDAN PRESENTS

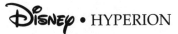

Los Angeles New York

First Edition, January 2021
1   3   5   7   9   10   8   6   4   2
FAC-021131-20332
Printed in the United States of America

This book is set in Palatino LT Std, Adorn Roman,
Stone Informal ITC Pro, Palatino LT Std/Fontspring
Designed by Jamie Alloy

Library of Congress Cataloging-in-Publication Data
Names: Chadda, Sarwat, author.
Title: City of the plague god / Sarwat Chadda.
Description: First edition. • Los Angeles ; New York : Disney-Hyperion,
2021. • Audience: Ages 8–12. • Summary: "Thirteen-year-old Sikander
Aziz has to team up with the hero Gilgamesh in order to stop Nergal, the
ancient god of plagues, from wiping out the population of Manhattan in this
adventure based on Mesopotamian mythology"—Provided by publisher.
Identifiers: LCCN 2020002173 • ISBN 9781368051507
(hardcover) • ISBN 9781368066631 (ebook)
Subjects: CYAC: Heroes—Fiction. • Mythology, Assyro-Babylonian—Fiction.
• Iraqi Americans—Fiction. • Diseases—Fiction. • New York (N.Y.)—Fiction.
Classification: LCC PZ7.C343 Ck 2021 • DDC [Fic]—dc23
LC record available at https://lccn.loc.gov/2020002173
Reinforced binding

Follow @ReadRiordan

Visit www.DisneyBooks.com

To my wife and daughters

YOU WANT MYTHOLOGY?
LET'S GET OLD-SCHOOL!

It doesn't get any more "old-school" than Mesopotamia.

Without a doubt, the stories of Sumer, Babylon, and the rest of the Fertile Crescent are my favorite myths that I've never written about. Fortunately, I don't have to. Sarwat Chadda knows the stories better than I do, and he is about to take you on a thrill ride you will never forget!

If you've ever wondered how mythology can be important and relevant, even thousands of years after it was written, you only have to look at current events. This book was entitled *City of the Plague God* long before the recent outbreak of COVID-19. When he wrote it, Sarwat Chadda had no idea we would soon be facing a new sort of plague that would affect the lives of everyone on earth. He was just telling a fantasy story about Nergal, the plague god from ancient Mesopotamia, and imagining what would happen if Nergal were still around today. Now, because of the coronavirus, his story feels *very* real and close to home.

At Rick Riordan Presents, we talked a lot about *City of the Plague God* after the virus became a global challenge. The book had been written and ready to go for months. Still, we didn't want anyone to think we were trivializing or capitalizing on a worldwide crisis by releasing this type of story. In the end, we decided that this book and Mesopotamian myths have a lot to teach us about dealing with major upheavals—about fear of the unknown, courage in the face of danger, and the importance of family and community working together to solve problems.

Mesopotamians were just as worried about and affected by disease outbreaks as we are today. The fact that they had a *god* of plagues tells us how seriously they took the issue. *City of the Plague God* is a timely story that gives us a chance to reflect on how much we have in common with our ancient ancestors. Like Gilgamesh, like Sikandar Aziz, the hero of this book, we are called on to be heroes, each of us in our own way, and stand up to a plague that threatens our community. Together, we can succeed!

So . . . back to Mesopotamian mythology and what makes it awesome. Just the term *ziggurat,* for one thing— is there any cooler word? When I was a kid, I loved learning about those step pyramids. I marveled at the mysteries of cuneiform writing. I stared at pictures of winged lions, freaky dragons, and dudes with righteous curly beards and massive hats and wondered why I couldn't be awesome like the Mesopotamians.

Fast-forward a few decades, to when I became a teacher: Every year, my students and I would embark on a unit about Mesopotamia. It was always one of their favorite subjects. We would roll out the clay and practice writing in cuneiform. We'd make our own signature seals so we could sign clay tablets like pros. We would hold trials based on the Code of Hammurabi, meting out harsh punishments like cutting off hands (with red markers. Ah, I'm bleeding!), drowning in the Euphrates (with water guns), or stoning (with wadded-up paper balls). The kids would also reenact *The Epic of Gilgamesh*, complete with Nerf weapons and fake beards. The Mesopotamians would have been proud . . . or possibly horrified. Anyway, we had fun.

As for the gods of Mesopotamia—wow! Those were some crazy deities. Ishtar, goddess of love and war. Nergal, the god of plague and war. Ninurta, the god of hunting and war. (Notice how all those gods are of something *and* war? They had a lot of conflicts back then.) Their stories offer a glimpse into one of the oldest known civilizations, which had a huge influence on Egypt, Greece, Rome, and the whole world.

How excited was I when Sarwat Chadda offered to write a book bringing all this wild, wonderful mythology into the modern world for the Rick Riordan Presents imprint? Yeah, I was pretty excited. I've been a fan of Sarwat's books for years—Ash Mistry, Shadow Magic—and I knew he was the perfect guy for the job.

City of the Plague God does not disappoint. Our hero, Sikander Aziz, is an American Muslim kid born and raised in New York City. His parents are refugees from Iraq. His colleague, Daoud, is an aspiring actor who can only seem to get TV roles like "terrorist henchman." His older brother, Mo, died two years ago, and Sikander (Sik) is still processing his grief and resentment. Sik is doing his best to help keep his family's deli afloat when it is attacked one night by two rat-faced fellows who claim to be ancient demons. Things just get weirder from there.

Soon, a strange disease grips New York City. (Spoiler alert: Plague gods gonna plague.) Sikander's parents fall ill along with many others. In order to stop the sickness and save Manhattan, Sikander has to plunge into a world of ancient gods, demigods, and monsters, and find out the truth about his own secret powers. There will be tears and snarky jokes. There will be a badass ninja girl, a chariot pulled by big cats, and a demon with really bad breath. I can also guarantee you will not want the adventure to end. I know I didn't!

Welcome to the world of Mesopotamian myth as interpreted by the brilliantly creative, wonderfully offbeat mind of Sarwat Chadda. You may never want to leave!

Rick Riordan

Mankind can number his days,
Whatever he may achieve, it is only wind.
Do you fear death on this occasion?
Where is the strength of your heroic nature?

—*The Epic of Gilgamesh*, translated by Stephanie Dalley

ONE

———◆———

"GIVE ME A HAND WITH THIS SHUTTER, DAOUD?" I
asked, and not for the first time that night.

Daoud raised his finger as he continued his phone conversation. "You're kidding. From Hollywood? What time?"
He checked his watch. "Cool. I'll be there."

"At last." I sighed as he put the phone away. It was creeping toward midnight, and we should have locked up the deli
an hour ago. I tugged at the unyielding roll-down security
shutter.

Daoud flexed his biceps. "You need some real muscle
behind this." He grabbed the other handle.

"On three . . ." I tightened my grip. "One . . ."

"Three!"

The slatted steel grille rattled down thunderously and
slammed on the sidewalk. Daoud snapped on the padlock.
"Yallah, cuz. I've got places to be."

𒀯𒌋𒈦𒌋𒆠 𒊩𒁹 𒂗𒌋𒁲𒅎 𒐏𒊑𒂠𒉺 𒂍𒌋𒆠 𒈾𒐏

Cuz? Daoud acted like he was one of the family, but he was just a guy my brother had brought home when they'd met in fifth grade, a decade ago. I'd never understood why Mo had liked him so much. Maybe it was because there weren't many other Iraqi kids at school. Since then, Daoud had hardly been out of my life, but he was still no "cuz."

"Another party?" I asked.

"Not all of us want to spend our lives grilling kebabs."

"Nothing haram about it. People gotta eat," I replied. "So, who's in town? Spielberg? The head honcho from Disney?"

He grinned. "A big-shot casting agent out of LA. She'll be attending the *Hamilton* after-party. That's where I've got to be in exactly one hour."

We set to pulling the second shutter down. "Wouldn't it be easier if you actually learned acting?" I asked. "And, I don't know, appeared in something?"

Daoud scowled. "In case you've forgotten, I was in *Homeland*. Twice."

"Yeah, and spent it with your face covered by a keffiyeh. What was the part again? Terrorist Henchman?"

"*Head* Terrorist Henchman." One big pull and the grille rattled down into place.

I put on the padlock. "So when are you gonna play a hero?"

Daoud laughed. "Guys like us don't get to be heroes. You know that."

"Why? 'Cause you're an Arab, or 'cause you're a Muslim?"

𒀭𒈹𒄿𒈾𒃶𒂊𒁲𒍑𒌉𒆠𒈨𒊩𒄿𒌋𒐊

"Take your pick, cuz. Take your pick."

Why did Daoud still bother? I couldn't understand it. How could he be happy with always being the bad guy?

It made more sense to keep both of your feet on the hard concrete. In the real world.

We reentered the deli from the rear, through the cramped kitchen and into the dining area. Mo's didn't look like much. The tables didn't match and some of the chairs wobbled, but the place had *sizzle*. And I'm not just talking about the onions in the pan or the shawarma turning on the skewer, but the crowd. We were on the corner of Fifteenth and Siegel, so we got constant foot traffic. We specialized in Arab and Mediterranean, basically the best food in the world.

We opened at six a.m. to fuel the office workers with fresh pita and Turkish coffee thick enough to stand a spoon in. Mid-morning brought the locals, who came for a chat and to break out the backgammon, or to just sit by the windows with a pot of mint tea and watch the rest of the world rush by.

I took the late shift. Yeah, I know thirteen-year-olds aren't supposed to work, but Mama and Baba needed the extra hands. Our block had plenty of pop-up music clubs and art galleries, and there was no better way to kick-start an evening than with a falafel sandwich topped with a spoonful of our famous Baghdad chili sauce. On good nights, our deli's sizzle would become a *blaze*, and it felt like the whole city was in there with us.

The trouble with sharing your home with a thousand people was it needed a serious wipe-down at the end of every day, and that was left to me and Daoud. But mostly me.

I triple-locked the front door from the inside and left the keys on the countertop while Daoud continued to explain his career plan, for the thousandth time.

"It's not about talent—just look at the people who get all the parts—it's about getting spotted. And you get spotted at parties. The right parties."

"If you say so."

"Look at this face, Sik. Just look at it."

I dipped the mop into the bucket for a soak. "I know what you look like, Daoud."

"Look. Really look."

Okay, I need to fess up. Daoud was stupidly handsome, the emphasis on both words. Chiseled jaw, high cheekbones, a mop of wavy black hair, and a deep brow that only magnified his light brown eyes. His physique was gym-sculpted, his skin as flawless as only a three-hour daily cleansing routine could manage. He was more vain than a Real Housewife of Beverly Hills and blew most of his salary on top-of-the-line bodywash and Versace aftershave. Me? I *liked* smelling of sautéed onions.

Daoud pointed to his chin. "I've only got another five years and then it's over, Sik. I'll be too old."

"Too old at twenty-five?"

He sighed. "Twenty-one if you're a girl."

"Is that why you wanted Botox gift certificates for Eid?"

He double-checked himself in the window reflection. "Beauty's got to be preserved."

I peered at him. "Is that a zit?"

"What?" he exclaimed, horrified. "Where?"

"Middle of your forehead. You can't miss it."

He wailed and dashed off to the bathroom to inspect every single one of his pores.

Finally, some peace. I dragged the bucket to the center of the room and got to work, sliding the mop over the floor in long, easy strokes.

Mopping used to be Mo's job. I'd be in bed, and the cleaning fluid's citrus smell would rise through the apartment and I'd fall asleep to the bittersweet scent of lemons.

We'd changed the brand once, but customers had complained that Mo's no longer smelled as friendly, so we'd gone back to the lemon stuff. You couldn't escape Mo—this was his deli.

Photos of him plastered the wall, the biggest being of his high school graduation, right under the framed takbir, and alongside the Iraqi flag. He'd been born there, and though my parents had immigrated to the US when he was little, Iraq had always remained home for him. Which is why he went straight back there during his first college break. And the next and the next.

I paused to look at the collage he'd made of his trips to places that were already ancient when Rome was just a village. There he was, grinning in front of the Ziggurat of Ur, sitting on a camel at the ruins of Nineveh, and dusty from his motorcycle trip to the brick mounds at Lagash, remnants of when the country had been known by its ancient name: Mesopotamia.

The cradle of civilization. Yet as I looked at the photos of Mo helping out at the refugee camps, rebuilding bombed-out villages, and replanting farms, I couldn't help but think of how that birthplace had suffered over the centuries. Why couldn't it have been left in peace?

I was in some of the pictures on the wall. Birthday shots, us dressed up for Halloween. Typical sibling stuff.

The space wasn't big—twenty-four feet by ten—but it displayed Mo's life, from beginning to its end.

But it was the flowers that really made it Mo's. Being born near barren desert had made him appreciate plants all the more, which was why he'd chosen to major in botany. He'd started the local community garden down the block and preserved his favorites in frames, decorating the deli's white-washed walls with the brightest colors nature could provide. Roses ranging from the deepest crimson to the snowiest white ran above the windows. Lush purple orchids hung beside the explosive pink, gold, and orange petals of countless wildflowers.

A car swept by, and its headlights stroked the far wall, stretching out the shadows, bringing them to life.

The lemon scent, the photos, the flowers, the quietness of the night, and the swaying shadows combined to bring him back. It was like my brother was sitting at that table.

"Hey, Mo," I said.

Asalaamu alaikum, Yakhi. You should be in bed. School tomorrow.

"And leave lock-up to Daoud? No way." I sank the mop back into the bucket and gave it a twist before starting under the windows.

Actually, shouldn't you be crashing at Aaron's? Wasn't Thursday always game night with him and the other guys?

"You know I don't have time for that anymore, Mo. The deli needs—"

There's life outside the deli, Sik.

"The deli suits me fine," I snapped. I shoved the mop back into the bucket for a soak. "I wouldn't have to do this if you were around to help out. When was the last time you mopped?"

You tell me.

"Two years, three months, and fourteen days." As if I

didn't know. "So when are you coming back?"

Come on, Sik. . . .

"This place you're staying, it must be some sort of paradise. Better than home?"

You've got Daoud.

"He was always your friend, not mine," I said. "He's moved into your room. Can you believe that?"

That's better than leaving it empty.

"He takes your clothes. Remember that leather jacket? He wears it everywhere."

Why are you doing this, Sik?

The memory flashed across my mind. The worst day of my life. Sitting near the landline with my parents as they learned what had happened. I knew it had to be bad news. Three a.m. phone calls are always bad news. Mo had been riding his motorcycle in the dark, a truck had swerved into his lane and . . . That night I had watched Mama and Baba grow old in an instant as their futures crumbled to dust.

"Someone's got to look after our folks," I replied.

And the garden? You looking after that?

I scowled. "I'll get around to it, inshallah. Maybe this weekend."

You haven't weeded it in months.

"Figures you would know *that*."

You know everything I know.

"That's not true. I don't know why you went and never came back."

I had to. It was the right thing to do.

"No, it wasn't. It was wrong."

Iraq was my home. Saving your home is never wrong.

I didn't want to argue with him—that wouldn't get me anywhere. "They miss you so much, Mo. I see it in Mama's eyes. Baba's, too, but he's better at hiding it."

Don't forget me, Yakhi.

"Never." I looked up suddenly, hoping to catch a glimpse of him at our table, even just for a slice of a second, but of course he wasn't there.

Why did I do it? Try to bring him back, night after night? Why couldn't I just forget about my brother and get on with my life?

The school counselor had called it a "coping mechanism," my way of dealing with the tragedy. She'd assured me I'd adjust to him being gone, but two years later Mo still felt as real as ever. And even though he was just a mismatched collection of memories, he still disagreed with me—over everything. Strange, huh? I guess you just can't control some people, even when they're only figments of your imagination.

I entered the kitchen to rinse out the pots, starting with the leftover Lebanon and Cairo sauces. I sniffed the pot of Baghdad sauce from a wary distance, and despite it being almost empty, that alone was enough to make my eyes water. The deadly chilies my dad put in it were part of the reason our deli was so popular. Everyone, at some point, tried the Baghdad—"pure shock and awe to your taste buds," Baba always said. Only the hardiest came back for more.

"For you, Yakhi," I said as I emptied the thick red sauce into the sink. Mo had loved the Baghdad. He used to pour it over his cornflakes.

I heard a cat shriek in the back alley, followed by the crash and rattle of a trash can falling over.

The dumpster lid banged. What was going on? I opened the rear door a crack, but I couldn't see anything in the dark.

Then I heard voices.

Someone grunted with satisfaction. "Look at that, Sidana, me old mate. Fancy a bite?"

There was a fear-filled squeak.

Another someone smacked their lips. "What a sweet, delicious rat! All juicy and oh so fat!"

Were they hunting a *rat*?

There were two people, at least. I couldn't make them out. So I listened.

The squeaking got more desperate.

"Manhattan vermin—ain't nothing tastier."

The rat gave one final squeal and then there was a snap, followed by a sickening crunch. And a loud, satisfied burp.

Okaaay, things were getting weird.

The reply was a snicker. "Allow your mem'ry to linger, dwell on the taste of a finger. To suck on marrow, crunch on bone . . . what food delights we both have known!"

Really weird. And in rhyming couplets no less.

I put down my mop and, after a second's hesitation, unhooked our big cast-iron wok from the wall. Then I slipped outside to take a look.

That, as it happens, turned out to be a *huuuge* mistake.

TWO

THE ALLEY BEHIND OUR DELI *STANK*. WORSE THAN usual, I mean. A putrid, hot stench lay as thick as syrup. Funny that I hadn't noticed it a few minutes ago, when I'd entered through the back door. Had a sewer pipe burst or something?

Flies swarmed over the food that had spilled out of two torn-open garbage bags. Rotten vegetables carpeted the bare concrete and maggot-infested meat smeared the brick walls. I heard movement from within the dumpster.

I crept closer and almost slipped on a half-eaten rat. Yeah, that was exactly as disgusting as it sounds.

A feral-looking tabby cat watched me from the fire escape. It had scars across its body and one completely white eye, which, I swear, winked at me. Then it sprang up and hissed as a guy stuck his head up from inside the dumpster, waving a wedge of old pizza. "Maggot topping, all slimy and nice! I shall devour it in a trice!"

I ducked behind a trash can as the tabby leaped away into the darkness.

I say *guy*, but I mean it in the loosest sense of the word. He had a head and two arms, but aside from that . . .

His dented top hat did nothing to hide the deformed length of his skull, or his long, hairy ears. A pair of cracked pince-nez balanced on the end of his twitching nose. Wiry black whiskers sprouted from either side of a mouth crowded with yellow teeth that jutted out at all angles. He heaved the slice into his mouth and chewed loudly, his beady red eyes rolling in delight.

His companion rose beside him. He wore a battered bowler hat, pulled down low over his huge toadlike eyes, and he licked his wide lips with a tongue as thick as my arm. His belly rumbled loudly as he chewed on a length of rotten sausage. "Leave room, chum. There are plenty of tasty morsels to be had."

More flies gathered. Ugly, shiny bluebottles darted by me, as if trying to determine whether I was a tasty morsel, too.

These dudes were seriously into their roles. Were they cosplayers gone bad? Or burglars in seriously weird disguises? I should have gotten Daoud or woken Baba before coming out here. I couldn't run for help now. Messrs. Strange and Unusual would see me the moment I raised my head from behind the trash can. So I crouched lower and tightened my fingers around the wok handle. It wasn't exactly Thor's hammer, but it was big and heavy and would leave a big dent in their faces if need be.

The rat-faced rhymer picked at his teeth with a dirty claw as he turned his attention to the darkened windows of our upstairs apartment. "The family sleeps up there. Shall we two give them a scare?"

That didn't sound friendly.

Toady licked his lips with a disgustingly long and slimy tongue. "We only need the boy."

"Oh, him we shall take with ease. The rest, handle as we please." Ratty straightened his top hat and reached for the lip of the dumpster.

Not friendly at all.

Did *the boy* mean me?

I was afraid, verging on terrified. I wanted to run and hide. I wanted to be anywhere but here, but they were threatening Mo's and I wasn't going to let that happen, not now, not ever. So even though the wok trembled in my sweaty grip, even though I could hardly breathe for the fear gripping my chest, I charged.

I swung the wok—missing them both—but they ducked, and that was good enough. I grabbed the lid of the dumpster and slammed it down onto their hatted heads. I flipped the latch just as one of them tried to shoulder the lid back open.

I smacked the wok on the side of the metal container. "You freaks stay right in there!"

The dumpster rocked as the pair crashed against it. I could hear their muffled, furious shouts from inside.

"Daoud!" I yelled. "Call the cops!"

Where was he?

"Daoud!"

The dumpster hopped, and bumps appeared in its steel lid. But that didn't matter—as long as the latch was secured, the lid was going to stay exactly where it was.

Then there was a flapping, and a wet whistling. A stomach-churning stench hissed through the narrow gap between the dumpster's lid and rim. I held my breath to avoid inhaling it.

A pair of beady crimson eyes peered out through the gap. "Sikander Aziz? Well, well. For this I'll see you in hell," he said with a snarl.

I stepped back. "You know who I am?"

Ratty snickered. "Know you? That would be a yes. You're famous, we must confess."

A fist slammed against the inside of the dumpster wall. "You, mate, are gonna suffer when Sidana and me get outta here," said Toady. "I promise you that."

"Sidana?" I asked Ratty. "What sort of name is that?"

"It's not a name—it's a curse," said Toady. "As is mine: Idiptu. Remember them well."

𒐕𒉌𒆠𒂗 𒐕𒁹 𒂊𒌅 𒅆𒍢𒌅 𒈨𒂊𒊏 𒆠𒅀𒂊 𒈨𒐕𒁹

"Sidana and Idiptu, eh?" I asked. "Think I'll just stick with Ratty and Toady."

Ratty—sorry, Sidana—hissed angrily. Clearly they were not fond of nicknames. "This will not bode well for you. We shall wreak revenge, we two."

"Yeah? It's boding okay so far." Where was Daoud? Was he still checking his pores?

"You have courage," admitted Idiptu.

"I have a wok." I banged it hard on the lid, and it rang loud and proud.

"Who does this boy think he is, Gilgamesh reborn?" Sidana taunted. "We shall correct that, and leave him tattered and torn!"

Nice. It's not every day you get compared to the world's first and, IMHO, greatest hero. Just think King Arthur meets Heracles with a dash of Thor and multiply that by fifty thousand.

Toady pressed his face right up to the crack. "Do you know who we are, mate? *What* we are?"

"I find myself not caring a whole lot." I glanced at the trash can. Could I use it to weigh down the lid of the dumpster so I could get inside to call 911?

"We are the Great Misfortunes of Mankind, the Asakku," said Idiptu. "Or, in common parlance—"

"Demons," I replied. I was up on my mythology. "Uh-huh,

yeah. More like trick-or-treaters with no sense of time."

Idiptu's eyes glowed a sickly yellow. "We've come from Kurnugi."

"Kurnugi?" I rolled the trash can toward them. "Is that near Michigan?" I knew he meant the netherworld, but I was enjoying having the upper hand.

Speaking of hands, mine were busying swatting the flies that swarmed all over. And not only flies—I slapped a mosquito on my neck. My palm came away smeared with blood.

"Bugs are quite nasty, my dear." Sidana tutted. "They carry disease, I fear."

"Is bad rhyme a thing in Kurnugi? Listen to this." I started tapping a rap rhythm on the dumpster. "Sik's my name, and I play a mean game/What makes you think you can bring your stink/To threaten my fam and our fine deli meat?/Get out now before I call the heat."

Idiptu grunted. "Not bad."

Why wasn't Daoud out here already? Hadn't he heard my banging?

No choice but to keep on vamping. "So, demons, eh? Nice angle. But I don't think the cops are going to go for it. This is the real world, and here demons don't exist. Neither does the Tooth Fairy. I've got a bad feeling about Santa, too."

Sidana snarled as if I'd insulted his parentage. "No demons exist, you cry? Then pray tell me, what am I?"

"In need of some serious dental work?"

Despite the sass coming out of my mouth, my legs were shaking. Whatever these guys were, they were not the type you wanted to meet in a dark alley.

The swarm of flies around me grew thicker, buzzing in my ears, biting my skin. I swung the wok, splatting a few, but more and more gathered. "Bug off!"

"All yours, Idiptu, my love," said Sidana. "Can't you give the latch a shove?"

Idiptu unrolled his slimy tongue through the narrow gap. Three feet long, it slid down the side of the dumpster and began darting from side to side. It found the latch and flicked it open.

And then the falafel really hit the fan.

The lid crashed open. Idiptu sprang out and landed on the ground in front of me with a heavy thump. He was squat and barrel-chested, with thick bowed legs that strained the seams of his checked pants. Sidana, wearing a tattered old tuxedo jacket, scrambled out and limped over to Idiptu. He polished his pince-nez and fixed them to the end of his hairy snout. "Master Sikander, how do you do?" He grinned, giving me a good view of his crooked yellow fangs. "We have some cruelties prepared for you."

This was bad, really bad. And I don't just mean the verse. I backed away, waving the wok in front of me. "Don't come any closer."

"Or what? You'll stir-fry us?" Idiptu gestured at a shifting black cloud at the far end of the alley. "It's not us you need to worry about, mate. . . ."

An immense figure stood within the whining swarm. Over ten feet tall, even hunched over, he shuffled through the mass of insects. Instead of dispersing, they coalesced *into* him, clustering in the folds of his ragged cloak, disappearing into his mouth, and flying around his head like a screaming halo.

Idiptu doffed his bowler hat. "It's the boss."

THREE

———✦———

"YA ALLAH . . ." I SHOOK MY HEAD, HOPING FOR A REALITY reboot, but the giant fly guy in the cloak just continued to . . . exist.

The whining of the millions of insects intensified, rattling the windows overlooking the alley. Any louder and I thought my ears would start bleeding.

I still had my wok. I had to do something.

So I ran.

Straight through the kitchen door, slamming it behind me.

"Who's . . . What's out there?" asked Daoud, his face ashen.

"*Now* you show up?" I shoved the dead bolts into place. "Grab the biggest knife you can find." I backed away as Idiptu charged the door, shaking the hinges. "We've got to stop them—"

"What?! No, we've got to call the police!"

𒀭𒈹𒌋𒁶 𒋃𒁲 𒂗𒋫𒉺𒈨𒅕 𒁲𒋫𒀀 𒋗

"A little late for that now!" I snapped. "Arm yourself—hurry!"

"Just let them take whatever they want!" Daoud cried. "We can hide in our rooms upstairs." He tried to pull me through the swinging door to the seating area.

"Leave the deli to them? No way!" I snapped, wrenching myself out of his grasp. "I'm not abandoning Mo's. This is your chance to be a hero, Daoud. A *real* one."

He stared at me as if I were insane. "I can't be a hero, especially not a real one!"

"What's the point of all those muscles if you aren't going to use them to smash bad guys?" I needed to get him on board before the back door was destroyed. So I spoke in a language he understood: "Think of this as a movie, Daoud. The good guys always win, right?"

"A movie?" Daoud kept retreating. "That makes me the token sidekick! We always die in act two, right after the jock!"

The back door jumped in its frame under another charge from the hulking Idiptu. It wouldn't hold for long. We needed to block it with something stronger.

Daoud glared at me. "This isn't about the deli."

"You in or not?"

The metal door bulged under the latest assault.

"Come on, Sik!" Daoud fled into the seating area, and I heard him leave to go toward the upstairs apartment, slamming the security door behind him. That door was three inches of solid oak with an auto lock; you'd need a chain saw to get through it. Then again, I'd thought the metal door was impenetrable. . . .

I grabbed the landline in the kitchen and punched in three numbers.

Ring . . . ring . . . ring . . .

"Yallah, pick up!" I yelled as Idiptu continued his battering.

"Which service, please?" the dispatcher asked.

"Police," I replied. "Right now. Sooner."

"Please hold while I transfer you. . . ."

"Tut-tut, that won't do at all." Sidana peered through a newly created space between the warped metal and the door-frame. "I think it best to end that call."

The phone receiver *squirmed* in my hand. Something tickled my lips. Something slimy.

Fat white worms wriggled out of the mouthpiece. Maggots. I dropped the phone and spat furiously. How was this even happening?

"I do hope you didn't swallow any," said Sidana. "They might—"

"Just shut up!" Who were these guys? *What* were they? I didn't want to admit it, but the word *demon* was beginning to sound . . . right.

My heart raced as a hundred panicky thoughts battled

for the top spot. The security gates were down in front, so I couldn't run. *Scream for help? Beg them to stop? Let them take whatever it is they want and hope they'll leave? Hide under the counter? Fight them for all you're worth?*

I had options, but they were all just different levels of bad.

The best choice was to keep them out, but the door wasn't going to last much longer.

I wedged my spine against the wall, pressed both feet against the big refrigerator, and pushed. Seven feet by four and made of stainless steel, it would be the perfect blockade. "Come on," I snarled. My legs trembled as I forced out every ounce of power I had. The refrigerator tilted slightly.

The middle hinge came off the back door. Idiptu stuck his head through the bigger opening and his tongue rolled out, searching for the dead bolts.

"Move!" I roared as I gave the refrigerator one final, desperate push. The thing had sat in the same place ever since we'd bought it, and it wasn't ready to budge even an inch, but . . . but it groaned as it leaned sideways across the back door and then fell, crashing with thunderous impact, rattling all the pots and pans. The refrigerator door swung open and out poured tubs of hummus and tzatziki sauce. Lemons and oranges rolled away in all directions.

There, that would hold them. I snatched up my wok as I ran into the seating area and scrambled over to the door that led to the apartment. "Daoud? Are you there?"

𒀭𒈾𒂊 𒀸𒉌𒌷𒐊 𒋛𒈨𒊑 𒂍𒐊 𒈝

"I've got the police on my cell!"

"When are they coming?"

"Er . . . I'm third in line."

Great, just great. With any luck they'd make it over by lunchtime.

I heard scraping from the kitchen. Like the sound a heavy metal object, say a refrigerator, might make if it were slowly being pushed across ceramic tile.

"Sik? What's going on down there?" It was Baba. He shook the handle of the security door. "Where are the keys?"

I glanced over to them, lying on the countertop. "Er . . . here?"

"Mina, get the spare set!" Baba yelled, not giving up on the handle. "Get out of there, Sik!"

I know it was crazy to stay. The deli wasn't much, but it was all we had.

"Sik . . . habibi. Please, please run."

I wiped the sweat off my hands and took a fresh grip on the wok.

The kitchen had fallen eerily quiet.

Had they given up? *Please, ya Allah, please,* I prayed.

A sudden blue flash illuminated the seating area for a second as the fly zapper on the ceiling took out a bug. The electric hum lingered, then it flashed again as another fly went straight into it.

The swinging door between the deli and the kitchen creaked as if something were gently, ever so gently, pressing against it, testing it.

Cockroaches poured from under the door, spreading over the floor like an oil spill.

Then the door was blown apart and a shock wave hurled me over, forcing all the air out of my lungs. The wok spun out of my hands and clanged against the far wall.

A screaming tornado of insects swirled around the room, coating the walls in glistening black, purple, and green. They curtained the windows and crawled over me, trying to enter my mouth and ears even as they stung me.

"Where is it, boy? Where is it?" roared the giant "boss" creature, his hulking, fly-infested body bent over so his head wouldn't scrape the ceiling. He snatched up an empty vase on one of the tables, sniffed at it, and then threw it on the floor. He opened cabinets and flung their contents left and right like a dog digging for a bone. Next he ripped down one of Mo's pressed flowers and broke the frame into splinters. He plucked out the plant and held it between his finger and thumb before grinding it into dust. Then he yanked down another, and another, his fury rising with each one. "It has to be here!"

No, no, no! In that awful moment, I didn't care that he was twice my height and had ten times my strength—I had to save those pictures. The wok had rolled to the opposite side of the room, too far for me to reach. With teeth clamped and fists tight, I hurled myself at his back.

The giant spun around—lightning fast—and grabbed me in midair. His fingers locked around my neck like an iron collar. He drew me nearer. "Tell me where it is, boy."

Leathery patches of skin hung off his face, among patches of raw red flesh seeping with pus and crawling with flies. Gaping holes in his cheeks exposed the sinews of his jaw, and his nose was a pair of rotten holes. But nothing matched the darkness of his eyes—pure black and overflowing with hate. I shivered, unable to escape their drowning, endless depths. He squeezed my throat. "Where is it?" he hissed, his stench poisoning what little oxygen I had left.

What is he talking about? I kicked out feebly, my strength all but gone, like the air in my lungs. Blackness crawled in from the edges of my vision.

"Let him go," said a voice from behind me.

Through the haze of semiconsciousness, I was expecting a cop, but instead I got . . .

A ninja?

Sure, why not? Things were crazy enough, so why not a ninja? She stood in the doorway, dressed in midnight black with her face hidden by a ski mask, carrying a gleaming scimitar.

The sword's single edge shimmered with exceeding sharpness, but I wished she'd brought a bazooka. She raised her blade. "I said, let him go."

The giant dropped me with a hard thud. He gestured at his two minions. "Deal with her."

Idiptu was crouched on a dining table, grinning. "My pleasure, Boss." His thick legs catapulted him at the girl.

The ninja threw her whole body into a blinding spin, swinging her right foot up in a high arc. Her boot heel smashed Idiptu in the side of the jaw like a wrecking ball. Teeth burst from his mouth as he sailed into our shelf of syrup jars. His bowler hat spun over the countertop.

The ninja paused, her foot poised in the air. Then she lowered it back to the floor as lightly as a ballet dancer. She turned to Sidana and, I swear, arched her eyebrow. "You next?"

Maybe she didn't need a bazooka after all.

Sidana scurried over to his unconscious, toothless friend. "T'would be unwise after that performance," he said ingratiatingly to the ninja. "Not to mention your mother's importance."

Mother? Wait . . . they know each other?

The ninja gripped her sword in both hands and turned back to the boss. Things were about to go epic.

The giant scowled. "Do you really think you have a

chance against me? Even with Kasusu?"

The ninja pointed her scimitar at him. "Let's find out, Uncle."

Uncle? *Uncle?!*

"Just hang on, habibi!" Baba began smashing at the security door lock from the other side with what sounded like a fire extinguisher.

"No!" I cried. "It's not safe!"

The giant exploded into a roaring hurricane of insects and rammed the front windows. The glass shattered, and the security gates were torn clean out of their frames. The steel clattered on the sidewalk as the whirlwind rose into the night sky.

"I'm coming!" yelled Baba.

Sidana heaved Idiptu out the now-demolished windows, leaving only my sword-wielding savior. She flicked the blade into a round leather sheath and headed for the back door.

"Wait . . ." I said.

She paused.

"You have to tell me—" Sirens wailed nearby. I turned my head to see blue-and-red police lights illuminating the street and a crowd gathering outside. "What's going on? He . . . He was looking for something. . . ."

But when I turned back to hear her answer, no one was there.

The apartment door crashed open, and Baba barged in, wild-eyed and waving the fire extinguisher, with Mama beside him. Cowering behind them was Daoud.

"They're gone," I said, collapsing to my knees. Without adrenaline to keep me going, all my terror turned to pure exhaustion.

Baba froze, gaping at the devastation, while Mama said, "Habibi, oh, habibi . . ." and wrapped her arms around me.

Baba stumbled over the wreckage and knelt down beside me. "What were you thinking, facing them all by yourself?"

Why did he even need to ask? "The deli, Baba . . ."

Mama squeezed me tighter. "The deli, Sik? The deli doesn't matter!"

They didn't get it. They just didn't.

"Look at what they've done. . . ." Daoud picked up one of the broken frames and tried to gently lift the flower out. It crumbled in his hands.

𒀭𒈦𒌆𒉿 𒀸𒆠𒌁𒈨𒊏𒌁𒉿 𒂗𒈦 𒈾𒀸

FOUR

THEY'D DESTROYED OUR HOME.

I thought it had looked bad at night, but in the glaring light of morning, I could see the whole extent of the damage. Mama shuffled around the carnage, dazed, whispering, "Laa, laa, laa . . ."

The police had come and gone. They'd taken pictures and statements and had scheduled a time for us to go down to the station to look at mug shots. See if we could recognize the guys behind the attack.

Recognize them? How could I ever forget guys who looked like toads and rats, and a giant made of a billion flies? But somehow I doubted they'd be in any police database.

Had it *really* happened the way I remembered it? I'd tried to explain what I saw, but the police officer just shook his head and said I was in shock. Mama and Baba didn't know what to make of it, either, and Daoud . . . he claimed he hadn't seen anything. It was too dark in the alley. He hadn't even stuck around to help us clean up, saying he was "too upset." Typical Daoud.

I went down the counter with a big trash bag, adding the cabbage to the rest of the mulched vegetables. Everything had gone bad—vegetables, fruit, meat, everything. Maggots had somehow even found their way into airtight jars. There are few things fouler than watching huge white maggots writhe inside jars of apricot syrup. And the decay wasn't limited to food. The wooden tables had rotted overnight—one had collapsed into sawdust. The gas pipes to the cookers had a worrying coat of rust on them.

"Pizza! Hot outta the oven!"

Our across-the-street neighbor Mr. Georgiou barged in with four big pizza boxes—two-footers. He swept his gaze over our deli—or what was left of it—and for a moment, his face fell. Then he slapped his mighty belly, holding his pizzas aloft as if he were carrying the Super Bowl trophy. "Who wants a slice?"

"For breakfast?" I asked.

We cleared space on a table, and he laid the boxes down, glancing over at my parents. "How they doing, Sik?" he whispered.

Baba sat at the other remaining table with all his papers

out, on the phone with the insurance company. "Six months?! We need to restart the business *today*, not in half a year!" He rustled through the sheets. "What do you mean, health code violations?" His knuckles whitened as he gripped the handset. "No—don't you dare . . . Hello? Hello?"

Mr. Georgiou shook his head. "This place'll be up and running again before you know it. Better than ever."

"How?" It hurt seeing our home so . . . contaminated. I wanted to bulldoze it flat. "How do you know?"

Mr. Georgiou grinned. "This time your parents have you to help, Sik."

Me? How was I going to fix any of this?

But I had to. This destruction was my fault. I hadn't fought hard enough. And what had Boss Bug been after? It made no sense—we didn't have much. I gazed at the wreckage. And now we had even less.

Mr. Georgiou rested his big hands across his bigger belly. "Leave supper to us. Livia's cooking up a lasagna for you guys. Halal, of course."

"Of course." The pizzas smelled delicious—he'd been generous with the garlic and anchovies—but I had no appetite. "Thanks."

"Look after your folks," said Mr. Georgiou, and then he headed back across the street to his pizzeria.

"Don't I always?" I said to no one.

Mama sighed and continued sweeping up the broken

glass, dead flies, shattered frames, and Mo's flowers. She put all the dried blossoms in a separate pile and gazed at them, fighting back tears. Those pressed flowers were worthless to anyone but us. They were all we had left of Mo, and they'd been destroyed out of pure maliciousness.

She caught me looking at her and offered a smile. A sad, fragile one. "It'll be fine, habibi. Inshallah."

"Yeah, Mama. Inshallah."

God willing.

Mama and Baba were refugees. They knew what it was like to lose everything overnight, and ever since the first time, they'd lived with the dread that it could happen again. Now that fear was back in their eyes—they couldn't hide it. I felt it, too, a black mass clogging my throat. It would choke me if I wasn't careful.

I *would* make everything better for them. Somehow I'd fix this. I reached for her broom. "Let me help."

She looked me over and frowned. "Are you still itching?"

Oh, that. I was lathered up in calamine lotion and had swallowed a bucketful of antihistamines with my morning orange juice. My face was a volcanic red landscape of bites and stings with blue patches of bruising under the eyes. I should have been in a coma, but I barely felt a thing. "It looks worse than it feels."

"Fine, in which case there's no reason to miss school," she said.

"School? What about here? We haven't even started on the kitchen yet. You need—"

Mama fixed her gaze upon me. "To school, young man."

"I could—"

"Now."

I snuck into the back of the classroom halfway through social studies. Mr. Grant didn't notice my late arrival—he was too busy arguing with one of the other students. Good. Maybe I could sit quietly and think up a way to save our deli. After all, you went to school to get smarter, right? I took the empty seat next to Jake.

He stared at me, horrified. "What the heck, Sik? You infected?"

"Bad night at the deli." I flicked up my hoodie. I could do without the whole school staring at me.

"You missed an epic game last night! We're level twenty now—we're fighting demons! Can you imagine that?"

"Actually, I can," I replied. "Whoa. Level twenty? We were only fifth when I last played. . . ."

"It's been a long time." Jake nudged me. "You should come back, Sik. There's always room for another hero."

"My folks need me at the deli right now. You know how it is."

I could see his disappointed resignation. I'd used that

excuse a hundred times, maybe a thousand. We didn't need to go over it again.

I glanced up front. "What's all the drama?"

"Belet."

I should have guessed.

How could someone make so many enemies so quickly? She'd been here only a few days and was adding Mr. Grant to her already long list.

Despite being Iraqi like me, Belet spoke in a snooty British accent. It was obvious she belonged in some uptown prep academy, not a run-down public school like Hudson Square. Her baggy gray pants did not look cheap, and the same went for the tight top that covered her from wrist to neck. Her sneakers were plain white, but I bet they cost more than our monthly rent.

Rumor had it that she'd been kicked out of every decent school in the city until only we were left. Watching her in action, it was easy to believe.

She suddenly turned and looked straight at me from under the bangs of her tight bob. She wore kohl around her dark eyes—the only makeup she bothered with—amplifying their brooding intensity. Belet seemed stunned by my presence, or perhaps it was just my face. It had drawn a few strange looks on the subway. Then she focused her attention back on Grant.

"Jefferson stole all his best ideas," she declared. "And from one man: Cicero."

"Jefferson's *inspirations* were wide and varied," said Grant wearily.

Belet rolled her eyes. "If your knowledge of history stretched back farther than 1620, you'd know that I am right and you are wrong."

Grant chewed on his mustache, never a good sign, and the vein in his temple throbbed, an even worse sign. "Careful, young lady. I have been teaching this subject for twenty years."

"Incorrectly," Belet replied matter-of-factly.

I winced, almost feeling sorry for Grant. Belet fought dirty.

His vein turned deep purple. "I didn't quite catch that."

Belet hooked her thumbs into her pockets. "Cuiusvis hominis est errare. Nullius nisi insipientis in errore perseverare."

Now, I didn't understand Latin, but I understood that someone had just gotten burned.

"I beg your pardon?" said Grant through gritted teeth.

"Any man can make a mistake," said Belet. "But only a fool keeps making the same one."

I laughed. I didn't mean to, but it slipped out, louder than it should have. What can I say? It had been a tough night, and I needed something to lighten my mood, even if it was Belet.

Grant took off his glasses and wiped them on his tie. "Do you have something to add, Mr. Aziz?"

Uh-oh.

"No, sir. It's just I'm a big fan of, er . . . Latin."

I know, I know. Of all the dumb things to say, that was perhaps the dumbest.

"Really?" Mr. Grant grinned like a shark about to have a big, juicy meal. "Perhaps you could share your enthusiasm with the rest of us?"

"Nope. I think Belet's doing fine without me."

Grant's smile widened. "I insist. Stand up."

Okay, I was caught. Might as well try and make this as painless as possible. Everyone turned to me, and the shock of my cream-covered battlefield of a face ran all the way from Belet to the back of the classroom. A few even flinched.

Latin . . . What did I know about Latin? Math was my specialty—you spend enough time at the cash register and you learn to love numbers, because each and every one means dollars and cents, and enough of those mean business is booming.

That gave me an idea.

"We're all waiting," said Mr. Grant, enjoying bringing everyone else into my public torture.

"Okay. Here's my favorite quote." I took a deep breath. "E pluribus unum."

𒀭𒈾𒃶 𒀭𒅀 𒂖𒆪 𒅈𒐉 𒍝𒈲 𒂠𒆤 𒌋𒄀

Grant's jaw tensed, and his gaze narrowed. "And do you know what that means?"

"Sure do." I grinned. "Another satisfied customer."

Someone giggled. Grant snapped his fingers and pointed at the door. "The principal's office. Both of you."

"The principal's office is thataway," I said, pointing left.

"Which is why I'm going thisaway," replied Belet, pointing right. "Enjoy your detention."

"You'll get in even more trouble, Belet."

"Oh, I think I can handle it." Then she turned around slowly, frowning. "But thank you for your concern."

"Okaaay. I see the concept of human interaction is new to you, but if you don't come to the principal's office, she'll blame me, and I don't need any more grief right now."

"Why aren't you in hospital? You look hideous."

"I'm fine, but thank you for your concern." How did things get so awkward so quickly?

She just stood there staring at me. Then her phone rang. She ignored it.

"Aren't you going to answer that?"

"It's just Mother," said Belet. "She's the only one who has my number."

"No friends, huh?" Now, that didn't surprise me at all.

There was a strange tension between us as we faced each other, and it kept building as the phone kept ringing.

"Just answer it, will you?" I snapped.

At last she did. "Yes, Mother?"

It was a very smart-looking smartphone. The screen shimmered as though coated in a pearly oil. Like everything else she owned, it appeared insanely expensive.

"Nothing out of the ordinary," Belet said. "Just a regular day."

So, getting sent to the principal's office is pretty routine for you?

"No, Mother. Do not collect me. I can make my—" Belet scowled. "I'm sure I can use the subway. It's not complicated."

She'd never taken the subway before? Some people . . .

"Fine. You can pick me up, just this once." She turned her back on me to whisper, "No, Mother, it's not like that. . . . Yes, yes, I love you, too. Obviously."

Belet ended the call and dangled the phone between her fingers, clearly not happy about what she just agreed to.

"I know I'm going to regret asking this, but why don't you want your mom to pick you up?"

Belet's scowl deepened. "I don't see how this is any of your business."

"You're ashamed of her?"

"Not ashamed, but parents can be embarrassing."

"C'mon, there must be something she—"

"Look who it is."

We both turned as three guys headed toward us, one of them punching the metal lockers as they approached.

Great. Zack and his gang of two. You must know the type. Big everywhere except in the brain cells. "Hey, raghead. Your parents still serving dog meat?"

"Only on Wednesdays," I replied.

Zack pulled off my hood and grimaced. "Jeez, you mutating, or what?"

Hobbs stepped back. "Don't get too close to him, Zack. It's Ebola for sure."

I know I should have been more bothered, but I'd heard this sentiment more often than you'd think. The comment pricked but didn't hurt much more than that. Not really. "Had enough? Now why don't you move before I sneeze all over you?"

Then Belet's phone rang again. All eyes went to it, and Zack's widened. "That is swee-eet. What model?"

"Model?" replied Belet. "It's a one of a kind. Tim Cook gave it to me."

"Really? The Apple guy?" Zack asked.

I would have called anyone else a liar. Anyone but Belet.

I nudged her. "Just hand it over to him. It'll save time, effort, and pain."

Zack snapped his fingers. "You heard the raghead. Hand it over."

"I think not."

"Give it," ordered Zack.

"No." It was subtle, but Belet rose to the balls of her feet. Guess she was getting ready to run. I hoped she was fast. I also hoped I was faster.

"Think you get a pass 'cause you're a girl?" Zack's beady eyes locked greedily onto that exclusive phone. "I'm not sexist. I believe in equal pain."

Hobbs and Clyde planted themselves on either side of Zack, blocking any possible escape.

I stepped in front of Belet. No, it wasn't bravery. I was just sick of violence. "Listen, the phone will attract the wrong attention. How are you going to explain having one when no one else in the world has it? I'm doing you a favor, Zack."

Hobbs laughed. "Careful. Sik's about to go full jihadi on us."

Sometimes the whole Islamophobe thing gets tiresome. "There's no need for—"

"Outta my way." Zack shoved me aside.

And then it happened.

Belet spun. She twisted her whole body, from the hips to the waist to the shoulders, then unwound it like a spring, throwing her left foot around high and fast. Like a wrecking ball.

Her heel smashed into Zack's temple. He crashed into the lockers and tried to hold himself up, but his legs jellified and down he went.

Belet's pirouette completed, she slowly lowered her foot like a ballet dancer. She faced Zack's petrified chums and raised an eyebrow. "You next?"

Whoa. Now what did *that* remind me of?

Belet tucked her phone away and stepped over the groaning Zack. Clyde and Hobbs pressed themselves flat against the wall to clear the way.

I jumped over the sprawled lump and caught Belet at the outside steps. "What's your story, Belet?"

"Story?"

"Yeah," I said. "You did the same fancy kick when you knocked out Idiptu's teeth." I gestured back down the corridor. "And what was that? Karate? Kung fu?"

"Ballet."

"Ballet is not a martial art."

"It is the way Mother teaches it."

Sarcasm? With her accent, I wasn't entirely sure. "No, I think you'll—"

Belet raised her hand to stop me. "Wait. This discussion, and any subsequent discussions, will go *much* quicker if you just assume I'm always correct."

I frowned. "About ballet?"

"About everything."

I stared, waiting for her to laugh, or smile, or acknowledge that she'd made a joke. But she didn't, so I guess it wasn't. "Wow. No wonder you don't have any friends."

"Friends like you? Er, no thanks." She gazed at the passing traffic. "Now if you would just go away. Mother will be here soon."

"First, tell me what you were doing at our place last night."

"Besides saving you?"

"From your *uncle*," I said.

The roar of a car engine drowned out her reply. A gleaming jet-black top-of-the-line Jaguar coupe performed a tread-melting illegal U-turn, much to the horror of the cab coming head-on. The two cars missed each other by an inch, and the Jaguar wedged itself between the school bus and the principal's 1970s Cadillac, tires smoking. The cabdriver rolled down his window and began yelling.

Belet went pale. "Oh, Mother."

The Jaguar's horn blasted once, twice, and was followed by a cheerful shout: "Belet, sweetheart!"

Belet's groan was louder than Zack's had been.

"She can't be that bad," I said, feeling the need to stand up for all the moms of the world, but a picture was forming in my head of a hulking female boxer with a busted nose and cauliflower ears.

Belet elbowed me in the ribs. "Just don't stare."

"Ow! Of course I won't. Why would I . . . ?"

The car door swung open, and Belet's mom stepped out. I stared.

The woman stretched up, tall and lithe. She wore an

emerald-hued wraparound silk dress that emphasized her curves, and her wavy raven-black hair cascaded loose over her shoulders and halfway down her back. She removed her sunglasses, and her smile hit me like a thunderbolt, electrifying every atom. The taxi driver stared, too, agog.

Belet met her mom halfway down the school steps. "You could have waited in the car."

Her mom patted Belet on the cheek. "Sweetheart, don't scowl—it does you no favors. Now tell me . . ." Then she strode past her with those long tan legs to where I stood, still staring. I smelled lemons warmed by the summer sunshine, my favorite scent in the whole world. "Who is this dashing young man?"

Her husky voice was irresistible, and I glimpsed starlight in her dark, mysterious gaze. "I'm . . . I'm . . . I'm . . ." What was my name? It was hard to think while looking into her eyes. Then it came to me. "I'm Sikander Aziz, Mrs. . . . ?"

"Sikander? How delightfully heroic." She offered me her hand. "And no need to be so formal. You can call me Ishtar."

FIVE

"ISHTAR?" I ASKED. "LIKE THE GODDESS?"

"So handsome and clever," she replied. "Yes, like the goddess."

She'd just called me handsome *and* clever. My millennium couldn't get any better. "My brother taught me all about the myths of Mesopotamia. He was a—"

"Hey! Get that rusty tin can outta my way!"

We turned to see the traffic at a standstill along Hudson. Ishtar's fancy move had forced a cab across the lanes, blocking a pickup truck.

"Take a detour, pal!" the cabdriver shouted. "How about right up your—"

I missed the rest as the truck blasted his horn long and loud.

Belet stood by her mom's Jaguar. "Can we go now?"

Ishtar held up her hand. "In a moment, dear. I think they're going to fight."

The cabbie flung his door open, and the pickup guy jumped down out of his seat and flicked a cigarette butt at him.

Ishtar winked at me. "Exciting, isn't it?"

Judging by Belet's groan, this wasn't the first time her mother had caused trouble.

The two guys stood chest-to-chest, nose-to-nose. Pickup guy had a few extra inches in height, but the cabbie was built like a bull and already pumping his thick, hairy arms.

My money was on the cabbie. His ham-size fists—haram, I know—could crush rocks.

"Mother! Stop it!" snapped Belet.

Now, that wasn't going to happen. Both of the men were rolling up their sleeves, huffing and posturing like a pair of alley cats. A small crowd surrounded them, enjoying the morning's street theater.

Ishtar sighed. Then she put two fingers between her lips and whistled. Like, shake-the-teeth-out-of-your-jaw whistled.

The two would-be boxers looked over at her.

"Boys!" shouted Ishtar. "There's no need for violence! All you need is love!"

I swear I am not making this up. That's exactly what she said, and I could not believe it, but the two of them paused and looked at each other, slightly bewildered, and then hugged.

"Now that's strange," I said, keeping an eye on Belet and Ishtar. "How did you do that?"

"Do what?" asked Ishtar. She smiled, and I think the word for it is *beatific*. It made you forget what you were thinking as it warmed your very innermost innards. Ishtar made it hard to stay focused on . . .

Wow, she had the longest eyelashes.

Now the cabbie and trucker were sitting on the cab hood exchanging phone numbers.

"Satisfied?" said Ishtar as she joined Belet by her car. "It would have been much more dramatic if they'd spilled a little blood first."

"Do you really need more drama in your life, Mother?" Belet held the driver door open for her. "Time to leave."

Something weird was going on. I pulled myself back to the main question. "You need to tell me . . . who was that guy last night?"

Belet crossed her arms. "Or what?"

How could she be related to Ishtar? Belet may have had serious fighting skills, but she didn't have a single molecule of charm in her whole body. "Your mom's right about the scowling—it's a little one-note."

"Ha! I like him!" said Ishtar as she nudged Belet. "I told you to leave it to me, darling."

"I would have handled it if he hadn't got in the way," snapped Belet.

𒀸𒈨𒅗 𒊍𒅇 𒂗𒀭 𒂍𒐈 𒅅𒅗𒈾 𒂍𒍑 𒈨𒀸

I turned to face Ishtar. "You know what's going on?"

She responded with a vague, dismissive wave. "Oh, it's family business."

"Your family business destroyed my family business," I replied. I wanted to sound angry, but I couldn't bring myself to raise my voice to her. "That bug guy . . . he's your brother?"

Ishtar looked shocked. "Brother-*in-law*. But my dear sister, Erishkigal, always did have a terrible taste in gods."

"In gods?" I repeated. "Did you just say she had a terrible taste in gods?"

"No, you're hearing things." Belet took her mother's hand and tried to pull her, gently but firmly, toward the driver's seat. "Come on, Mother. We'll be late."

"For what, darling?"

Belet paused. "Er . . . ballet lessons?"

There was a sudden smattering of applause from across the street. The crowd cheered as the cabbie went down on one knee before the trucker, who was wiping tears from his eyes.

Ishtar clapped, too. "This is the kind of moment that makes me realize it's all worth it. Now, Sikander, how can I help you?" She took my hand, and her whole demeanor transformed as she gazed into my eyes.

I'd never felt so seen, so attended to. It was as if she really, truly, deeply cared for me. I wanted to tell her everything. "I . . ."

"Enough," said Belet. "He doesn't need to be involved. I can just watch out for—"

"Nonsense," said Ishtar. "Sikander's already involved." Then to me she said, "We'll explain everything, but not here. Come along with us."

I glanced back at the school. "I can't. I've got to go to the principal's—"

"Do you want to know or not?" Belet asked. "Last chance."

She wanted me to back down—I saw it in her eyes. She wanted me to go to the office, get my detention, and stay out of her life. Me? I wanted to return to the deli and never see her again. But I had to find out, to understand why giant fly-infested monsters and demons had trashed our home.

"Yallah," I said, meeting her gaze. "I want to know everything." I could get identities for the police, learn who to go after for damages, and maybe even find out what their relative had been looking for.

"My chariot awaits!" Ishtar gestured to the Jaguar. "Why don't the two of you snuggle into the back?"

Belet's lips tightened. "I can think of nothing worse." She pushed the front seat up so she could climb into the rear and then, firmly and decisively, pulled the seat back into place. Leaving me to ride shotgun with Ishtar.

Not so bad.

Ishtar settled herself into the driver's seat. "It's been so

𒀀𒈾𒆠 𒀭𒈨𒌍𒌋 𒍢𒐀𒄑𒐀 𒁲𒌋 𒈨

long since you had a friend over."

"Oh, joy," said Belet.

Even with her posh British accent, I was pretty sure that was sarcasm.

The seat was comfier than a leather recliner, and the dashboard looked like it had been designed by NASA. Ishtar drove stick, and the engine purred to life. One thing stood out, though: a button with a strip of tape across it marked DNT. As in *do not touch*. Ishtar caught me looking at it and tutted. "I really wouldn't, Sikander."

"What's it for?" I asked. She'd guessed right about my intentions. Buttons like that almost demanded pressing. "Turbo boost?"

"Something like that." She smirked as she twirled the steering wheel. "It's for when I really need to fly."

SIX

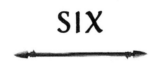

"YOU LIVE HERE?" I ASKED.

"For now," said Belet. She slammed the passenger door behind her. "Come on."

We were somewhere on the Upper East Side—way out of our school district—and we'd gotten here in no time, thanks to Ishtar taking a few illegal shortcuts, including one across a playground. Tall, elegant town houses and a few fashion boutiques lined the street, and there was a fancy florist shop on the corner. Birds sang from the branches of the fruit trees growing near the curb. Actual fruit trees. I stood on the sidewalk and let the perfumed breeze blow over me, free of construction dust and exhaust fumes.

This was epically upmarket, but I couldn't let Belet know I thought that. "Nice."

Ishtar's phone rang, and she tucked it under her chin as

she fished around in her Chanel purse. "Ah, Bee! I've been expecting your call. The twins are gorgeous! How quickly they've grown! Yes, yes, the babysitter . . ."

Vines rose from the lower corner of Belet's brownstone and climbed up and across the exterior, sprinkling the front with lush red flowers. Butterflies of different vivid colors danced from petal to petal, and they seemed to cloud around Ishtar as she ascended the stairs to the front door, still on her call. "Give her six months' severance and put her on the next flight back home. I'll send over someone less . . . distracting. Svetlana is older, a grandmother type, and utterly brilliant. Her goulash is to die for." She tossed her phone back into her purse. "Another marriage saved. I live for victories like this."

A large tabby cat lounged on the top step, watching us. Belet smiled at it as she tickled its chin. "All safe and sound, Sargon?"

"Wait a minute," I said. The cat had scars all over it and one completely white eye. "I know this kitty. It was outside our deli last night."

"Of course he was." Belet stroked his head. "Now pay attention, Sargon. This is Sikander, and he's a guest, so you can't kill him. For now."

Ishtar shook her purse. "Now, where are those keys? I swear I had them last—"

"Use mine." Belet dangled a bunch off her forefinger.

"Oh, darling! What would I do without you?" A moment

later, the door swung open and Ishtar casually tossed her handbag into the corner. "Welcome to my humble abode."

Humble? Ishtar's abode made the White House look like a tin shack.

The hall led to a sweeping spiral marble staircase that went up a whole lot more floors than seemed possible. Cats prowled around the hallway and upon the staircase, and a sleek black one sprang up into Belet's arms. A huge chandelier hung down from on high. Portraits lined the walls, and statues filled the alcoves. Massive bunches of fragrant flowers covered every mahogany table. Mo would have loved this place—those orchids looked rare. Ishtar gently brushed the sapphire-blue petals with her fingertips. "Arrived fresh from the Amazon this morning."

"Amazon does flowers?"

Belet looked up from the black cat she was tickling while I was ogling the room. "The Amazon *rain forest.*"

"Yeah, I knew that. Obviously, the rain forest." I hoped I wasn't blushing too much. A tawny cat sat upon a couch, gazing at me. I reached down—

"I wouldn't," warned Belet. "Simba's a biter."

"I think I can handle a cat." But I left Simba where he was. Those fangs did look longer than normal.

A pile of wafer-thin bronze business cards lay on the nearest table. Ishtar handed me one.

I read the text engraved into the metal, "'The Two Rivers

Matchmakers.' You run a dating service?"

"Not just any dating service, darling boy, but the first and very best. Established in 2635 BCE."

"Riiight." Every business needed a gimmick, I suppose, and hers clearly worked if she could afford a pad like this. I tried to calculate how many kebabs we'd need to sell to live here. Several times infinity.

The black cat sprang out of Belet's arms and onto the marble stairs to join his half a dozen or so companions on the landing.

Two more came through one of the doors, a ginger and a tortoiseshell. "How many cats does your mom have, exactly?"

Belet looked confused by my question. "All of them?"

Why did she insist on making no sense? "Er . . . okay. Must be a lot of maintenance."

"No. They know how to look after themselves."

"I feel a celebration is in order," said Ishtar. "Now, tell me, Sikander, what's your favorite meal? I'll whip it up in no time."

But before I could answer *Kofte wrapped in homemade pita*, Belet interrupted. "Can't we order takeout as usual, Mother? You know you can't cook."

Ishtar frowned. "You really don't think much of me as a mother, do you . . . ?"

"*Belet*. My name's Belet."

"Of course it is." Ishtar paused at a door. "Kitchen?"

"That's the coat closet, Mother." Belet pointed at the third door on the right. "The kitchen is downstairs, next to the pool, remember?"

Okay, officially impressed. "You have a swimming pool?"

"Just a normal one, not quite Olympic-size." Belet peered at her mother. "And before you ask, no, we are not getting dolphins."

I laughed. "Dolphins? You've got to be joking."

"Belet rarely jokes. It's part of her charm," said Ishtar. "Darling, give Sikander a tour while I cook something delicious."

"Do I have to?"

"Yeah, does she have to?" I replied. "I'd much rather hang with—"

But Ishtar was already gone.

Two cats prowled around us. The tabby—Sargon—and the jet-black one wove between my legs, purring softly. "At least your *pets* are friendly," I said.

I stopped at the nearest portrait—a beautiful dark-haired woman lounging on a high-backed chair with a pair of big cats, one a tawny lion and the other a smoky black panther, resting on either side. "Nice."

"That's a da Vinci. It's a little more than 'nice.'"

"She looks a lot like your mom." I peered closer. The colors had faded and the paint was cracked, but those eyes were the same. "I mean a *lot*."

Turns out all the artwork in the foyer looked like Ishtar. A framed charcoal sketch by Toulouse-Lautrec showed her sitting at a café, fingers idle on a cup. Beside that hung a somber, dark painting of her in black silk . . . yet Ishtar, or her historical doppelgänger, smiled amusedly at me, as if remembering a joke only she understood. It was a strange collection. Had Ishtar picked these out of vanity?

Belet made her way down the hall. "Come on, then."

I didn't move. "When are you going to tell me what's going on, Belet? Girls like you don't go to schools like mine."

She stopped. "And what sort of girl is that?"

With a fun mom like Ishtar, she'd had to grow up being the serious one in the family. That must have sucked. I almost felt sorry for her. Almost. "Complicated."

"And that's a bad thing?"

I shrugged. "I'm a straightforward kind of guy. What you see is what you get."

"Somehow I doubt that." Belet barged through the far door. "Hurry up."

I turned to the cats. "She always like this?"

The cats, being cats, kept their opinions to themselves.

I went through the door, and guess what? No Belet. The corridor branched to the left and right, which didn't make a whole lot of sense given how narrow the house was. Had they knocked through the building next door?

"Hey! Belet?"

No response. Just great. I had so many questions, and both Belet and Ishtar had disappeared on me.

There was a pair of big double doors on the right, so I headed for those and went through.

Whoa.

Dimly lit glass cabinets filled the room, displaying swords, clubs, pistols, and every type of weapon in between, going back in time to a flint ax someone might have used to take out a mammoth. Along the walls, suits of armor stood at attention. Medieval chain mail hung next to ornate layered samurai outfits and richly inlaid steel-plate suits. It was a history-of-war parade in a single room.

Why would someone like Ishtar spend her fortune on this? I would've expected a room full of designer shoes instead.

In the middle of the space, a single spotlight illuminated a curved sword, its blade bare and supported by two silk-covered wedges. It was the scimitar Belet had brought to the fight at the deli.

What was so special about this one? Why pick it when there were Japanese katanas racked up nearby? Maybe because it wasn't behind glass like the rest?

It did look ridiculously sharp. Working in a kitchen every day made you appreciate a keen edge, and this edge was keener than most.

Every hero from *The Arabian Nights* carried a scimitar. Those had been my favorite tales as a kid—you didn't come across many Arabian heroes anywhere else.

I'd never even held a real sword.

I double-checked that Belet was nowhere nearby. Nope. I had the room to myself.

I'd just give it a few swings and then put it right back. I reached out. . . .

"Hands off, Private."

I stopped dead and looked around. "Who's there?"

"You touch me and you're going to regret it for the rest of your short life."

I gritted my teeth. The voice had a nasty, ear-aching, metal-scraping-metal pitch. "Come out. This isn't funny."

"I gave you an order."

A couple more cats now prowled about the room, led by the white-eyed Sargon, who sprang up to the top of a suit of armor to watch. The others slinked behind the displays or perched themselves on the cabinets. One of them hissed at me.

They did not want me in here.

Claws clicked on the marble floor. A soft, deep growl rumbled from the shadows, but instead of the lion I was expecting, out came a Siamese. Someone had once told me that a group of cats was called a clowder or a glaring. These were definitely a glaring.

Was it my imagination, or had the cats grown in the last few minutes? Their claws looked longer and their fangs sharper. I heard the fluttering of wings. The green eyes of the black cat glowed and its snarl was something out of the jungle, the threat of a panther.

I picked up Belet's sword.

"What do you think you're doing, Private? I am off-limits to enlisted men!"

"Belet! I know you're in here!" I shouted.

"This is a court-martial offense, soldier!"

The cats encircled me, hissing, growling, and scraping their claws on the floor, leaving deep, clean grooves. A big, fluffy Persian leaped, and I thought I glimpsed . . . *wings* as it sailed over me and landed by the door, blocking any escape. Wings?

This was ridiculous. I was freaking out over a bunch of cats! One squirt from a water bottle would be enough to deal with them, so why did I feel like a trapped mouse?

"Call that a fighting stance?" the voice continued. "Where did you learn swordsmanship, in the circus?"

"Shut up, whoever you are!" I swung the sword in front of the black cat that was getting too close.

"Careful, Private Clown. Another move like that and you'll slice off your own ear."

"Shut up!" I tightened my grip on the handle. I loved cats—they kept the deli rodent-free—but if any of these fleabags so much as hissed loudly, I was going to—

"Sik!"

I spun around, the sword swinging in a horizontal arc . . .

At Belet.

I stopped barely an inch from her neck. She hadn't even blinked.

She held out her hand. "Didn't your parents teach you not to touch things that don't belong to you?"

"Ya Allah, Belet." I was dripping with sweat. "Never creep up on me like that." But I opened my hand and let her take the blade.

The cats lost interest in me, just like that. The lights brightened, and they went back to licking their paws. They seemed smaller again, and I didn't see any wings on the Persian. Must have been my nerves playing a trick on me.

"I'm sorry," said Belet.

I shrugged. "No need to apologize. I just took a wrong turn."

"I wasn't talking to you, Sik."

"That door was supposed to be locked," said the unknown metallic voice.

Belet wiped down the sword hilt. "Mother invited him unexpectedly."

"Who are you talking to?" I asked.

She put the scimitar back on its stand. "Kasusu."

"Yarhamkum Allah," I said, thinking she had sneezed.

Belet pointed at the scimitar. *"That's* Kasusu."

Okay, okay. I needed a reality check. *Get a major grip of yourself, Sik,* I thought. "You have a talking sword?"

"All great weapons have voices, Sik," said Belet. "Some are just louder than others. And more obnoxious."

"I am not merely great," said . . . *Kasusu?* "I am *legendary,* boy. You've heard of Excalibur?"

"Wasn't that King Arthur's sword?" I couldn't believe I was actually talking to a piece of metal.

"Me. Ah, the fifth century. Those were the days. . . ."

I looked at it again. "I thought Excalibur would have been a bit . . . bigger?"

Kasusu huffed. "Size is not everything."

Belet continued. "The greatest weapons evolve to suit the warrior. Kasusu is the first sword. It can take any form since they are all, originally, based on him. You must have noticed how perfectly it fit in your hand?"

"Okay, okay, okay." I laughed at myself. A talking sword. As if!

"Something's amusing you?" asked Belet.

"I've realized what's happening. I'm having a stress-related breakdown. Or at least a minor psychotic episode brought on by the trauma of last night's attack."

The far door swung open, and Ishtar strode in. "Belet,

why did you bring him in here?"

"He found it himself, Mother. And where's the food?"

Ishtar tapped her chin. "I honestly could not find the kitchen. Are you sure we have one?"

I'd had enough. "Look, I love all this domestic stuff, but I came here to find out why a fly-infested giant and a couple of freaks destroyed my home last night. What were they looking for? And how did they know me? Tell me the truth. Like normal people."

Ishtar stood beside me, and there, surrounded by shadows and deadly weaponry, she came across very differently. It was the difference between seeing a tiger on the other side of the fence and then on your own. Suddenly I wished I'd never accepted their ride. No one would know where to look for me. . . .

"Sikander . . ." said Ishtar. "I suppose you know where your name comes from?"

"It's Arabic for Alexander. Pretty common in the Middle East."

She nodded. "It means 'defender of the world.'"

That, I admit, I did not know.

Ishtar sighed. "He died in Babylon, in my arms."

"Who?"

"Alexander of Macedonia. Alexander the Great. Only thirty-two years old and ruler of much of the ancient world.

How much more he might have achieved if he'd only listened to me."

That was impossible. Alexander the Great had died more than two thousand years ago. Yet she sounded so sincere, as if she were recalling a memory.

Ishtar glanced over her shoulder. "He cut the Gordian Knot with Kasusu."

The sword grunted.

Ishtar gazed at me. "When I learned your name, I thought it was an omen." She laughed lightly. "But then I remembered that we gods *send* omens—we don't observe them."

"*We?*" I asked. "You're a god?"

Belet raised her head proudly. "My mother is Ishtar, the goddess of love and war."

Between the freaky cats, the talking sword, and now this, my mind was turning to hummus. I faced Belet. "And that makes you . . . ?"

"Adopted."

"Well, that's great, but I want to go home now." These people were obviously deluded and probably dangerous. "I'll find my own way out."

Somehow, in a blink, Ishtar moved to block the door. "But we owe you an explanation, dear boy. You need to know the truth. You're caught in a little drama, and I think you have a part to play. Whether you like it or not."

"Why do I think I'm *not* going to like it?"

Belet spoke. "How much do you know about ancient Iraq? When it was Mesopotamia?"

"Not much. It was all destroyed when—"

Belet shook her head. "Not all of it. The gods survived. A few of them. My mother, her sister, and Nergal, the god of plagues. You met him last night."

Ishtar joined in. "I thought I'd caught him in Iraq, but somehow he and his demons have managed to get themselves to New York. This will be our battleground."

I backed away. "Do you hear yourselves? Gods and demons? They're not *real*. All that—it's just fairy tales. Stories to explain the sun and the moon, from back in the days when people believed the world was flat."

"Some people still believe the world is flat," said Belet.

"Yeah, and they're crazy, too."

Ishtar tapped her lips, thinking. "What would it take to make you believe?"

"You can't. The world *isn't* flat."

She laughed. "No, child. That I am who I say I am. That you are caught in a war between gods."

"It'll take more than some fancy parlor tricks, that's for sure."

Ishtar stepped nearer. "You know they say the eyes are the windows of the soul?"

"Mother, don't," pleaded Belet. "You'll break him."

"Hush, sweetheart. Mother knows best." Ishtar drew me close, right up close. I couldn't resist her.

Her eyes were huge, dark, and deep. "Look, Sikander. Look into my soul."

I did. I gazed into the soul of Ishtar.

And reality shattered.

SEVEN

———◆———

AN AVALANCHE COMPRISED OF A HUNDRED THOUSAND
memories, experiences, sights, smells, sounds, and feelings swept over me. My mind screamed. It was too raw, too
real, too much. I was buried, crushed, under the soul of the
goddess.

Ishtar sings as she stalks through the battle. On the dusty
plains before the walls of Troy, thousands upon thousands of
soldiers take part in the dance of death. Bronze weapons are
an orchestra of destruction and bloodshed, and the screams
of the warriors are her choir. Most beautiful of all are the
emotions: She feels the tides of fear, bloodlust, despair, and
blind fury like a swimmer in a stormy sea, overwhelming
yet thrilling.

Men, smooth-limbed, muscular, tanned, and beautiful
in their youth, offer their lives at the altar of love. For one

another, for their kings, their people, and, most of all, for the Spartan queen, Helen, who watches from the battlements of the impregnable city.

To the east is gold-haired Achilles, his armor shining like the sun, his face a mask of raging battle madness. Around him men seem to melt, the light of their lives darkened under his long-shadowed spear.

To the west strives the Trojan prince Hector, his armor stained with the lifeblood of many Greek nobles. His dark eyes cannot hide the passion burning inside his heart; Ishtar has to shield hers to look upon him. Hector's love powers every swing of his sword. Troy is his home, and within its walls live his wife and infant son. Should he fall, then they are doomed.

Thus love fuels war, turning it into an inferno whose heat and smoke rise to the heavens.

Ishtar cries out, and her voice rolls like thunder across the plain. She cannot contain her joy.

Children scream and mothers sob inside the classroom as the Luftwaffe continues its attack. The huddled townsfolk cannot contain their fear. A dreadful, chilling whine is heard as the bombs are released overhead. The sound pierces the dull drone of the aircraft engines, and then there's an ominous pause before the thunder of another explosion.

The school building shakes again and tiles tumble off the

roof. The windows have long since been blown in, and shards of glass are scattered across the floor. Pages from textbooks drift in the smoke.

A little girl clutches Ishtar with all the strength she has in her thin fingers. "When will it end, Mama?"

Ishtar smiles softly at the small blond girl, Florence. The goddess took her in when Florence's parents were killed. This is not the first time Ishtar has gathered a war orphan from the ruins, and it won't be the last. It lifts the guilt—at least some of it—from Ishtar's shoulders. She strokes her new daughter's hair. "It has just started, ma chérie."

The bombings began at dawn and have continued unabated. But why? This little French town has no factories, no supplies, and it is far from the front line. The men have all gone to their battalions. Only the elderly, the women, and the children are left, huddling in the smoke-filled ruins of their homes.

Hitler's war machine, the blitzkrieg, knows only destruction.

Where is the magnificent combat? Ishtar wonders. *Where is the holy sound of clashing swords? Where are the warriors determined to test their pride, their honor, and their skills one-on-one? Where are the heroes whose battle cries are my hymns?*

Ishtar gently frees herself of her daughter's grasp. "Wait here, Florence."

"Mama!"

Ishtar winks. "I won't be long."

Down the block, she climbs over the burning ruins of her home, a small maisonette on the corner. Flames lick her, and the walls hiss and spit molten plaster. She brushes fiery debris off her shoulders and sighs as she tiptoes through pieces of broken furniture and chinaware. She pushes aside a splintered dresser and sees a glint of metal on the floor.

Ishtar blows the brick dust off her sword.

"At last," complains Kasusu. "This is just like the time you left me at the bottom of that lake in Wales. I had to wait fifteen hundred years to be found! The humiliation."

"Hush," says Ishtar.

Another squadron of German bombers appears on the crimson horizon, lit by the burning trees like a false dawn. *They will be overhead in minutes. Why? What is left to destroy?*

"Where is the glory?" she asks aloud.

The smoke thickens around her as she climbs out of the wreckage of her apartment. Then she sees him, picking over the mangled bodies of those who didn't get to safety in time. He digs out a victim's eyeballs and tosses them to his waiting pack of demons, igniting a tussle.

"There is nothing for you here, Nergal," she says.

"That is where you are wrong, dear sister." He wheezes with each step. Patches of jaundiced skin dangle from his face, and the rest is covered with weeping sores. His rheumy eyes narrow. "There is plenty for me."

The bombers pass through the clouds of black smoke. They know there are no soldiers here and the remaining people are defenseless. They know that the school contains only women and children, and they do not care.

"You should have retired, Ishtar," says Nergal as he crawls over a mound of pale corpses sniffing for juicy morsels. "Beautiful, isn't it?"

"You call this beautiful?" Ishtar tightens her grip on her sword. "You were golden and glorious once, Nergal. What happened?"

"Unlike you, I was not sustained by the love and worship of mortals," he growls. "I was left to feed on their hatred. Fortunately, they hate for the most inconsequential reasons, as you must have noticed. If someone looks different, speaks with an accent, prays at one house rather than another . . . anything, really." He shakes his head in wonder. "It is marvelous."

"There are heroes still," Ishtar replies.

He laughs. "The age of heroes has long passed. This is a time of monsters and monstrous deeds."

The planes' bomb hatches open overhead. . . .

"It is my time." Nergal digs out the plump heart of a freshly killed young man and begins to chew it, letting the blood dribble down his chin. "Courage does not matter. Honor is a poor joke. Pride has given way to terror. This is an era of machines and meaningless death. And there you stand, with a sword. Do you know how ridiculous you look?"

Ishtar flips her blade from one hand to the other and sees Nergal's eyes widen. He cringes, and his demons snarl. "You wouldn't dare. . . ."

She might dare, one god killing another. Kasusu hums with eagerness. . . .

But not this time. "Instead of making humans in your mold, Nergal," says Ishtar, lowering her sword, "you could raise them up. They could be great again if we inspired them to be so."

"Sounds like too much trouble." The plague god sneers. "And just how would you achieve that miracle?"

"Watch and learn."

Ishtar runs. Her divine powers surge as she leaps up to the roof of the old café. The structure crumbles, but she launches herself higher, flying through the smoke and fire.

"Ishtar!" screams Nergal.

The first bomber is in her path.

Steel screams against steel as she slices a wing with her blade, and the plane goes into a spin. Ishtar sprints along its fuselage and launches herself at the second bomber.

The cockpit window shatters as she plunges through it.

The pilot only has time to blink before she flicks Kasusu across his neck. The copilot fumbles for his sidearm, and Ishtar rips him from his seat and tosses him into the sky. The plane nose-dives, but she is already out, back among the smoke and the gunfire blazing from the squadron around her. Bullets that would obliterate mortals shatter against her skin as she tears open the hull of the third bomber. Men tumble out, and their cries and prayers fade away swiftly.

The old warrior hymns swell in her heart. Ishtar shines with the joy of battle, and she remembers what it is to be a goddess, to hold mortal fates in her hands. The wind howls as Ishtar lands on the next plane. She slides along the fuselage, rips off the hatch, and enters.

The pilot stares. The copilot screams.

"Hello, boys," says Ishtar.

Kasusu begins to sing.

EIGHT

I COLLAPSED, GASPING. I WANTED TO CURL UP AND HIDE from the world, from everything, most of all the visions I'd just witnessed.

Belet looked anxious. "Are you all right?"

It had been a mistake to close my eyes. The bloodshed poured through my mind again, and the screams of battle echoed in my ears. But thanks to Ishtar, I'd felt, briefly, what it was like to have that inhuman power. To fly. To be able to tear metal with my bare hands. To have senses so sharp I could hear thoughts. Now I was back in weak, helpless flesh.

"See, Mother?" said Belet. "You've broken him."

I drew in a few slow, deep breaths, forcing myself to stop shaking. My heart rate calmed down, and I opened my eyes slowly.

There she stood. Ishtar was so beautiful, and so terrible. How many people had sacrificed themselves for her? How many cities had burned to the ground? How many cries had risen up to her ears in the fire and smoke? What bitter, cruel prayers had she heard?

"What did you do?" I muttered, still struggling to think straight. "What just happened?"

Then Ishtar took my hand. Those eyes that had witnessed so much horror softened with sincere worry. "You've just experienced a god surge. It will pass."

Belet crouched down beside me, curious. "You're lucky he's not been reduced to a gibbering imbecile."

"Tsk. Sikander is made of firmer stuff than you give him credit for." Ishtar patted my arm. "You're going to help us defeat Nergal, aren't you?"

Help? After what I'd just seen? "No way." I pushed myself to my feet, away from them. "You've got the wrong guy—all of you. I'm going home, and I never want to see any of you ever again."

"Oh," said Ishtar, surprised. "It's not often anyone refuses me."

Belet pushed her mom aside. "What did you expect? You've scared him witless."

I really wanted to prove her wrong on that point, but my flight instinct was stronger. "Outta my way, Belet. I mean it."

Belet didn't move. "Not till you tell us what Nergal was looking for. You have something he wants."

I could hear an accusation hanging between her lips, and

it made me angry. "How'm I supposed to know? He just busted in and . . ." Then it dawned on me, what she was suggesting. "Oh, I get it. You think we've got some great treasure, stolen from Iraq."

When American tanks had rolled in, there had been a lot of chaos and looting. I'm not talking about people stealing designer sneakers or seventy-inch high-def TVs, but priceless artifacts, thousands of years old. Smugglers earned millions overnight, at the cost of everyone else.

Ishtar joined the interrogation. "Your brother worked all over the country. What was he doing?"

How had she heard about Mo? "Helping to repair villages and grow crops," I said, trying not to sound defensive. "He even had a certificate from the Department of Agriculture for importing and exporting plants and seeds."

"You can use a shovel in many ways." Belet's eyes narrowed. "Maybe he wasn't just planting vegetables. Maybe he was digging up treasures from ancient Mesopotamia to sell on the black market. Maybe he—"

I gritted my teeth and glared. "You know nothing about Mo. The guy was the best person you, or anyone, would ever meet. The only thing he was interested in was rebuilding his homeland, one farm at a time. All he sent me were flowers, and your uncle destroyed them all last night."

Belet wasn't finished. "Relatives can keep big secrets from one another."

"Yours, maybe. Not mine." I raised my palm. "Look, this is not my problem. You all can sort out *your* family squabbles and leave *my* family way out of it."

"It's not that simple, Sik," Belet insisted. "If Nergal is here, this affects everyone."

"Then you'd better grab your mouthy sword and take care of it."

Ishtar reached into her pocket. "It is tragic what happened to your delightful home. And as Nergal is family, it *is* our responsibility to repair the damage he caused. How much do you want? Is a million enough?"

I stared at her as she drew out a checkbook. "You're joking, right?"

"Ah. Two, then." Ishtar took out a silver pen. "In dollars?"

I don't know why I said the next thing, but I did. I couldn't help myself. "In exchange for what?"

Ishtar held the pen poised over the checkbook. "That would be entirely up to you."

I know, I know! Who in their right mind would pass up two million dollars? The money didn't mean anything to Ishtar—I doubted it would make a dent in her account—but make a deal with a god? I'd seen what Ishtar could do, how she'd led humans to their destruction over all those centuries. "La, shukran. We'll manage on our own."

"I'll show him out, Mother," said Belet, heading toward the door. "Come on, Sik."

I admit I looked back at Ishtar. With just a few scratches of her pen, our deli would be saved. But then I found myself at the front door.

"Do you want an Uber to take you home?" asked Belet. "I'll order one."

"I'll take the subway." I didn't want anything from either of them.

The train couldn't move quickly enough. The moment the doors opened at Fourteenth, I burst out of the car, sprinted along the platform, and took the steps up to the street three at a time. I ran all the way home. I wasn't sure whether I was running away from Ishtar and Belet and their world or toward Mo's. I was needed at home. That was where I belonged, not on some ridiculous adventure with a crazy rich woman and her high-kicking daughter.

I stopped dead when I saw the ambulances parked in front of the deli, lights flashing. People had gathered in the street to watch. I pushed them aside, trying to get to the front. "What's going on?"

A man glanced down at me. "It's the family that runs the deli."

My heart froze. Had Nergal come back? I felt sick. I'd wasted time with Belet and Ishtar when I should have been home.

Just then two paramedics came out our front door wheeling

a gurney. They were wearing N95 masks and rubber gloves.

"Mama! Let me through!" I yelled, and ran up to her. "Mama!"

She was in an oxygen mask, unconscious, and I'd never seen her so pale. Only then did I notice that Baba was already loaded in the second ambulance. He looked like he was in just as bad shape.

No, no, no! What was happening? They'd been fine this morning. . . .

"You related?" asked one of the paramedics.

"They're my parents." I stared as they slid Mama into the ambulance. "What's wrong with them?"

He peered at me curiously. "How are you feeling, son?"

"Me?" Why was he asking? "I'm fine. Where are you taking them?"

"Manhattan General," he said. He grabbed my wrist and took my pulse. "Your folks been abroad recently?"

"The last vacation we took was in Florida. That was ages ago."

"You'd better come along so we can run a few tests."

"Tests? What kind of tests?"

The expression in his eyes was awful. My blood ran cold. He led me to the waiting ambulance. "I want you up front. Let's get you a mask and gloves, too."

"Why can't I sit with my mom?"

"We need to keep her isolated from germs as much as we can. Until we know what's wrong with her. With them both."

"Are they going to be okay?" I was almost too scared to ask.

He paused before answering. "We're going to do our best, son."

That wasn't a yes. That wasn't anywhere near a yes.

𒀸𒅕𒆷𒂊 𒀸𒁉 𒂊𒈝 𒂍𒐲𒐲 𒐲𒊺𒌋𒍝 𒂍𒐲𒂊 𒌋𒀸

NINE

I WAS WRONG.

I used to think Mo's death was the worst thing that could ever happen to me. Part of me figured that, having survived the loss of my brother, my hero, I couldn't be hurt anymore, would never feel that level of pain again.

I was so, so wrong.

Petrified, that's how I felt now. Scared stiff. I couldn't think about anything except *What'll I do if my parents die tonight?*

By the time we'd heard about Mo, it was over already. *Bang!* and he was gone. Past tense. No promises, no wishes, and no prayers were going to make any difference. This wasn't like that. My parents were still alive, and no one knew what was wrong with them.

I prayed hard. I lost count of the suras I recited all

through the night. I'd be a good Muslim—the best—if Allah just let me keep my parents.

Each was put in an airtight isolation room; the staff had to wear hazmat suits to go in. I could only look at them through the anteroom windows. I watched as Mama and Baba lay there in medically induced comas with ventilators breathing for them because their lungs were full of fluid.

As for me, I was whirled from one test to another. This doctor and that doctor took blood samples, put me through X-ray machines and even an MRI scan. They poked and prodded me all through the afternoon and evening until finally the doctors shook their heads in amazement and told me I was totally okay.

I didn't feel totally okay. Not even close.

I had my own room. The doctors wanted me under "observation" for at least twenty-four hours, just in case. I paced around in my hospital gown and socks, too tired and too wired to do anything but worry. It was eerie, silent except for the beeps and pings of the equipment, the walls and ceiling lit by the cold blue glow of the monitors. Finally I lay down on the bed, scared and despairing, staring blankly out the window as the sky began to turn purple, then pink, with a new day.

At dawn, I had visitors. How they got in, or how they knew where to find me, I had no idea.

Belet and Ishtar burst in, followed by an angry-looking nurse. He jumped in front of them. "You can't come in here. The boy's under quarantine. He could be infectious."

Ishtar dismissed his worries with a flick of her hand. "Ridiculous. Just look at him—the very picture of rosy-cheeked health."

The nurse cleared his throat. "I'm sorry, but you—"

Then Ishtar did her thing. I don't know if it was a "god surge," but I felt the atmosphere change. She put her hand delicately on the nurse's arm. "No need to be sorry, Duncan, unless it has to do with your feelings for Jessica."

He stepped back, stunned. "What? How do you know about that?"

Ishtar leaned in close, as though confiding with him. "Jessica's not the right match for you. Now *Alice*, on the other hand . . . she's perfect."

"Really? Alice? The one who works in the morgue?"

Before he knew what had hit him, Ishtar had guided him into the elevator out in the hallway. She handed him her business card just before the doors closed.

Belet picked up the plastic bag holding my street clothes and emptied it onto the bed. "Get dressed. You're leaving."

"I can't leave my parents! And the docs may want to run more tests tomorrow. I've gotta stay until they know for sure what's going on."

"Tsk. You know exactly what's going on, Sikander," said Ishtar, stepping back into the room. "Nergal is behind all this, and you can't help your parents if you're stuck in here."

"Nergal . . ." I almost choked on his name. He'd given them a disease—probably an ancient one the doctors didn't know about. "Is he . . . Is he going to kill them?"

"If he did," Ishtar said coolly, "he'd have no bargaining chip with you, now, would he?"

"But why does he need one? I haven't—"

"We told you," said Belet, holding out my jeans. "He wants something he thinks you have."

I felt so frustrated, so helpless. "Can't you cure my parents?" I asked Ishtar, hating how pitiful I sounded. "If you are what you say you are."

She smiled sympathetically. "Healing's not my forte, but I'll slow the illness as much as I can."

I thought back to the isolation rooms and the two pitiful husks that were my parents. They'd done no wrong in their lives. They'd lost their homeland, their son, and their business, and now they were fighting for their very survival.

Ishtar put her hand on my shoulder. "Sikander, Defender of the World, I am calling upon you."

"We need you to help us fight Nergal," Belet translated.

"Fight? But how . . . ?"

"This is war," said Ishtar, "and I need you on my side."

"No, not war. My parents have had enough of war." I pictured them trapped in their comas. "They would call this a righteous struggle, and there's a better word for that." For when you had to struggle for something you believed in. When you had to face terrible odds, whatever form they came in. When you had to fight with all your heart to save those you loved. "A jihad."

TEN

SOMETHING WASN'T RIGHT. NO THICK SCENT OF TURKISH coffee brewing. No smell of pitas on the grill. No clitter-clatter from the kitchen and no Mama singing Arabic love songs by her favorite artist, Fairuz.

This wasn't home.

I'm at Belet's.

I'd been so exhausted, I barely remembered the journey from the hospital, being greeted by the cats, and Belet showing me to this bedroom, which looked like it had come straight out of *Vogue*. Gold-embroidered cushions were scattered over the crimson-and-navy Persian rug that covered a spotless white-marble floor. The furniture was straight out of a sultan's palace: ornate and inlaid with silver and mother-of-pearl.

And it was the first time I'd ever slept on silk sheets. But instead of lying on a bed suited for a king, I'd have preferred to be at home on my rickety pallet with bedding from the discount aisle at Target.

I was surrounded by comfort while Mama and Baba were comatose in the hospital. Maybe they'd gotten better overnight? Yes, that was it. They were waiting for me to show up and take them home so we could put this nightmare behind us.

No. I knew that wasn't possible. It was up to us to save them. I just hoped Ishtar had a plan.

The cats ignored me as I padded barefoot along the marble corridors. They slumbered on plush chairs or lurked among the vases and pedestals. I went down two flights of stairs, and the scent of pancakes drifted from a door on the right.

Ishtar must have finally found the kitchen. Good, I was starving. And more important, I needed to talk with her about how to get my parents *saved*. I went straight through and found . . .

"Daoud?"

"You're up at last, mashallah." Wearing only his pajama bottoms, he gently flexed his abdominal muscles as he filled the espresso machine with water.

"How did *you* get here?"

"I met Ishtar and Belet at the hospital last night," he said. "After I'd been waiting there for *hours*. Ishtar told me she's putting you up and I could crash here, too." He pointed to his portfolio resting against the wall. "Ishtar says she has a lot of connections in Hollywood, so I brought that along. Who am I to refuse an offer like that?"

I sighed and said in a low voice, "Be careful who you trust, Daoud."

He looked confused. "C'mon, Ishtar just wants to help."

"Yes, but . . ." Worried that Ishtar might somehow be listening, I changed the subject. "Did you get to see Mama and Baba?"

"The receptionist wouldn't let me up, because I'm not *family*," he said. "But I called the hospital an hour ago. My friend says they're stable, but the docs haven't figured out what's wrong with them yet."

"Who's your friend?" What right did he have, knowing before me? They were *my* parents.

"Rita, the hospital charge nurse. She's in my improv group."

Typical Daoud, always working the system. But this time I was grateful for it.

He flipped the pancakes, then looked at the metal spatula to check his eyebrows in the reflection. "By the way, she says the doctors want you back ASAP. You're supposed to be in quarantine."

"There's nothing wrong with me."

"Yeah. Those bug bites cleared up pretty fast, didn't they? What'd you use? Vitamin E cream?"

I hadn't even thought about them, but he was right. I didn't itch anymore, and the swelling had all but disappeared. Maybe Nergal wasn't as dangerous as he seemed.

"I need to get back in to see my parents," I said, "but the moment I set foot in Manhattan General, they'll lock me up in a lab."

"I could help," said Daoud. "We actors know how to change our appearance."

"You mean go in disguise?"

He nodded. "You'd be surprised at what I can do with my makeup kit."

"That's what you salvaged from home? Your portfolio and makeup kit?"

"Hey!" complained Daoud. "They're important! Remember what they said on the *Titanic*? Models and children first!"

"*Women* and children, Daoud."

"Ya salam, Sik. That's pretty sexist of you. I'm surprised. And a bit disappointed."

Why did I bother? I'd forgotten Daoud lived on planet Daoud in the galaxy of Daoud in the universe of Daoud, of which he was the absolute center.

I stared at him. "What. Are. You. Doing?"

He held up a bag of apples. "Making a smoothie? The pancakes are for you."

"No. With your face. Stop it. It's freaking me out."

He gestured at his eyebrows, which he was raising one at

a time while simultaneously puckering his lips. "It's the latest thing out of Beverly Hills—Face Pilates. Gwyneth swears by it."

"Face Pilates is not a thing, Daoud."

He started in on cheek lifts. Really. "It is. How do you think they all look so good after thirty?"

"Plastic surgery?"

He sighed. "You're way too young to be so cynical. Try it. It'll stop those frown lines from getting deeper."

"I do not have frown lines!"

Daoud moved on to nostril flares. "Mo always said you worried too much. Told me I needed to make sure you didn't go gray before high school."

"Mo said that? To you?" I don't know why I was so surprised. Mo and Daoud had always hung out together. "What else did he say about me?"

"What do you think? He wanted me to make sure you were okay. Why d'you think I moved in with you? You think I like working at the deli? Promises were made, cuz."

"To Mo?"

He took a deep breath. "Wow. First set done. Back to the eyebrows."

"Daoud! Tell me about Mo and these promises!"

"Check this out, Sik." He pinched the skin on his waist. "Less than ten percent body fat. That's not easy with your mom's cooking all around me, and your dad grilling up all those delicious kebabs. You don't understand the sacrifices I've made to look this amazing." He put the pancakes on a plate and handed it to me with a wistful expression. "So long, carbs."

"You could always give yourself the weekends off. You could have the odd baklava. What damage could that really do?"

"A single zit could destroy my career, Sik. I only have one shot to get noticed."

This was the longest conversation we'd ever had. I couldn't believe he was only working at the deli because of a promise he'd made to Mo.

I sat down to eat my pancakes while Daoud poured his fruit sludge into a tumbler. "So, where do you think Ishtar's money came from? Daddy an oil sheikh? Maybe an arms dealer? War's good business."

"You have no idea."

The door crashed open, and Ishtar gazed around, stunned. "You were right, Belet. We do have a kitchen." She smiled when she saw us. Belet, coming in behind her, didn't. "And the boys are already making themselves at home. How wonderful."

How could these two be mother and daughter? Ishtar stood there in silver high heels and a dress that shimmered as if made of starlight. And Belet? Well, she looked like she was about to overthrow a dictatorship in her black T-shirt, combat pants, and boots.

Daoud held out his portfolio to Ishtar. "You said you would take a look. There are some stills from a play I did, off-off-Broadway, called *The Wife, the Thief, and the Hijacker.* There's a review from—"

She gently pushed the portfolio aside. "Which I'm sure is fabulous. But you and I have an appointment with Monsieur Bertrand at ten."

"Designer to the stars?" Daoud bowed. "Your whim is my command, goddess."

Belet glared at me accusingly.

What? I hadn't said anything to him! How did he know?

Then Daoud tapped his nose. "Goddess. It's the new perfume from Versace. It suits you."

We all breathed a sigh of relief. He was as oblivious as always.

"Why, Daoud, you are full of surprises," said Ishtar, her eyes sparkling. "Now hurry. Bertrand has to be back in Paris tonight."

Daoud bowed again and, with a wink to me, left.

Ishtar sniffed her coffee, grimaced, and poured it down the sink. "Well, now that he's gone, perhaps we can get down to business."

"And save my parents," I stated.

Ishtar smiled gently. "Dearest Sikander, to do that, first we must find Nergal. He is the key to all this."

"Okay. And what happens when we find him?" I asked. "Just ask him to heal everyone and go home? Somehow I don't think he's going to play along."

Belet flipped a knife and chopped up a banana into neat slivers. "We destroy him, once and for all. With his presence gone, life will return to normal."

I looked between them. It might have been my imagination, but I thought Ishtar looked uneasy. "You can do that? Kill a god? How?"

Ishtar sighed. "It's easier than you'd think. Gods die in so many ways. They lose worshippers and they just fade away, or they can become . . . irrelevant. There was once a god of wild donkeys and . . . I can't even remember his name myself."

Belet dissected an apple with two swift knife strokes. "And, of course, a god can be slain by another god, or by a weapon like Kasusu. It was forged for that very reason."

"Where do gods go?" I asked. "When they die?"

Ishtar smiled wistfully. "Some dwell in Kurnugi now, but not many. Nergal's doomed, though. He broke out of Kurnugi once too often. He faces utter annihilation."

That wasn't the best news. "So he's got nothing to lose."

Belet looked over at her mom. "We need to find Nergal fast."

"I have people looking for him," said Ishtar.

"What people? Gods?" I asked. "You have Gilgamesh on speed dial?"

Ishtar grimaced. "Gilgamesh was only part god, on his mother's side, though he pretended otherwise."

Belet laughed. "It's been four thousand years, Mother. Get over it."

I looked between them. "Get over what?"

Belet put a fist on either side of her head, her forefingers up to look like horns. "Gilgamesh killed Mother's cow."

Ishtar glared at her daughter. "It was the Bull of Heaven, and you know it."

Belet shrugged. "Anyway, Gilgamesh is long gone."

"Too bad. With his strength, he could have solved all our problems," I said.

How many versions of *The Epic of Gilgamesh* had I read over the years? Probably every one there was. It was the world's oldest story, and I'd grown up with it, first with Mo reading me big-and-bright picture books. Then I'd found it in comic book form. More recently I'd read translations and modern adaptations.

"Mo was a big fan," I told them. "He once dressed up as Gilgamesh for Halloween. I was his sidekick, Enkidu—no surprise there."

They were the original dynamic duo: Gilgamesh the demigod warrior king, and Enkidu, the wild man with hair down to his knees and kin to the animals. While Mo had dressed in gold lamé and gotten to wield a huge plastic ax, I'd been stuck with itchy fake fur, a wig that had boiled my head, and no weapon, just my cuddly lion. Hey, I'd only been five at the time.

Before Mo got too old for it, we used to pretend Central Park was the dreaded Cedar Forest, home to all the great demons. In the subway, we imagined we were delving into the netherworld to fight monsters and to commune with the spirits of our ancestors. Mo got the glory, of course. But I didn't care. I would have followed him anywhere, just like Enkidu had happily trailed Gilgamesh. And I got to end each day with a grand, tragic death. Who could've asked for more?

Yeah, we could have used an epic hero about now. "So how long will we have to wait? Mama and Baba are in intensive care, in case you've forgotten."

Belet looked irritated. "You need to understand the scale of the problem, Sik. We're dealing with a renegade god."

"Nergal." Like I could forget. Every time I closed my eyes, I saw him. "The rotting god."

Ishtar sighed. "He was once much more than he is now, Sikander. He was a war god. You should have seen him in his glory days. There was rarely a sight more splendid. I suppose that was when Erishkigal fell in love with him. She and I would visit the battlefields together, and Nergal would be there, covered in gore."

"Erishkigal?" I asked. I should have listened more closely to Mo when he'd rambled on about Mesopotamian mythology. I'd never imagined it would become such a matter of life and death.

"My older sister, the goddess of death. She and Nergal rule Kurnugi, the netherworld."

"I suppose it makes sense that the goddesses of war and death would be sisters," I said. "But how can you be the goddess of love, too? That *doesn't* make sense."

"The *goddess of passion* would be a more accurate term, and what generates more passion than love and war?" Ishtar raised her eyebrows. "If you look even slightly into the ancient past, you'll see how love has driven many a war. Just ask Helen."

"As in Helen of Troy?"

"Not quite as attractive as you'd imagine, but she tried so very hard," continued Ishtar. "I knew them all. Alexander and Hephaestion. Antony and Cleopatra, Napoleon and Josephine, who had such terrible teeth. I used to tell her—"

"Mother . . ." said Belet.

Ishtar waved her hand dismissively. "So love and war overlap more than you think. Thus I took dominion over that aspect of war, while Nergal took mastery and power from the disease that follows. He—"

Belet interrupted. "After World War I, more people died

of the Spanish flu than in the entire war. All those infected soldiers, shipped home to all corners of the world, not realizing they were bringing death with them. Millions perished."

"That was Nergal's doing?"

"He likes to play his cruel little games," said Ishtar.

A dreadful thought crept into my head. "And we're only getting over the last pandemic. You think he was behind that, too?"

"Who knows? But you understand why we need to stop him fast, before this goes global."

I shuddered, then shook my head. "All this talk about gods and goddesses—it's hard to take in. Y'know, I was brought up as a Muslim, to believe in the Shahada." I closed my eyes. *"La ilaha illah muhammadun rasulu llah."*

"There is no god but Allah, and Muhammad is His messenger," said Ishtar.

"Muhammad, peace be upon him," I added. "So what are you, Ishtar?"

Ishtar's expression changed, going from her usual playful, slightly not-too-serious to deep and thoughtful. "I am very old, Sikander. Old and powerful, but not *all*-powerful. When humanity first encountered me and my kin, they called us gods, and gods we were back then. Nowadays, we might well be called something different."

Belet handed over a slice of apple. "I call it the Thor

Conundrum. What is he, a god or a superhero?"

Ishtar laughed. "That is one way of looking at it."

I got it, sort of. But it still didn't help me get over the fact that there was a supernatural being sitting opposite me.

Ishtar must have seen my confusion, because she continued. "People worshipped us, and we drew power from that. But there are mysteries, wonders far greater that even I don't understand. I am not omniscient, nor omnipotent. Those are attributes of this greater power. After all, someone created *me*."

"And does this power have a name?" I asked.

"In the culture I once belonged to, we called it Ea. But each culture has given the power a name that suits it best. The name you use is as good, and as profound, as any I have ever known."

"My imam is gonna love meeting you," I said. "It's a lot to take in."

"The universe is a complex place," said Ishtar. "I don't pretend to understand even a fraction of it."

"And speaking of things I don't understand"—I gestured to the portfolio—"what about Daoud? What's his part in all this?"

"Simply to be fabulous." Ishtar glanced at her watch. "Which reminds me. Bertrand does not like to be left waiting."

I frowned. "How is taking Daoud shopping gonna help us find Nergal?"

Ishtar collected her purse. "We gods have our ways. Most of them mysterious."

"Why can't I come?" said Belet. If I didn't know any better, I'd have said she was almost pleading.

But Ishtar wagged her finger. "Remember Paris?"

Belet turned pale. "I honestly thought she was a demon! She was so skeletal!"

"She was a supermodel! They're all like that!" snapped Ishtar. "To be banned, and by Chanel of all people! Let me remind you, it was I who—"

"Who gave Coco Chanel the idea for the little black dress. I *know*, Mother," said Belet, rolling her eyes. "Your great contribution to civilization."

Ishtar's gaze went cold. "Ah, that famous teen sarcasm. No parent's life is complete without it."

"Mother . . ."

"No. I must be firm. This is going to require tact, charm, and subtlety, Belet."

I stifled a laugh, but not very well. Belet glared at me before turning back to her mother. "I can be those things."

Now I laughed out loud. "C'mon, Belet. Your talents are extreme violence, being rude, and, er, more violence."

She swiveled so fast I flinched, expecting her to give me a personal demonstration of her first and third talents, but she only narrowed her eyes at me. "Rude? Only to idiots who don't stay out of our business."

I spread out my hands. "Aaand I rest my case."

"I'm not spending my day babysitting Sik, Mother. Why can't I at least—"

I finished off the last mango in the fruit bowl. "She's already gone, Belet."

Her spirits seemed to drop a hundred feet.

"She's always pushing me away," Belet said to herself. Then she remembered she wasn't alone. "Not that I care. I'm perfectly good at looking after myself. At least *I* knew we had a kitchen."

For the first time, it struck me that Belet had to be very lonely. Then why did *she* push everyone away? "It must be weird having a goddess as a mom."

Belet blinked rapidly. Like you would if you were trying to hold back tears. But that couldn't be the case, right? Not with Belet.

"I don't blame you for wanting to go with her instead of being stuck here with me," I said. "I'd rather be with my parents, too. I didn't ask for any of this."

She let down her shoulders, as if melting a little. "I know. I just . . . want to be useful."

I heard that. I didn't want to sit around waiting, either. I stood and zipped up my hoodie. "C'mon. Let's go find Nergal on our own."

Belet arched her eyebrow, which was clearly talent number four. "And how exactly are you going to find him when my mother hasn't?"

"You don't know New York like I do," I said. "You and your mom are uptown girls living in your uptown worlds. You won't find Nergal at Tiffany's, or Chanel's, or wherever it is that beautiful people hang out."

"Is this wealth shaming? If so, it won't work. I'm not embarrassed by being fabulously rich." Then she looked at me quizzically. "You *really* know how to find Nergal?"

"Actually, yeah." Why hadn't I come up with this right away? I'd been too busy worrying about Mama and Baba, that's why. "You remember Saddam Hussein, the old Iraqi dictator?"

"Where is this going, Sik?" asked Belet.

"The guy had a hundred palaces and solid-gold toilets. Statues on every street corner. He lived the life of an emperor. Or a god." Slaving away in a deli six days a week, I had learned a few things. Okay, nothing as cool as how to deliver kicks to the head, but I learned how people worked. "Then the war hits, and he's overthrown. Saddam goes into hiding, and when he's eventually found, months later, he's filthy, dressed in rags, and living in a hole in the ground."

"And this relates to Nergal how?"

More than she could imagine. "Grab your coat, Belet."

ELEVEN

"WELCOME TO LITTLE EGYPT!" I SAID. "MAKES YOU FEEL right at home, doesn't it?"

Manhattan was only a few miles west, but each of the boroughs had its own unique identity, and none more so than Steinway Street in Queens.

Middle Eastern restaurants lined both sides. There were tables outside them with men playing backgammon, and long-necked shishas bubbled and puffed out rose-scented smoke. Arabic street signs could be seen everywhere, and Arab newspapers and magazines covered the stands. *El-Mizan*, Mama's favorite Egyptian show, blared from one of the cafés.

"I left Iraq when I was a week old, Sik," said Belet.

"But heritage, right?"

"You don't strike me as someone who cares much about your heritage."

"I started caring a lot when it came crashing through my back door," I replied. "We're heading to the Dar al-Islam masjid off Thirty-First. It's running the kebab kitchen tonight."

"Kebab kitchen?" she asked.

"It's like a soup kitchen, but spicier." We made our way down Steinway. Instead of English, we heard a babble of accents from every corner of the Middle East: slang from Egypt, Lebanon, and Syria, as well as some in Farsi—the music store was run by Iranians.

Belet took out her fancy phone and started taking photos. "Mother would love it here."

"Did Tim Cook really give you that? As in the head of Apple?"

She handed it to me so I could have a better look. It was very sleek, exactly the sort of phone the daughter of a goddess would have. "Mother knew Steve Jobs. He was of Mesopotamian descent—his father was Syrian. Heritage, right?"

The phone was more than nice—it was a work of art. Then I noticed the alerts on her screen. Lots of them. All with my name in them. "Why am I all over the school message board?"

Belet snatched back the phone. "I wouldn't worry about it."

"Hey! I *am* worried about it! Why is everyone talking about me? And why do I feel it's not in a good way?"

She let me read the posts. "Sorry, Sik."

"I'm a biohazard risk?" I read some more. "Zack ended up in the hospital because he caught something from me? The only thing he caught was your boot!"

On and on the messages went, each one escalating the last. Mama and Baba had been taken away by ambulance because of some unknown disease. The deli had been closed down and sealed off. So far, so true. But then I'd apparently broken out of the hospital in a rabid rampage, and every student with a cough or runny nose was now a suspected plague carrier and being rushed to the doctor. Parents were demanding that the school be closed down and decontaminated. On the other hand, vaccination rates for other diseases had skyrocketed, so it wasn't all bad news. Just *mostly* bad news.

"Fear is a disease, too," said Belet, taking the phone back. "It spreads fastest of all. We're going to need to shut it down before it becomes a citywide epidemic."

"Guess it's gonna be homeschooling for me from now on," I said. "If I *have* a home, that is." I felt almost as helpless as my parents lying in their isolation rooms and didn't know whether to punch someone or cry.

Fortunately, before I could do either one, I was distracted by our arrival at the masjid.

"Sikander? Alhamdulillah!" A man in splattered white coveralls stood outside it, apparently taking a break from painting the exterior. He wiped his forehead with a cloth, leaving a gray paint smear across his skin. "Haven't seen you around here for a while, young man, not even for Jummah prayers. How are you doing?"

I blushed. It was the imam. He ran the masjid, and my attendance hadn't been that great for a while. Quite a while, actually. "Salaam, Mr. Khan." His son Farouk was on a ladder next to him. "Are you redecorating?" I asked.

"Cleaning up the graffiti," said Mr. Khan, tugging at his beard. "Some . . . bad words were painted on our walls. There was some damage, too." He gestured to the second floor, and I saw two smashed windows.

Farouk turned and spoke through gritted teeth. "They also threw a pig's head over the wall. If I knew who did it, I—"

"We reported it, Farouk," his father cut in. "Leave it to the police."

Farouk snorted, clearly not impressed by his dad's restraint.

Mr. Khan shook his head, then smiled. "And you've brought a friend, yes?"

Had I? It took me a moment to realize who he meant. "Oh, yes. This is Belet. We came to help serve lunch."

Belet's face said, *We did?* but her mouth stayed closed.

Mr. Khan nodded. "Mashallah. We have a big crowd today."

I could already smell delicious foods cooking. "We would have been here earlier, but Penn Station's shut down because of a water-main break. And they've closed the Brooklyn Bridge because of some cracks in one of the towers."

Belet arched her eyebrow. "Doesn't take a lot to paralyze a city, does it?"

She was sure both things were Nergal's doing. I was sure it was just life as usual in New York.

"Farouk and I will join you as soon as we get cleaned up," said Mr. Khan. "I want to hear about your parents. We are all praying that they will be fit and well very soon."

"Inshallah, Mr. Khan," I said.

I said a hasty good-bye to him and walked around to the small parking lot at the back of the masjid. Brown picnic tables ran in neat rows along the asphalt, and people lined up at buffet tables with their paper plates, each collecting a pile of food from the cluster of stalls.

"Best free meal a person can get this side of the Tigris," I said to Belet. "Curries from our Pakistani brothers and sisters, Sudanese dura, and that whole corner is Malaysian. Baba says his jihad is against bland food."

"Do we have time for this, Sik?" she asked.

"You said you want to be useful," I pointed out. "And serving others is a great way to take your mind off your own problems."

"I knew I'd regret coming," Belet muttered.

She and I collected clear plastic water pitchers and moved from table to table to pour.

𒐓𒐊𒈨𒈨𒑊 𒐓𒐋𒀜 𒂍𒅆𒈨𒊏𒈨𒑉𒐥 𒂊𒐊𒈨 𒈨𒐓𒐥

There were salaams from the benches as people I knew from masjid inquired about Mama and Baba, told me that du'as had been made for their health, and asked if I needed anything. There were a few smiles at Belet, too, as nosy folks tried to meet my "new friend."

Among the regular worshippers were many poor and homeless people from the neighborhood. Food united us as much as religion. Gathered there were individuals from all over the world, from all walks of life, come to break bread and say a few prayers together. It made me feel better about things, if only for a brief time. "This place helped my parents when they arrived in America. So Mama and Baba usually bring over a pot or two to pay it forward."

"I know about zakat," said Belet, referring to the obligation to help the needy. "But you said we were going to find Nergal."

"My guess is your god of rot will not be hiding in high society. He'll be among those less fortunate. The ones already struggling."

Belet surveyed the diners. "It makes a vague sense, I suppose."

Then I spotted a figure at the gate. Small and wearing a patched-up parka that went down to her ankles. She had her hood on, but there was no mistaking her. "There she is."

Belet followed my gaze. "Who?"

"Hey, Ada!" I shouted across the parking lot, waving to

get her attention. She looked up abruptly, startled.

"Let me introduce you," I said to Belet.

As we approached Ada, there was a moment when I thought she'd run—she'd done that a couple of times—but then she relaxed . . . until she saw Belet.

"Hey," I said, trying to be as casual as possible. "Been looking for you."

Ada stood there, encased in her coat of patches. Some were wallets she had decorated with shiny candy wrappers; others were sequined purses she had found. She had glued, sewn, or pasted them on as outer pockets, and in the sunlight, she shimmered as if dressed in fish scales. Like a crow, Ada liked shiny things, and with them she had transformed her dull, ragged coat into a sparkling work of art. She had never told me her age, but I guessed she was only a couple of years older than me. We all kept an eye on her, but she wasn't interested in getting too close.

"Ada is happy to see Sik." Then she looked over at Belet, wrinkling her nose. "Ada is not happy to see Sik has brought someone . . . else."

"And salaam to you, too, Ada," I said. "This is Belet. She's my friend. Apparently."

"Salaamu alaikum, Ada." Belet held out her hand. "It's good to—"

Ada looked Belet up and down, clearly not impressed. "Is Belet Sik's girlfriend? Sik could do better. Much better."

𒁹𒌷𒆬𒂊 𒁹𒈠𒉌 𒄑𒃻𒐌 𒅆𒈨𒌝 𒂍𒐌𒊏 𒁹

"Your friend's remarkably rude," said Belet.

"I like to think she's refreshingly honest."

I steered Ada toward the kebab table. "What do you want, Ada?"

"It's Saturday," she said firmly.

"One Saturday Special coming right up."

I asked old Ali if I could take over for a little while, and after washing my hands, I got behind the grill. Making kebabs is my one and only superpower. I glanced over at Belet. She nodded. "I'll have one, too."

"How hot do you want it?"

She recognized a challenge when she saw one. "Try me."

Ada hovered nearby. "Just make sure—"

"Relax, Ada." I flipped over the warming pitas. Ada liked her kebabs a *very* particular way. I started with the onions.

And a few minutes later, we sat around a table with a kebab roll each. Belet took a bite, and there was a flicker of shock on her face. She reached for the yogurt sauce. "That's . . . quite spicy."

Ada nibbled, holding the roll lightly with her fingertips. She ate carefully, taking pains not to let a single piece of lettuce or drop of sauce fall. "Ada wonders if Sik's friend Daoud will be here tonight. Ada likes Daoud. He gives her a funny feeling in her belly."

"That's just indigestion." I poured Ada a cup of water and then let her eat in peace. My parents and other adults at the masjid had given up trying to "save" her by getting the authorities involved. She always ended up back on the street. I'd known her for a while now; she came around the deli on Wednesdays—at eight thirty exactly—and Mama would always give her a meal and bag of fruit. Ada usually showed up at the kebab kitchen on Saturdays, but the rest of the week? That was her business.

"The tomatoes are different," said Ada, pausing mid-chew.

"Fresher, right?" I replied.

She nodded and continued eating. You had to be careful around Ada. If anything wasn't exactly right, she'd take off.

"I need your help, Ada," I said.

Ada's focus remained on her roll. "Is it Sik asking for help, or this Belet?"

"Both of us. There's something strange going on, and we wonder if you know anything about it? You are a very observant person, and you . . . go many places. Did you hear about what happened at our deli?"

"Ada likes Sik's parents."

"Do you know about anything, Ada? Anything unusual?"

She hesitated, looking around before speaking. "The stranger arrived thirty days ago."

Belet sat up. "Stranger?"

Ada shivered. "He came by boat, in a shipping container."

I looked over at Belet. "Didn't your mom say Nergal smuggled himself here? Easy to do in a shipping container."

"Not easy," said Ada. "Everyone died."

"Died? Who?" I asked.

"Refugees. Some from Africa. Some from the Middle East."

I frowned. "Oh, I think I read about that online. They suffocated, right? Pretty sad."

"They didn't suffocate," said Ada quietly.

Belet leaned over the table toward Ada. "How do you know this?"

Ada shrank back, and her gaze flicked to the gate. She was thinking about running, and if we lost her now, that would be it.

"Ada, this is really important," I said quietly while giving Belet a *just back off* glare. Belet was scaring her, but we needed to learn what Ada knew. "Just talk to us for one minute. That's all."

Ada took a step toward the gate, but I got up, nice and slowly, and stood beside her. "I'm your friend, Ada, but Mama and Baba are in a bad way, and I think this stranger from the ship is behind it. We need to find a way to stop him before more people suffer." Then I stepped back. "It's your call, either way. Where's this container?"

Ada chewed the inside of her cheek. "Gravesend Dock."

TWELVE

"GRAVESEND DOCK. THAT DOESN'T BODE WELL, DOES it?" said Belet.

No, it did not. I looked around, half expecting to see vultures perched on the lampposts. The dockyard was vast and isolated—the ideal place for, say, a renegade god and his horde of demons to settle in. And if they weren't there, the container might still hold a clue that could help us find Nergal, something the police might have overlooked because investigating ancient monsters wasn't part of their job description.

We stood at a ten-foot-tall chain-link fence. Beyond it lay a city of shipping containers, all part of the Gravesend marine terminal. They formed multicolored skyscrapers, spreading high and wide. Forklifts rumbled along the steel-lined chasms.

I searched in both directions for an opening in the fence, to no avail. "Guess we're climbing."

While Belet practically flew over the fence, I tore my sleeve getting over, but in only a few minutes we were hiding behind a tower of crates. We needed to keep a low profile—if movies are to be believed, dockworkers have a reputation for punching first and asking questions later, if at all. We sprinted to the first wall of containers. If there were security cameras, we couldn't see them. Perhaps this was why the human traffickers had picked this dock in the first place.

The layout was simple: The dock was divided into zones, just like a parking lot. We needed zone 12; we were in 20.

"I should have brought Kasusu," said Belet.

I scanned the direction we were headed in, and we both ducked as three guys walked past. They were big and mean-looking and exactly the type we needed to avoid. "You cannot carry a five-foot sword around New York. Not unless it could disguise itself."

"Disguise a sword?" she asked. "Like cosplay?"

"I'm not saying tie ribbons to it and pretend we're in a parade, but you said it could change shape. Perhaps it could turn into something smaller? Pocket-size maybe? I don't know, like a pen or something."

Belet laughed. "Now that would be handy."

It didn't take long to find the right container—it was still sectioned off with police tape. Even without knowing what had happened inside, looking at its exterior made my guts churn, like when I was working in the deli late at night and heard something out back. . . . Never mind. Didn't need to be thinking about *that* just then.

Even Belet looked wary. "You want to go first?"

"La, shukran," I replied. "I think we need to get one thing straight: You're the action heroine. You lead."

Belet didn't disagree. Humility was not part of her personality. "So what does that make you?"

"The comic sidekick."

She gave me her "arched eyebrow" glance. "But you're not actually funny. Or even mildly amusing."

"Ouch. I give you a compliment, you give me a verbal kick to the face. We are gonna have to seriously review your people skills when all this is over."

Even though it was only mid-afternoon, zone 20 was draped in shadow, and deserted. Nobody wanted to be around here, and that made life easier for us as we made our way to the container doors. While the other containers were brightly colored and marked with company logos, this one was black with big patches of orange rust. It was as if the metal itself was diseased.

Once we were there, I was not at all interested in looking inside. But Ada had sent us here for a reason, so . . .

Belet wrinkled her nose. "What's that smell?"

A sharp whiff burned my nostrils. "Cleaning fluid. Industrial-strength."

The rusty hinges cried as we dragged the doors open

wide enough to slip through. The acidic stink of the fluid hit hard, stinging my eyes and attacking the back of my throat. I hauled the door wider to get some fresh air in there.

Smartphone flashlights on, we looked in.

Empty. Empty, empty, empty.

Except for the ghosts.

It wasn't hard to imagine the refugees, huddled together with their meager belongings. Desperate families hoping they'd made the right decision to leave their war-torn homes and everything they knew for the wild gamble of a better life here, in the Land of the Free and Home of the Brave.

Mo had worked with a few refugee families, helping them get settled in New York. He'd told me all about human traffickers who offered to deliver people to the safety of the West—for a price. How much had these poor victims paid to spend months living in this steel box?

I heard Mo in my head: *They came here to start afresh, and this is how it ended.*

The left corner had been scrubbed spotless. I tried not to imagine the bodies.

This is just the beginning, Yakhi. Nergal's out there, planning something terrible.

The smell of disinfectant was stronger in the back. The cleaning crew must have used gallons of it. It had stripped the paint off a portion of the metal floor.

I remember when we fled Iraq. I was only allowed to bring one toy with me. It was a monkey. I wonder what toys these children had with them.

"Shut up!" I snapped.

Belet looked at me. "Pardon?"

"Sorry. Just talking to myself. The fumes are getting to me, I guess."

"Look," said Belet, beaming her flashlight on the walls.

"Ya Allah." They were covered in scratches, but they were too neat and regular to be random. I looked closer and realized what they were—words. Cuneiform. It didn't have the glamour of Egyptian hieroglyphs—it was made up mostly of dashes—yet it was from these marks that history had officially begun. But cuneiform was found in museums, displayed in glass cases and preserved as something precious, not scratched into a steel slaughterhouse. This was graffiti, scrawled at all angles and in different sizes, the lines overlapping each other, as if the writer had been so filled with fury he couldn't stop himself from attacking the metal. There had to be thousands of words crisscrossing the walls, even the ceiling.

"Can you read it?" I asked Belet.

"There's so much. . . ." She swept her light from corner to corner. "Wait a minute. It's all the same thing, only in different languages—ancient Sumerian. Akkadian. Babylonian, Assyrian . . . All the cultures from Mesopotamian history that used cuneiform. Just two words, over and over again . . ."

"Which two?"

"'Gilgamesh lied.'"

"Lied about what?"

Belet passed the light over the wall from side to side. "It doesn't say."

I'd grown up with the tales of Gilgamesh—there had to be hundreds. About fighting demons and monsters, saving princesses, and going on adventures with his best bud, Enkidu. Until a few days ago, I'd always assumed they were fairy tales. I'd never taken them literally.

Belet got down on her knees to look more closely at the bottom corner of a wall. "Wait a minute—there's something else here. Just a few lines. Strange. I think it's a rhyme."

"In cuneiform? What does it say?"

"Let's see. . . ." She cleared her throat as if doing a classroom recital. "'There is much goodness to savor, as mortals have so much flavor. Kidney from the Ivory Coast tastes best when it is served on toast, but my—'" Belet covered her mouth. "The rest is really disgusting."

"Sidana." Who else? "So at least we know this is how Nergal and his demons got here. Still doesn't tell us why, though. Or where they are now."

I gazed at the wall of scratches. This was the work of an obsessive. Nergal couldn't get the thought of Gilgamesh lying out of his mind, and it was driving him insane.

Belet got to her feet and snapped a few photos with her phone. "I'll speak to Mother. She'll—"

"Now what do we have here?"

Uh-oh.

The three dockworkers we'd seen earlier now stood in the doorway.

"Maybe one of us should have kept an eye out," I said.

"Thanks for stating the blatantly obvious, Sik," replied Belet.

"Let's just remember it for next time." I put up my hands and said to the men, "This isn't what it looks like."

Dockworker One, a big guy with tattoos from his wrist all the way up to his neck, shook his head. "You're trespassing. And in here, of all places. You kids nowadays have no respect."

His companion, with a boulder-like chin thick with black stubble, cracked his knuckles. "You need to be taught a lesson."

Okay, this was escalating way too quickly. "We're not stealing anything. We just wanted to take a look. Maybe help find out what happened. Who was behind it."

The third guy scratched his cheek and gave us a smile made of a row of black teeth, the top middle pair missing. "And what business would that be of yours?"

Tatt Man blocked our way out. Somewhere he'd found

𒀀𒈾𒂊 𒀭𒐊 𒌉𒈾𒐊𒌐 𒅖𒈨𒐕 𒁹𒌉𒐊 𒂷

a length of chunky chain, each iron link the size of a brick. "What should we do with 'em?"

Stubble Chin drew a hammer from his tool belt. Belet clenched her fists.

I had one chance before this all got totally out of control. "Listen, now, I know this might sound strange, but that girl there"—I pointed at Belet—"is really good at ballet."

Black Teeth scowled. "Funny guy."

"See, Belet? *He* thinks I'm amusing." I turned back to Black Teeth and pointed as he screwed up his face. "There's something under your eye."

"It's nothing." He rubbed the bag under his left eye, and it *squirmed*.

"Seriously, it looks infected."

He rubbed harder, and something squeezed out of his tear duct.

An ugly bluebottle crept along his cheek before buzzing off.

"Now, that's not good," I said.

These were no ordinary dockworkers. I wondered, fleetingly, if demons had their own union.

Belet jumped to the same conclusion. "Nergal did this to you, didn't he?"

Now, up close, I saw they weren't demons, but seriously infected humans. Egg-size boils covered their faces, thick

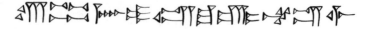

green veins pushed hard against sickly yellow skin, and a decaying stench emanated from them, almost as bad as the one from that night I'd met Sidana and Idiptu. Tatt Man's grotesquely bulbous knuckles cracked noisily as he made his fists.

"Why?" I asked. "Why did you let him turn you into monsters?"

Tatt Man passed his hand over his deformed face. "This? This is nothing. You just wait and see what he's got in store for the city."

"Kill them." Black Teeth grinned as he pulled out a knife, taking us from *not good* to *far worse*. Another fly emerged from the gap in his teeth and took off. More spilled out of his eyes, ears, and mouth, and the container echoed with their evil, unnaturally loud buzzing.

Far worse was now officially *super bad*.

"What was it you were saying about weapons, Sik?" Belet asked with forced nonchalance. "Remind me."

Any one of the guys was equal to our combined body weight, and there came a point when it didn't matter how hard you hit, some things were just too big to be taken out with a spinning hook kick.

But no one had told that to Belet. She was all the weapon we needed.

She skipped sideways as Black Teeth slashed downward.

𒀭𒌓𒁕 𒀭𒅎 𒂍𒉌 𒌉𒈨𒊏 𒁇𒐊𒐊 𒀭𒋾𒋾

She bobbed below the next chop and sprang straight up, her boot catching him in the throat. He croaked and stumbled back. Belet didn't pause but, grabbing his ears, pulled his head down into her knee, delivering a thunderous *crack!*

Ouch.

As Black Teeth sank to the floor, Tatt Man swung his chain at her unprotected back.

"Belet!" I jumped forward. I couldn't stop myself. Not to fight—I didn't know how—but to put myself between the oncoming chain and Belet's unprotected back, even if it meant—

—getting smashed across my arm and ribs, and being hurled across the container into the wall, hard. My lungs felt as if they were on fire, and breathing suddenly became impossible.

Belet shot me a worried glance, then twisted around and rammed her fist repeatedly into Tatt Man's kidneys. Three times in a second. The fourth took him off his feet.

Stubble Chin roared as he charged, his eyes blazing with berserk fury. But he ran past Belet and raised his hammer over me. I crossed my arms over my head, as if that would do any good. I could see his whitened knuckles around the handle and the thick veins standing out in his forearms, but I couldn't do anything to stop him.

Belet leaped off the flattened body of Black Teeth. I thought she would spring out a kick, but instead she wrapped her leg around Stubble Chin's throat, catching it in the crook of her knee. The entire momentum of her body went into a sharp twist, literally forcing Stubble Chin into trying a backflip. Except he didn't land on his feet. He landed on his head with a heavy thud. So much for Stubble Chin.

I sat slumped against the wall, panting. How could I hurt this much and still be conscious?

Belet rushed over to me and snapped her fingers in my face. "Sik? Say something."

"Stop doing that. It's irritating."

My arm was all pins and needles, but I could move my fingers. I carefully unwrapped the chain, then winced as I saw the damage underneath. "It can't be that . . . Oh." I almost threw up. Splotchy purple bruises ringed my upper arms.

I sucked in a single deep breath, my lungs pushing painfully against the vise trapping my chest. Gritting my teeth, I forced in more air and something inside me relaxed. At last. My heart raced, but the ache in my lungs lifted. I wiped my mouth. There was a slight red smear of blood on my hand, but when I spat, it came out clear. Belet helped me up, and after a moment of wobbling, I stood up straight. The dizziness began to recede.

Belet's face was pale. "I thought you were dead."

"It looks worse than it is. Honestly." I thought I was dying, too, and yet there I stood, battered and bruised but more or less fully functioning. I gently moved my swollen arms. The nerves sent pure fire through me, but it swiftly receded to a dull, constant ache. I wiggled my fingers. "You were great, by the way. Those ballet lessons have really paid off."

Belet laughed. Honestly laughed. I must have been staring at her in shock, because she quickly pulled herself back under control. But I think there was still a tiny smirk on her lips when she said, "And you're tougher than you look."

THIRTEEN

GOLDEN SUNLIGHT STREAMED DOWN THROUGH
the skylight into the armory. It shone upon the rows of
armored suits, the edges of the swords and axes, and on spear
tips and a thousand other pointy objects designed to spoil
your day permanently.

"It's seven in the morning. I should be in bed, recuperating." I held up my lilac-tinged arm. "Look, bruises. And I
think I have a cough." I coughed twice. "Hear that?"

"What I hear is whining, and you seem perfectly fine,"
said Belet, expressing zero sympathy. "All things considered."

Yeah, all things considered I should have ended up in
the hospital after the previous night. I still felt as if I'd been
stuffed in a dryer and spun around at a thousand rpm, but
as Belet said, I seemed fine. Nothing broken, cracked, or split
in two. Ishtar had given me a *very* cursory once-over when
we'd gotten back and declared me fit and well, all the while

telling us about the nightclubs she and Daoud had visited. Apparently, he'd made quite an impact, and the city was all abuzz about this "dashing Arabian prince." Annie Leibovitz was going to do new headshots for his portfolio.

Which reminded me . . .

"How come Daoud gets to sleep in? He wasn't beaten up by a trio of god-cursed dockworkers last night."

"Mother says he needs his beauty sleep," Belet answered, and to give her credit, she didn't sound entirely happy with her mother's strategy in finding Nergal.

"And I don't?"

"No amount of sleep is going to help you, Sik."

"Gee, thanks, pal." And here I thought we'd bonded during the fight for our lives.

Belet picked up a battle-ax while our audience, the cats, found suitable spots to watch the action. Sargon settled himself on top of a Napoleonic cannon. "What I mean is, Mother thinks more people will probably try to kill you."

"Is that what you think?"

"No. Not at all."

"Cool, then why don't I go back to—"

"No, you don't understand." Belet plucked a hair and drew it over the blade's edge, slicing it neatly in two. "I think people will *definitely* try to kill you."

Great. Really, *really* great.

𒀭𒈾𒈨 𒁁𒊏𒈨 𒊭𒉌𒂗𒈨 𒊏 𒃲 𒌋𒁲

She swung the ax with worrying enthusiasm. "Do you have any martial arts training?"

"I've watched *Kung Fu Panda* like a hundred times. Does that count?"

She sighed as she put the battle-ax back, then flipped out a pair of nunchaku. "Come on. You must have a poster of Bruce Lee on your bedroom wall."

"Kenneth Lee. He's a celebrity chef."

"Any weapons training? At all?" She sounded both desperate and bemused, as if she couldn't understand why all parents didn't raise their kids to be ninjas.

"I'm pretty good with a wok."

"Okaaay. This may require a new strategy." Belet marched over to the sword stand. *The* sword stand. "Kasusu?"

Light rippled along the blade, refracting into a rainbow. Kasusu was sharp enough to cut light.

Belet picked it up gently, as she might if it were a sleeping baby. Or a cobra.

The sword hummed. "You want me to make him a warrior? Forget it. Never going to happen."

Belet shrugged. "Just try. He might surprise you. What's a good spot for you?"

"Over there. The column in the middle."

Belet swung Kasusu. She put hardly any effort into it, just a twist of the hips and a flick of the shoulders, but the steel screamed against stone as it cut halfway through the solid marble column. She left it there, the hilt sticking out.

Belet came over to me. "Don't let that lump of rusty metal bully you, okay?"

"Okaaay."

"I'm off to get a few pieces of equipment. I won't be long." Then she turned back to the sword. "Don't kill him, or Mother'll throw you in a lake like last time."

"I wouldn't waste my edge," said Kasusu.

She left and I reached for the sword. "Let's get this—"

"Do not touch."

"But Belet said you were going to teach me to fight."

The sword made a surly hum. "Why waste both our times? You haven't got it in you to be a hero. Believe me, I've taught the best. The very best."

"Yeah, I know about King Arthur and Alexander. Now how about we—"

"Beowulf. Tokugawa Ieyasu. The Rani of Jhansi. Heroes, every one of them. World changers. But even counting them, there was only one true legend: Gilgamesh."

"He was Mo's fave, too."

"Mo?"

"My brother," I said. "You can forget Superman—Gilgamesh was the boss. Mo worshipped him. Made us all go to the Metropolitan when they had the big exhibit. So, you were his sword?"

𒀸𒉌𒅆𒊏 𒁉𒌗𒌁 𒂍𒉿𒂊𒈨𒊏 𒊍𒌁𒁉

"At the beginning." The sword sighed. "Then he gained Abubu, the Sky Cutter. A weapon so devastating it could literally slice the heavens."

Mo's passion for the world's first hero had rubbed off on me a little. Okay, a lot. We didn't have much in common, but we had Gilgamesh. How many pictures had we drawn of him? Thousands for sure—enough to cover the deli walls ten times over. Big black beard, huge muscles, and armed with a gigantic ax, fighting hordes of monsters or legions of demons.

Gilgamesh lied.

Nergal was obsessed with that idea. Lied about what? Who better to ask than Kasusu?

"So, you were with Gilgamesh for a while? On his adventures? I read all the stories, so I know about how he defeated demons, slew the Bull of Heaven, and searched for immortality. Did all that really happen?"

The sword scoffed. "Those stories don't tell the half of it. The scribes wrote them down centuries afterward. They didn't know the truth."

"Are you saying his exploits were exaggerated?" Maybe he'd lied about his successes. . . .

"The opposite. The storytellers watered them down. Gilgamesh's life was too extraordinary to be believed, so they made his accomplishments more . . . modest. More relatable. As if anyone could relate to a man like Gilgamesh. He was one of a kind, an original."

𒀹𒈦𒉡𒂊 𒀹𒉌 𒁹𒉌𒀸𒐂𒊹𒌍 𒁹𒈦𒐀𒉌

"So there's nothing Gilgamesh failed at and pretended to have done?"

The sword made a screech, like the sound of a bow being drawn shakily over the strings of a violin. "Listen, Private Clown. Gilgamesh succeeded at *everything*. Every demon he fought, he vanquished. Every princess he set out to rescue, he got. Every kingdom he battled, he conquered. We're talking old-old-school heroism, where a good day was one when you came home soaked in the blood of your enemies. None of this caring-and-sharing garbage or rescuing-cats-out-of-trees nonsense. There's no—"

"Okay, okay, I get it."

"Well, maybe there *was* one thing . . ." Kasusu said in a quiet voice.

"Yes?" I prompted.

"He didn't save Enkidu," said the sword. "He was like a brother to Gilgamesh, more than a brother, and the king was devastated when he died. I think it broke him, truth be told. Gilgamesh became so terrified of death he even went on some foolish quest to become immortal, and that didn't work out, either. Then there was"—the sword's voice dropped to a whisper—"Ishtar."

"Yeah," I said. "She still hasn't gotten over that bull thing."

"There was more to it," the sword dished. "He rejected her."

"What?!" I said. Reject the goddess of love? "How could anyone turn down Ishtar?"

𒀭𒈦𒄩 𒁁𒂊𒂖 𒁹𒋾𒁲𒂖𒈨 𒅅𒐊𒋾 𒀊

"I'll tell you when you're a bit older, perhaps. For now, we've got some work to do."

I glanced to the door. "Belet will be back soon, and so far you've only given me gossip."

The sword paused. "Belet. *She's* got the potential to be one of the greats. Unlike you."

"Come on, give me a try. Belet said—"

"Fine, since you insist. I like to start with a song. Raises the spirits. You know, the Spartans sang when they went off to battle. Finest choir you could hope for. Now, listen, the lyrics are easy."

"Be my guest."

The sword cleared its . . . throat? Then it sang:

"My mother thinks I'm very brave,
But now I'm lying in my grave.
You can imagine my surprise,
When I caught an arrow between my eyes.
But I'm not down—"

I interrupted. "Do you have anything less . . . depressing?"

"I've got a song that was popular among the militia during the reign of Henry VIII."

"The one with all the wives?" I glanced at the blade. "Does it involve beheading?"

"You've heard it? Now, there's more to chopping

𒀭𒌋𒅗 𒀭𒌋𒂗𒐊𒋾𒐊𒌋𒐊 𒂗𒈠𒁉

someone's head off than giving them a healthy whack. A real master aims for the gap between the second and third cervical vertebrae. That's the sweet spot."

"Thanks for the advice. Also, I feel a bit sick." I slumped down onto the cold marble. "You're right. I'd be useless in a battle."

"No, I wouldn't say that."

"Really?" My hopes rose. Even learning a few simple moves would help, if I practiced enough? *Repetition teaches the donkey*, as the old Iraqi saying goes.

"Every army needs cannon fodder," said Kasusu cheerily. "Fine. Let's just get on with it. See that tabby over there?"

I did. The cat glanced at me with his mismatched green and white eyes. "You mean Sargon?"

"Grab that ax. I want you to fight him."

"I'm not going to hurt a cat!"

Kasusu hummed. "I'm sure you won't, but I want you to *try*."

Sargon rolled onto his back, wanting me to stroke his tummy. "I'm not using an ax."

"Whatever," replied the sword. "It's your funeral."

Sargon purred as I came closer, and he wriggled in anticipation of a sweet belly-rub.

"Nice kitty." I took another step, acting as casual as I could. "Pretty kitty."

Aw, he was swishing his tail.

𒀭𒈫𒌋𒐊 𒈬𒐊𒂖 𒀸𒋾𒄭𒈨𒐊𒌷𒄑𒐊𒌋𒐊

I reached down. "You want a cuddle? Come on—"

Sargon flipped onto his feet and *roared*.

The cabinets shook, and a suit of armor collapsed as the cat launched himself at me. He slammed all four feet into my face, claws tearing my cheeks. I fell over, and the cat leaped free.

Have you ever heard a sword laugh? It sounded like metal edges being scraped together, worse than fingernails on a blackboard.

I jumped back up, and the tabby prowled around me. "Wait a minute. He looks bigger."

"Lesson one in combat: Things are never as they seem," replied Kasusu. "So, do you want to go get the ax now?"

"La, shukran. I do not need an ax." I crouched, ready to duck, dodge, dive, weave, whatever was necessary to take this cat down. "Come here, you mangy fleabag."

He sprang.

Not like a small house cat, but like the kind of cat you'd find prowling the Serengeti. The beast slammed into my chest like a truck, sending me tumbling again. How could he have hit so hard? I tried to get up, but his claws ripped my forearm, and a swipe of his paw almost knocked out my molars. I threw my arms across my face as his teeth sank into my shoulder.

"The ax, Private!" yelled Kasusu.

"Get off me!" I yelled. I grabbed the tabby by the scruff of the neck and tried to push him off, with less than no success. How could he be so heavy?

Then Sargon leaped away, twisting in the air to land sure-footed on the marble floor among the fallen armor. He glanced at me—I swear he smirked—then settled down to lick his paws.

And that's when Belet returned, carrying a pair of wooden swords. She considered us warily. "How's it going?"

Kasusu gave his opinion. "The boy's going to die quickly and painfully in the first fight he's in. Though some of his enemies might also die . . . from laughing."

Belet sighed, then looked over at me. "At least we tried."

"That's it?" And here I'd thought she was smart. My bad.

"Ah . . ." Belet tossed the wooden swords in the corner. "At the very least I could turn you from a hopeless warrior into a merely useless one. But it would have the same result: You'd get killed in your first serious fight. Best not to encourage you. Next time you face an enemy, just shout really loud."

"I get it. To harness my internal strength, right?"

"So I might hear you and come running and save you."

That hurt, ego-wise. "Not even a pirouette hook kick?"

"You know what you'd get if you tried that?" she asked. "Groin strain."

FOURTEEN

IT WAS WEIRD NOT BEING ABLE TO GO BACK TO SCHOOL
on Monday morning. I thought I'd feel happy about it, but
when I tried to text my friends, they didn't even answer. It
was as if they thought they could catch something over the
internet.

I really wanted to go to see Mama and Baba, but I was
sure that the moment I walked back into Manhattan General
they'd seal me up in plastic and chuck me into deep quarantine for the rest of my life. I didn't know what to do with
myself. Belet was arguing with her mother—I think it was
about the dolphins in the swimming pool. Best to stay clear
of that family drama.

Instead, I found Daoud admiring himself in a standing
mirror. "Hey, cuz. What d'you think?" He turned slowly, his
arms spread out so I could admire his new suit from all
angles. The dark blue shimmered like the deep sea, as if there

were infinite depths within the color, and needless to say, it looked amazing on him. "You should have seen the price tag, but it's a Bertrand. Ishtar gave it to me."

"It's just a suit, Daoud."

"That's like saying a Ferrari is just an automobile."

"You going somewhere, or just wearing a hole in that carpet while you preen?"

He stopped. "What've you got in mind?"

What else was there? "See Mama and Baba. Somehow."

He nodded. "I'll go with. Let me change into something less fabulous."

The subway wasn't running, due to an electrical fire that had knocked out half the system. So we cut across Washington Square Park. From there it was a long walk east to Manhattan General. I didn't know how I'd get in to see my parents, but Daoud brushed off my worries. Apparently, he had a plan.

"Mo taught me how to ride a bike in this park," I said as we crossed the street.

"He tried to teach me the names of all the flowers," said Daoud. "In Latin, of course. I never got even one right. A flower's a flower, right? It's pretty and smells nice, and that's enough."

"Is that your feeling about people, too?"

"Beauty's got to be preserved, Sik."

"Don't you want to do something more . . . meaningful

with your life, Daoud? You and Mo were always hanging out together—you could have gone with him to Iraq. Helped people."

"He never asked me, Sik. Can you believe that?"

Actually, I could. He'd never invited me, either.

Then Daoud threw open his arms as if trying to embrace Manhattan. "But who could ever tire of all this?"

We reached the Washington Square Arch and stopped. "Something weird is happening here," I said.

Men were working with chain saws to take down the trees. Backhoes were pulling up stumps. People stared at the destruction, and one group was loudly confronting a police officer who was trying to make sure no one got killed by falling branches.

I stopped an elderly woman walking a small dog. "What's going on?"

"It's such a shame," she said, sniffling. "They say it's a blight—the trees are diseased. They have to chop them all down. Those beautiful trees."

And it wasn't just the trees. The flower beds had shriveled up and were crawling with the fattest, slimiest slugs I'd ever seen. Green gunk dribbled out of the fountain, and they'd cordoned off the arch with warning signs. A chunk had fallen off a corner and lay shattered into a thousand pieces on the ground.

"When did that happen?" I asked her, pointing to the arch.

𒀜𒌑𒅗𒂊 𒀜𒅀 𒃻𒊏𒅗𒐊 𒄩𒌍 𒀀𒐊𒅗 𒉌𒀜

"Last night, during a concert," she said. "It's a miracle no one was killed."

What had Ishtar said? *Nergal likes to play his cruel little games.*

Tears glistened on the woman's pale cheeks as a huge tree was heaved out of the soil. "My husband proposed to me by that oak."

"I'm sorry. I'm sure they'll replant."

She just sighed, and her dog pulled her away.

Daoud took my arm. "C'mon, cuz. It's too sad here."

"Leave all the talking to me, okay?" Daoud warned as we crossed the front lobby of Manhattan General. "We're just gonna act like we belong here."

I'd never seen it this crowded. People were camped out on the floor and along the corridors, and the line for any kind of vaccination was out the door and down the steps. Every staff member wore PPE, and I'd spotted two EMTs in full hazmat suits coming out of an ambulance.

Daoud nudged me. "Keep your head down and hood up."

I saw why. My face was on every health warning poster in the hospital. They'd used my school photo from last year, when I'd had the worst acne breakout imaginable. It had all cleared up suddenly afterward, but at that unique moment, my face was a mass of cherry-red—and cherry-size—zits. "I look like I'm about to explode."

"You have. You've gone viral—for real." Daoud handed me his phone. "You're trending higher than the Kardashian baby."

"What? Me?"

"Hashtag PlagueBoy. Mabrook—fame at last." Daoud frowned. "I must admit, I'm kinda jealous, cuz."

"Because everyone thinks I'm one of the horsemen of the Apocalypse?"

"Horsemen of what? Is that a Western?" Then Daoud punched the button for the elevator. "Fame is fame. Enjoy it while it lasts."

We got in and headed to the isolation ward at the top of the building. What would be waiting for us up there? A knot tightened in my guts. How would I even get to see my parents? "So, what's your plan, Daoud?"

He held out a pair of thick-framed glasses. "This. Geek Chic." He put them on and, using the mirror, parted his hair on the opposite side. "It's Archetype Number Fifteen: The Mousy Hottie."

"What are you talking about?"

"You know, the nerd in the front of the classroom who everyone ignores . . ." He rolled up his pants so they were way above his ankles. "But then, on the night of the prom, he has a makeover, takes off his glasses, does a hair flick"—which he demonstrated—"and suddenly . . . Ya salam! He's stunningly gorgeous! Who knew?" He adjusted the glasses so they were slightly askew on his nose. "Geek Chic is what I do."

The elevator stopped. We were on the top floor. "This is so not going to work."

"Trust me, I'm an actor."

Like I had a choice. I glanced around the corner. The nurse was a big, burly guy with tattoos on his hairy forearms. "I don't think he's your target audience."

"You'd be surprised about my target audience, Sik."

And in we went.

"You're not allowed up here," said the nurse. He didn't even look up from his screen.

Daoud cleared his throat loudly. "S'cuse me? S'cuse me? Need doctor?" He spoke in an unrecognizable accent. Sort of Mediterranean, sort of Indian, and sort of I-have-no-idea.

The nurse snapped his fingers and pointed back the way we came. "Press the big button with a one on it. You'll find all the doctors you want, pal."

Daoud turned and elbowed the vase of flowers off the countertop. He cried out and grabbed them just before they spilled all over the nurse's lap.

"Hey!" yelled the nurse, jumping up.

"S'cuse! S'cuse!" cried Daoud, still juggling the vase, each time almost dropping it on the nurse, no matter which way the guy jumped.

"Give me that!" The nurse reached out for the flowers and . . .

There they stood, both holding the vase, face-to-face, Daoud's specs precariously balanced on his nose.

"Your glasses are about to fall off," the nurse said softly.

"S'cuse?"

The frames clattered to the floor, and the nurse got the full impact of Daoud's big brown eyes and lusciously thick eyelashes, which he batted.

All the while Daoud's hair had fallen out of its neat side parting, and now it looked perfectly disheveled. I mean *perfectly*. He gave it a slight flick to shake his bangs out of his dreamy eyes.

The nurse actually sighed. "Look. I'll take you down to the first floor and find you a doctor."

He didn't even turn back to me—all his attention was on Daoud. I flattened myself against the wall and held my breath to be less noticeable.

Daoud put the vase back and collected his frames. He winked at me as the nurse led him to the elevator. Daoud held up the fingers of one hand just as the doors slid shut.

I had about five minutes. I needed to be quick.

I hardly recognized them. Mama and Baba lay within their airtight sterile chambers, buried under tubes and cables and lit only by the wall of monitors. IVs dangled next to their beds, respirators breathed for them, tubes fed them, and what little life they had left was kept going by machines. They'd lost weight and their muscles had withered on their bones. They were so pale.

I felt useless. I couldn't even reach out and touch them. I put my hands on the glass, hoping that some minute tremor, some tiny feeling, might travel through to them. My heart raced, and I wanted them to feel it beating. I'd tear it out for them right now if it would give them a chance to make it through another day.

"Salaamu alaikum, Mama. Salaam, Baba. I just want you to know I'm here. I'll get you out of here, I promise. You just hang in there a little longer. Please, you've got to stay with me. You have to."

I wasn't going to say good-bye. That would be giving up. That would be me saying I was a loser, and that my parents didn't have the strength to make it through. They did. They were the strongest people I knew.

I couldn't stand to lose the only heroes I had left.

"What am I going to do without you?" I asked them.

But it was my brother who answered. *You'll find a way to save them, Sik.*

"How? You were the smart one. My job is frying the onions. You should be here to save them, and then you could all live happily ever after."

They will *live happily ever after. You'll save them.*

"But how?"

The door swung open behind me. The nurse was back too

soon. "Listen, I'm sorry," I said, "but I got lost—"

A fly settled on the glass.

I spun around, fists clenched. "Get out, right now!"

The demon Idiptu took off his bowler hat as he waddled in on his thick bowed legs. He shivered. "I hate hospitals. Too many . . . cures."

"Get out," I growled.

"I ain't here for mischief, mate. I'm here 'cause the boss wants me to pass on a message." Then he shrugged. "Awright, a threat." He put his hand on the glass, smearing it with whatever foul fluid passed for his sweat. "Aw, ain't it tragic?" he said, peering at my parents. "And they were so peachy just a few days ago."

I could take a lot, deal with a lot, and turn the other cheek. I'd spent my life trying to avoid trouble, staying away from confrontation, but he was threatening my parents. I grabbed his head and slammed it against the glass.

Idiptu snarled and shoved me off. His eyes blazed with yellow fury, and his body quivered. "Normally I'd rip your arms off for that."

"Come and try it." I shook with a rage I'd never felt before. I could see my parents past his shoulder, and there was no way I was letting him get to them. No way.

Idiptu ran his long, disgusting tongue over his lips and face. The slime congealed on his cheeks and forehead, glistening sickly in the low light. He wasn't used to anyone standing up to him, at least not in a long while. . . .

"I know a story, but I'm fuzzy on the details. Maybe you can help me fill them in." I really wished I had my wok. "It's about Gilgamesh."

Idiptu twitched. His eyes narrowed to slits, and even through that thin gap, I could see his hatred for the name. "He's long gone."

"But there are tales of him wrestling Enkidu, killing the Bull of Heaven, and facing down some huge demon in a forest—cutting him clean in half, if I remember right." I smiled. "You must have met him at some point."

"And what if I did?" spat Idiptu. It might have happened thousands of years ago, but clearly the encounter still rankled.

"So tell me . . ." I leaned closer so I could whisper. "How hard did he kick your butt?" I could hear his teeth grinding. My smile broadened. "It still hurts, doesn't it? Is that why you walk like that?"

We glazed at each other until Idiptu, with difficulty, forced himself to relax. He brushed off his sleeves. "Give the boss what he wants and we'll leave your parents alone. You may be able to hide behind Ishtar's skirts, but these two? They're stuck here. The boss just needs to"—he snapped his fingers—"and it's bye-bye, dear old mum and dad."

He was bluffing. Reading demons is easier than reading people. People have so many things going on in their brain simultaneously that you have to work hard to figure out what they really want. Demons are much simpler. They only know how to make people afraid.

So I laughed. "Your boss can stuff his deal."

"What did you say?" growled Idiptu. Guess he wasn't used to getting back talk.

"You heard me." The fly crept along the glass as if looking for a crack so it could go in and feed on my parents. I slammed my palm on it.

Idiptu's eyes widened in shock. "How dare—"

"Shut up," I said matter-of-factly. "Now listen to me. If you or any of your fly-infested friends come within a hundred yards of my parents again, I will make sure your boss never ever gets his prize." I really wished I knew what that prize *was*, but I didn't want to reveal my ignorance to the toad. "From now on, I'm going to make it my life's work to be the"—I wiped my palm on his lapel—"fly in his hummus."

Idiptu ground his teeth. He was a degree or two from erupting, but I didn't care. I wanted to fight him. I may not have had any skill, but I had a belly full of rage.

"This ain't over," snarled the toad demon.

"You got that right," I replied.

FIFTEEN

"WHY WON'T YOU TELL ME WHAT YOU'RE UP TO, Mother?" yelled Belet from down the hall. "Or is it all just clubbing and shopping trips?"

"Please, Belet," replied Ishtar wearily. "It's all part of the plan."

"So how much progress *have* you made in finding Nergal?" Belet asked.

"Hush, Belet. Mother knows best."

"Why don't you share anything with me anymore?"

The kitchen door swung open, and they stared at me in surprise, as if it were unusual to find a teenage boy rummaging through the refrigerator at almost dinnertime. Ishtar rallied instantly by dropping her Dior purse on the countertop. "And how was your day, Sikander?"

"I saw my parents," I said. "And that toad demon, Idiptu."

"What?" exclaimed Belet.

"He must have been waiting there, knowing I'd turn up to see my parents sooner or later."

"Which is why you need to stay away," Belet continued. "You're lucky to be alive."

"What did he want, Sikander?" Ishtar looked intrigued. "To make a deal?"

"Yeah, er, how did you know?"

"That is Nergal's way," she said. "He'll fill you with self-doubt, fear, and paranoia, and even inspire betrayal. The mind suffers illnesses, too."

"So what happened?" asked Belet, looking amazed that I was here, all my limbs still attached.

"I slammed his head against the window."

Ishtar smiled. "There is a fighter in you after all."

"He was threatening my mom and dad." I tried not to tremble just thinking about it. "But if it had come to a fight, he would have torn me apart."

Ishtar looked around the kitchen, bemused. "Anyone know where the hot chocolate is?"

Belet sighed. "Third cupboard on the left."

"Ah." Ishtar took out the tin and handed it over to Belet. "Could you be a sweetie and make three mugs?"

Belet glared at her. "You don't know how to make hot chocolate? Really?"

"I'm sorry I don't know how to make hot chocolate! Does that make me a bad mother?"

There was a long and awkward silence after that. Belet was biting her tongue so hard I was surprised it didn't bleed. Then she huffed and headed for the teakettle.

"'Gilgamesh lied' . . ." said Ishtar as we gathered around the table with our drinks. "Why would Nergal write that? I cannot imagine what my brother-in-law is thinking. Gilgamesh wasn't the sort of hero who needed to lie about anything."

That wasn't exactly what Kasusu believed. I probably shouldn't have, but I asked, "Are you sure? I understand you two didn't get along very well . . . even though you're the goddess of love. It doesn't make sense."

Ishtar's eyes narrowed. "But that was how it was."

"Why would anyone reject you?" I asked.

"Why indeed?" said Ishtar. It might have been my imagination, but she looked a little tense. "Perhaps Gilgamesh *did* lie to Nergal about something, but whatever it was, it has nothing to do with me. What we do know is Nergal came to your home, Sikander, and he firmly believes that you, or more accurately, your brother, Mohammed, stole something."

"Are you sure he's got the right Mohammed? It is the most common boy's name in the world. There has to be a mistake. Mo would never steal."

"Perhaps he sent something home to you or your parents? To Daoud?"

"The only things he ever sent were seeds and plant cuttings for me to grow. I tried, but . . ." I blushed, thinking of all the pots that had remained barren and the fruitless work I'd done at the community garden. "Gardening's not exactly easy."

Belet scoffed. "You put seeds in soil and water them. Sounds exceedingly easy."

Ishtar patted my hand. "Not everything survives transplanting. What prospers in one place may wither in another."

That was pretty much the best description of my gardening efforts *ever*. "But Nergal thinks Mo sent me . . . what? The Holy Grail?"

"I can assure you the Holy Grail is quite safe in London," said Ishtar. "Now, I know you loved your brother, and we don't want to think ill of anyone we love, but this is important. Mohammed must have taken something precious from Iraq. I'm not saying he looted a museum, but he must have found something to drag Nergal out of Kurnugi."

"You're wrong! My brother never stole anything. Ever."

Ishtar sighed. "I know how love can make you blind. Your brother must have taken—"

"He did not!" I cried.

Ishtar stood up and the light seemed to warp around her. I could feel a tremor in my bones, and the mugs rattled on the table. "Sikander, do not—"

"Mother," snapped Belet. "Stop it. Right now."

She did. The mugs settled, and my pulse rate stopped heading toward a heart attack. I couldn't believe how quickly things had just flipped. I had to keep reminding myself of what Ishtar really was: a goddess of violence.

"If Sik says his brother never stole anything, then that's it," said Belet. "You need to have more faith in people."

That sounded funny coming from Belet.

But Ishtar didn't laugh. She poured her untouched hot chocolate down the sink and said, "Gods do not need to have faith in people. People need to have faith in their gods."

"This is ridiculous," I said, clutching one end of my mattress. "I do not need a babysitter."

"It was Mother's idea, not mine." Belet held the other end as we maneuvered it down the hall. "And she's sorry about losing her temper and nearly annihilating you."

"What? Did you say 'annihilating'?"

"She apologized, and that's what's important," Belet said hurriedly. "Look, I can't protect you if you're on the opposite side of the house."

I frowned. "And you're ready to fight dressed like that?"

Belet stopped. "Dressed like what?"

"You're wearing unicorn footie pajamas, Belet."

"So?"

"You have a tail and a horn. They're pink." I tried to be
diplomatic about this. "It's just not a look I associate with
you. I was expecting something more Xena, Warrior Princess
than . . . Disney princess."

She flicked the horn on her hood. "But unicorns are the
deadliest, fiercest, and most bloodthirsty of all creatures,
both mundane and supernatural. Their kill ratio is six times
higher than a dragon's."

"Really?" Wow, she really did have a different view of
the world.

"One stab with a unicorn horn and it's over. Doesn't matter how big and scaly you are. Mother had one when she
lived in Camelot." She reached for the knob of her bedroom
door. "In here."

The two of us struggled to drag in the queen mattress and
dropped it in the middle of the floor.

"My room's bigger," I said, looking around. "And has
actual furniture."

All Belet had was a small table, a single twin bed, and a
Louis Vuitton steamer trunk. Oh, and Kasusu on its sword
stand. It was worrying how inseparable they were.

"What's the point?" said Belet. "We'll be gone from here
soon enough. I think we're headed to Beijing after all this is
over."

"Oh." I'd just started getting, I dunno, used to her being

around. Then I reminded myself we weren't friends. Not real ones. Why should I be bothered if she left? "That must be cool, a new city every couple months. Your life's one big adventure. I wish I could go away, even for just a little while."

Belet handed me a pillow. "You don't take holidays?"

"Running a restaurant is hard. Spend a week at Disney World, and when you come back all your customers have gone elsewhere. Mo was the one who traveled. I stayed to, y'know, help out."

"You never wanted to go with your brother?"

"I thought I would. Inshallah."

"But he never invited you along?"

"I think he was waiting for when I was a little older." Whenever Mo had started planning a summer trip, I'd think, *Maybe this is the one. This time we'll go together and have our one big adventure.* "Flights are expensive, and we couldn't both be away from the deli." I shrugged. "You know how it is."

"At least you have a home, Sik." When Belet saw my expression, she added, "You will again, when it gets cleaned up." She tapped her massive trunk. "You'll have a permanent place to put out all your things and enjoy them. That's more than many people have."

"All you need are a few pictures." It didn't take much to make a home. Just memories.

"I have one. Right by the bed." Belet pointed to a small

photo in a frame on the nightstand. The photo had creases in it from being folded.

It looked much loved.

Belet picked it up and held it out to me. "The best picture in the world."

A man stood with his arm draped over his wife's shoulder, smiling easily. She was in the midst of laughing, her head thrown back and one hand catching a lock of hair that had slipped from her hijab. Behind them was a wall of emerald-green leaves sprinkled with white orchids.

"They look happy." I handed the precious photo back.

Belet brushed her finger lightly over the glass, as if she could still feel them. "My father was Dr. Faisal Amari. He worked at a children's hospital in Baghdad. My mother was Nadia, a civil engineer. Everyone told them to leave the city before it was too late, but they didn't. There were people who needed them." She paused as she gazed at the wrinkled picture. "They loved each other very much."

"Did you ever try and find any relatives? They must have had some brothers or sisters?"

She shook her head. "I never found any. They'd only been married a year and had a small apartment in the Mansour district."

"Mansour?" I laughed. "That's where my grandpa lived. How about that? In another life, we might have been neighbors. Hey, maybe they even knew him? He was pretty famous around there. Captain Heropants."

"Heropants? What are you talking about?"

"This was right in the middle of the war. The US army had taken Baghdad, but things were really dangerous." I pulled the tale from the memory bank, but it wasn't hard. Every refugee had a war story; this was the one my parents must have told me a thousand times over. "Our neighborhood had no water or power, but plenty of soldiers. It was all very tense, but we needed water and the Americans were controlling the supply. Grandpa decided to go speak to the soldiers, but they didn't trust locals to get too close. There'd been a suicide bombing a few days earlier. You can hide a lot under a kaftan."

"So what did he do?"

"Baba told me that Grandpa was a scrawny, short guy, just a lot of wrinkles and bone, and a mean temper. He wasn't scared of anyone or anything. So he went out to see the soldiers, dressed only in his underwear."

Belet laughed. "You're making this up."

"Bright red ones," I added. "Just like Superman. Grandma was scandalized and demanded a divorce there and then. He got the water running, though."

Belet gazed at her photograph. "Mother gave me this. She pulled it from the ruins of our home, along with me."

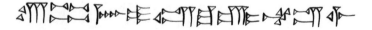

"I'm sorry," I said. "Still, it must be cool having a goddess for a foster mom."

"Is that what you think? Half the time she can't even remember my name."

"But she loves you, I can tell."

Belet scoffed. "She's the goddess of love. She loves everyone and everything. You should see how excited she gets over a new pair of Jimmy Choos."

I was starting to understand why Belet did everything so *hard*. She was always trying to be noticed by a distracted goddess, and to be worthy of her love.

Belet's demeanor changed. "I should be more grateful for her rescuing me. You have no idea what some girls have to do to survive war. I owe her my life. But how can I repay a goddess who already has everything?"

"It's not like that between parents and their kids."

"Could the both of you please shut up?" said Kasusu.

Belet stared at her sword. "You shouldn't be listening."

"Honestly. Do you think King Arthur sat at the Round Table whining like you two? No! He'd just pick up a shield, and we'd go out and kill a giant! That's how you deal with a problem, girl! You hit it very hard! Repeatedly!"

"Some problems can't be solved with violence," I said.

"You know what I call those problems?" sneered the sword.

𒀭𒈾𒄴𒂊 𒐀𒅍 𒄭𒈠𒅔𒊏 𒊕𒈨𒅗 𒂍𒐊𒂊 𒈾𒐊

"No. What?"

"Not problems," the sword declared.

"Life is simple when you're a weapon of mass destruction," said Belet.

Kasusu snorted. "Life's simple. Period."

Belet snored softly, and I stared at the ceiling.

I couldn't sleep. Too many thoughts were galloping through my head. Why was Nergal so convinced Mo had found something in Iraq? Had I been wrong about my brother? *Was* there some magical treasure hidden away back at the deli?

No, there wasn't. I'd trust him over a god any day of the week.

But I still couldn't sleep. I sat up. I needed to do something. Kasusu glistened.

"Let Belet sleep," I whispered.

"If you need help, just scream."

"Will do."

The cats prowled the moonlit corridors as I explored. One would pace beside me, as if keeping guard, then pass the duty on to the next. Everywhere I went, a cat's glowing eyes followed.

"Hello, Sikander."

I almost jumped out of my skin.

Ishtar stood in the shadows, smiling. It didn't look like

she was still mad at me. "Can't sleep? Me neither." She was dressed for a party, in a bloodred jacket, sleek embroidered pants, and six-inch high heels. "Gods don't."

"At all?"

She shook her head. "I wish I could. What a delight it must be to dream away the hours and wake up to a new day full of fresh possibilities."

"Sleeping's a waste of time," I said.

"I have time to waste. Endless amounts of it." She knelt down and stroked Sargon. "I use the quiet moments to listen to prayers."

"People still pray to you?"

She laughed. "What? Has love gone from the world? Are there no more heartthrobs left? No screen goddesses to adore or cheerleaders to pine for?"

"But you're the goddess of war, too."

"I no longer listen to those prayers." She patted a chaise lounge, and I sat down beside her. "I wish *I* could pray sometimes."

"What would you pray for?"

I could see words forming on her lips, but then she stopped herself. "What do you think of Belet?"

Uh-oh. I'd have to choose my words carefully. "She's . . . intense."

"I've tried to tell her to be a little more accommodating, but she's built a protective wall around herself. If she'd had a few siblings, perhaps she would have learned to trust other people. She still views herself as a war orphan."

"Orphans are tough. Just ask Bruce Wayne."

"Be her friend, Sikander. She will need you."

It sounded like Ishtar needed a friend just as much as her daughter did. "Er . . . how's Daoud?"

"Asleep. Three parties and a gallery launch tonight. He's attracting a lot of attention."

I scowled. Why wasn't she looking for Nergal?

She must have caught my expression. "Trust me, Sikander. I know what I'm doing. Well, except when it comes to Belet. You would have thought I'd have this down perfectly by now. It's hard being a single mother, even when you're a goddess. I cannot imagine how you mortals manage it."

I recalled the little girl I'd seen in Ishtar's World War II memory. "How many children have you raised? Before Belet?"

She stood up. "Let me show you."

SIXTEEN

WE WENT INTO A ROOM DOWN THE HALL WHERE PAINT-ings and photos covered the walls so completely, there was barely an inch of wallpaper exposed. Shelves overflowed with scrolls and books, and cabinets were stuffed with . . . toys?

In the nearest cupboard, I found a threadbare teddy bear and a G.I. Joe clutching a carved wooden rifle.

"Thought you might discover the corpses of my previous husbands?" She smirked. "Sorry, but I keep them in a ware-house in Queens."

I hoped she was kidding.

Hundreds of eyes, maybe even thousands, stared back at me from the walls. There were crude charcoal sketches on pieces of whitewashed plaster, carefully transplanted into a frame. On a piece of warped wood, I saw a faded painting of an old man in a toga. I paused at a yellowed photograph of a pair of Native American kids, one sitting on Ishtar's lap, staring blank-eyed at the camera.

"These are all your children?" I asked.

Ishtar picked a small rag doll from a shelf. "This was Fimi's. She was the only thing left living in her village—the militia had even killed the livestock. She'd spent two days hiding under her mother's body." She kissed the doll and replaced it gently.

I'd never heard her like this. Her voice sounded so fragile, nothing like the Ishtar I thought I knew.

She caught my gaze. "Not what you expect of a goddess, is it? I sometimes wonder what I truly am, how I came to exist. It is so easy to be called a god, yet I have my limits. More than you can imagine, Sikander."

"But think about everything you can do. The fact you're immortal. Who wouldn't want what you have?"

"Immortality is a sickness—a cancer. Your cells renewing and renewing endlessly." She stood in front of a small photograph in an oval frame. I could make out a smiling young man in a sailor's hat, posing in front of the USS *Arizona*. "Jacob always dreamed of being a sailor."

I heard a deep sadness in her tone. "No mother ever gets over the loss of her child."

"Why do you do it?" I asked. "Take them in, knowing you'll outlive them?"

"I am the goddess of love. How can I not?"

And the goddess of war. Was this her way of making

amends for that role? Every warrior who died for her on the battlefield had left a devastated family behind. And she'd been at it for *thousands* of years.

"The stories about you tend to focus on . . . other aspects of love."

Her laugh brightened the somber mood instantly. "Ah. You have to remember, many of the archaeologists were lonely Victorian men working far, far away from home and their wives. They tended to get . . . overexcited in their translations."

I looked at row after row of faces in photos, portraits, and sketches that stretched back in time—way, way back. Some were laughing, others gazed coolly at the viewer, others seemed distracted by something off to the side, not realizing that the moment would last forever. They came from all parts of the world. Some of her children weren't young. In one shot, Ishtar sat in the shade of a cypress tree, holding an old man's dark, wrinkled hand, his head as bowed as the branches. Yet he looked at me from beneath his red-checkered keffiyeh with eyes burning fiercely, refusing to be humbled by his age. Beside it was a photo of the same spot, though the paper had turned ocher with age, with a boy hanging upside down from those same branches while Ishtar laughed at his antics. I realized the old man and the boy were the same person—it was all in the eyes, the vitality undiminished despite the many decades.

Ishtar joined me in looking at it. "Ahmed at his family's orchard in Jordan. The boy wouldn't sit still. He'd had a good life, Sikander, but wanted me to be with him at the end of it."

"How can you bear the pain?" I asked.

She turned. "You tell me."

Tell her? How? I didn't know how to begin. Mo had been my world, and the day he'd died, all the memories, all the great moments, had turned into an ache that still lingered. "I don't have a choice. There are times I wish I could forget him. Forget what he meant to me."

"Listen to me, Sikander. There are only two things that are truly infinite, that transcend time and space. Love is one of them."

"And the other?"

"That is not for mortals to know." She gestured at a small frame. "Here's Belet."

She couldn't have been more than four or five, and she was glaring at the camera, her mouth turned down in a dangerous grimace. While dressed in a sparkly pink tutu.

"Oh, wow. She is never going to forgive you for showing me this."

"Isn't she sweet?" cooed Ishtar.

Sweet wasn't the word that sprang to my mind, but like all moms throughout history, Ishtar had a starry-eyed view of her child. And that's how it should be with parents, right?

The ballet teacher reflected in the mirror clutched her throat as if Belet was about to launch herself at her. Which, knowing Belet, was quite likely. "She hasn't changed much, has she?" I asked.

"Would you want her any other way?"

Belet's fierceness burned. You knew she would fight, no matter the odds, no matter how hopeless it all got. You wanted a Belet in your corner. As long as her blaze didn't get out of hand and destroy everyone and everything.

"I'm glad you are in her life," Ishtar went on. "She is going to need you."

"Why? She has you. . . ."

"Look after her, will you?" Ishtar patted my hand. "I know I can count on you to stick around."

"But Nergal is . . ."

Ishtar took something from her pocket. "I want you to have this."

She handed me a gold signet ring, and I didn't need to be an archaeologist to know it was ancient. The image was of a lion and a man facing each other.

"It's the king's seal," she said. "It might help you."

"Help how?"

"Return it to its rightful owner. You'll find him in Central Park."

The ring weighed more than it should. It was heavy with

responsibility and power. Judging by its extraordinary size, I had a suspicion the owner was just as extraordinary. "But who is—?"

She turned as Sargon entered the room. "Ah, the plan takes shape," she said to herself.

More cats arrived. Ishtar crouched down and gazed into the eyes of the black one.

"What's going on?" I asked.

While still communing with the cat, Ishtar said, "I didn't have the patience or enthusiasm to hunt down my brother-in-law. Instead, I ran around the city, attracting as much attention as I could. Daoud helped. Such a healthy-looking specimen."

Oh no. So much suddenly made a lot of awful sense. "You've been using Daoud as bait?"

"He is everything Nergal once was, and no longer is. I hoped to provoke Nergal, to attract him to me, and Daoud is *very* attractive." Ishtar stood up and the soft, reflective mother vanished. "Go tell Belet I need Kasusu."

"Are you really going to fight—"

She faced me suddenly. The eyes that had been so warm and compassionate just a minute before were now pitiless black stones, as dark and as dreadful as cold eternity. "Nergal is here," said the goddess of war.

SEVENTEEN

"BELET!" I RAN DOWN THE LONG HALL BACK TO THE bedroom. "Belet! Your mom needs you right now!"

"What's going on?" Belet rubbed the sleep from her eyes.

"Get Kasusu! Yallah!"

She went from three-quarters asleep to fully battle-ready in an eyeblink. Belet grabbed the sword, and the two of us dashed downstairs.

The cats wove around us in what could only be interpreted as feline impatience. Sargon stood by the front door, hissing, his back arched. The others looked just as agitated.

I sniffed. The foyer's usual rosy scent had been replaced by a hot, putrid odor.

Wrinkled, withered petals littered the floor, and all the huge bouquets were now just moldy stalks sagging in their vases.

A fly buzzed overhead. The black cat switched its tail and growled loudly. The fly took off.

Belet switched Kasusu from one hand to the other, her gaze darting to the big oak door.

A bad feeling was creeping up out of my gut. "Let's wait for your mom."

"Why? What's out there?"

I hesitated. Things were moving too quickly.

Belet started. "Nergal."

She swung open the door. The cats darted out first and leaped down the steps. Belet followed, rolling her wrists, and Kasusu made long whistles as it cut through the soggy air.

"Belet! Stay inside!" What was it about her? She constantly had to prove she was the best, even if it meant fighting a god.

She stood in the middle of the quiet, misty street in her unicorn pajamas. It was still a few hours before dawn, and beyond the small amber pools of light provided by the streetlamps, all else was dark. But creatures moved in that darkness.

Ishtar had asked me to look after her, so I joined Belet.

The huge creeping vine that cloaked the house had shriveled; the main trunk and stems sagged and dripped oily sap. The huge red flowers were gone, replaced with wrinkled, withered husks, the petals screwed up and decayed. Beady-eyed rats scurried along the vine, gnawing at it.

A hot, foul wind blew down the street, clogging my throat and making my eyes water.

Swarms of flies buzzed overhead, pulsating with anticipation. They gathered thickest at the north end of the street, around their god.

Nergal's pox-covered face peeled into a horrific smile. "Good morning, Niece."

Belet swapped Kasusu from hand to hand, her gaze locked on the monstrous giant.

Nergal's eyes fell on the sword, and he scowled. Then he pulled forward his own weapon, a twenty-foot-long steel scaffolding pole that had been converted into a crude spear. The tip had been hammered flat, and a jagged blade, three feet long and rusty, had been welded into place. He carried it as if it were made of straw.

One glance at Belet told me all I needed to know. She wanted to fight.

I had to stop her.

So I took a step toward them both. "Can you come back later? We're kinda busy right now."

Belet grabbed my sleeve and pulled me back. "What do you think you're doing?"

"Talking our way out of a painful death," I said from the side of my mouth. I didn't have any plan, but every second of not dying was a bonus. To Nergal I said, "It's just I was teaching Belet how to make a decent fatoush."

His cloak of flies buzzed angrily. "Fatoush?"

"Some things can't be rushed. Come back tomorrow? Maybe make an appointment?"

Nergal wasn't alone. Idiptu had gotten himself a replacement bowler hat, this one decorated with red ribbons. Sidana still had his top hat and was finishing off a pre-battle snack, which, from here, looked like a raw hot dog. No, scratch that—just plain dog. Behind them were another dozen or so monstrous creatures, no two alike. One even had the head of a fly and a stunted pair of semi-transparent wings.

This was the big showdown, so Nergal had brought all fourteen of his demons.

Still wearing my most confident smile, I whispered, "We're totally outnumbered. Let's run away."

Belet shook her head. "We've got the cats."

The kitties were between us and Nergal's crew, patrolling. This was going to be a short fight, and those cats were going to use up their nine lives pretty fast.

But the demons weren't making a move toward us. In fact, some of them seemed pretty worried about the cats.

Maybe the demons had good reason, because as I watched, the felines' hisses and purrs deepened into rumbling growls and they grew bigger, becoming . . . big cats. Literally.

The black one that had once sat on my lap had turned into a silky black panther, the gray tabby was a snarling leopard, and the tawny pair were now lions—one male, his head framed by a huge dark mane, and the other female. A hulking tiger stepped toward a cluster of demons, and its roar sent them scurrying behind Nergal.

And Sargon stood at the head of the lethal litter. He'd swapped his old, flabby shape for that of a lion the size of a rhino, fangs the length of cutlasses, and claws that could tear through tanks as if they were tin.

The odds were swinging waaay into our favor. "Now that is pretty special."

"You haven't seen anything yet," said Belet. "These are the lamassus."

"Lamassus?" I recognized the name. I vaguely remembered Mo showing me a picture of a lamassu in one of his archaeology books. "Weren't they guardian spirits or something? Didn't they have—"

Sargon shook his massive shoulders. Feathers sprouted through the fur. More and more gathered on his back, and a moment later, a pair of huge golden wings unfurled and flapped gently.

Any other day, any other week, I would have been really amazed. "Yup. Those."

Nergal sneered. "I've come too far, suffered too much to let a pack of feathered kittens get between me and my prize." He pointed at me. "Give me the boy and I will leave."

The demons gathered into packs, tensing for a charge.

The lamassus spread out. The panther perched on the roof of the house, muscles coiled and ready to swoop. The lions positioned themselves on either side of me and snarled.

"Give me the boy!" Nergal roared.

"He's under my protection, dear brother."

Ishtar walked down the steps and up in front of us. She moved with a feline, predatory grace, and I understood why the lion was her sacred animal: It was all about languid power. She looked lithe, elegant, relaxed, and deadly. Like the cats, she, too, had transformed. Nothing obvious and crude—she had too much style for vulgar displays of strength—but her entire being seemed more than human, as if her muscles were made of something far stronger than sinew and the heart beating in her chest pumped something greater than blood. Her skin shone as if bathed in moonlight. Ishtar certainly knew how to make an entrance.

She gave him an exaggerated frown. "Oh, dear. You look terrible. May I suggest moisturizer?"

The god growled. "Step aside, Ishtar."

She turned to Belet and held out her perfectly manicured hand. "I'll take it from here, sweetheart."

"Let me fight him, Mother. I know I can win."

"Belet." I spoke softly. "Please listen to your mom."

She looked at me, startled. Then, reluctantly, she held out the sword to her mother.

Ishtar smiled as she took the weapon. "I love you, Daughter."

"Now this is more like it." Kasusu hummed with contentment.

Ishtar walked into the space between us and Nergal. "You know how people say you can't fight in high heels?" She flicked the sword down once to her left, once to her right. The buckles fell from her Jimmy Choos, and Ishtar kicked them off. "They're absolutely right."

The air felt like it did before a severe thunderstorm: alive with unimaginable power. The asphalt under Ishtar's bare feet cracked, and everything around her and Nergal took on a hazy glow. The colors deepened, glorifying Ishtar and pushing Nergal into a darkness that verged on consuming existence. I swayed unsteadily, and Belet gripped my arm. "God surge. Reality is warping around them."

"So, Brother . . ." The buildings quivered at Ishtar's words. "Shall we show these mortals how gods fight?"

EIGHTEEN

"FIGHT, DEAR SISTER? WHY SHOULD WE FIGHT?"
Nergal lowered his spear. "You look tired, weary. There is no
joy in your face anymore."

"I have purpose," replied Ishtar.

Nergal scoffed. "Collecting orphans? Does that lift an
ounce of guilt? You have been among mortals too long. Gods
should not suffer guilt. You are the goddess of war. Cele-
brate!" He cupped a hand against his withered ear. "Can you
not hear the gunfire? The bombs falling across the world?
How many last breaths? Your name should be on the lips of
the dying." Nergal extended his palm. "You were great and
terrible in your beauty, Ishtar. Be so again."

Ishtar flinched. Each of his words hit her hard. Why?
Because they were all true. I had glimpsed her soul. I'd seen
her on the corpse-littered battlefields, filled with rapture. Part
of her wanted to enjoy the bloodshed, even now. She had

played the ditzy, glamorous mother to Belet, but now I realized it was all pretense. I saw what Ishtar was, or could be
again, and she was terrifying.

"Very well, Brother," said Ishtar, a cruel smile spreading
across her crimson lips. "If war is what you wish for, then
war is what you'll have."

Nergal's eyes narrowed. "Sister, you do not—"

She launched herself at Nergal, and the thunderous impact
shook the ground. Together they flew dozens of yards, crashing into a building. As they tore through the other side and
hit the asphalt again, the world warped and buckled around
them. Nergal hoisted a white van over his head, the metal
groaning in his grip, then hurled it at her. Ishtar leaped out
of the way. Barely tensing her legs, she shot up over one
of the apartment buildings, Kasusu shrieking with metallic
laughter.

God surge. That's how they did the impossible. You
couldn't jump hundreds of feet in a single blink unless dis-
tances shrank at your will. You couldn't lift a three-ton vehicle unless you adjusted gravity, and how could you survive
piling through a building unless you were able to manipulate
energy?

While most of Nergal's demons milled around warily, one
skittered into attack mode. It ran on too many legs and had
heads all over its torso, fanged and dripping with venom. It
pounced at Ishtar from behind—I yelled a warning—but the

goddess flicked Kasusu over her head and neatly bisected the monstrosity. Black bile oozed out of its sliced body.

Nergal roared as he flung another car at his sister-in-law. It missed her but took out the corner flower shop. The building began to totter.

I grabbed Belet's hand. "We've got to get people out of here."

Even as I spoke, doors were swinging open and residents, some still in their pajamas, were stumbling out. One old guy still had a bowl of cereal in his hand. "Is it an earthquake?"

I let go of Belet and waved people toward the far end of the street. "Just run!" I told them. Belet left me to direct others away from the monsters and destruction.

I dashed up to the next brownstone and began banging on the door. "Everyone out right now!" More people spilled out, dazed, confused, and frightened.

"Sik! Sik!"

Daoud shouted from Ishtar's doorway, looking frantic. Or as frantic as you can while wearing an avocado face mask.

"Run, Daoud!"

He staggered down the front steps to join me and stared in horror at the carnage. Then he gasped. "My portfolio!"

"Ya Allah!" I took both his arms and tried to shake some sense into him. "You have to be joking! Leave it! It's not important!"

"It's everything, Sik! You don't understand!"

The whole street trembled and cracks formed in the walls of Ishtar's house. It was going to come down and still Daoud was pulling toward the door.

"Listen to me, Daoud. Really listen," I dug my fingers into his arms. "I know how much Mo meant to you."

Daoud faced me, and for the first time, I saw the pain in his eyes. "More than you know, Sik."

"He'd want us to look out for each other, right?"

He nodded.

Phew. I loosened my hold. "C'mon. Let's get out of—"

Daoud tore away and ran back into the house.

"Daoud!" What was he doing? The front door splintered, and I saw the chandeliers swinging wildly in the foyer. Priceless artifacts tumbled off their pedestals, shattering on the marble floor. But I'd meant what I said. I had to go after him.

"Sik!" screamed Belet, running toward me.

Nergal dropped 12 Venus Street on Ishtar. It had little effect on her—she zoomed upward as though the bricks were made of Styrofoam—but number 10 began leaning into the already crumbling number 8, and the whole north side of the street was going to fall like a line of dominoes.

You know what people do when they face danger, death, and destruction? Yeah, they get out their phones and start recording.

"I don't believe it," Belet muttered.

"That's because you're not from around here." I cupped

my hands around my mouth and yelled at a twenty-something guy. "You! Run! Now!"

He didn't. He stayed exactly where he was, trying to find the best angle, right until the sidewalk opened next to his feet. *Then* he started screaming and running.

I took Belet's hand. "C'mon. Let's go and—"

Then we both turned as something crashed down behind us.

How can I describe this new demon? Start with a silver-back gorilla, remove the fur, add scales, and stick an extra pair of arms in the wrong places. It swung itself forward on its knuckles and snarled.

Belet stood her ground, fists raised high and close. "Long time no see, Saghulhaza. You still licking Nergal's feet?"

Of course she would be on a first-name basis with the monsters.

I tried to get past the gorilla demon, but it growled and two pairs of claws stretched out from its fists.

I stepped back. "Remember, Saggy, your boss wants me alive."

It smiled and said in a screechy voice, "Alive, but not necessarily whole."

The demon spun around as Sargon, now a giant winged lion, swooped down on it, burying his claws into its back and fangs into its neck. The two tumbled into the ruins, tearing out chunks of feathers, fur, and scales.

"Got it!"

Daoud stood at the doorway, waving his portfolio. He jumped down the steps as the house crumbled behind him and dashed straight for Ishtar's Jaguar, which was parked out front and, miraculously, had escaped damage. Had Ishtar gifted it to him? Regardless, he opened it with the key fob and tossed the precious portfolio in the back seat. "Yallah, guys!"

I wasn't leaving, not without Belet, and she wasn't leaving without Ishtar, and Ishtar wasn't leaving until Nergal was dead. So we were all staying put. I shot a look at Daoud. He bit his lip, unable to decide whether or not to go. His decision was made when Ishtar's brownstone collapsed, turning into a pile of rubble. Daoud slammed his foot on the gas pedal and roared away.

The nearest fashion boutique suddenly cracked in half as Ishtar smashed Nergal through the glazed facade and most of its support columns.

Ishtar paused and glanced back at me.

We had a deal. She wanted to know that I'd honor it.

Be her friend, Sikander. She will need you.

Belet saw me nod at Ishtar. "What's going on? Sik?"

The goddess smiled. She lifted her sword and went into the dense cloud of dust after Nergal.

Then the air was cut by a high-pitched keening, rising until my ears ached.

The building erupted. Belet and I jumped behind a car as the street was filled with millions of shards of razor-sharp glass. The sound was almost musical, as if we were under a waterfall of tinkling diamonds.

I glanced over the hood.

The fashion boutique was cloaked in dust.

Then Ishtar stumbled out of the ruin, dragging Kasusu along. Her clothes were bloody and torn and her hair disheveled. From the way she limped, it looked like her leg was injured.

Belet gasped. "Mother!"

Ishtar shook dust out of her hair and waved.

Where was Nergal? Was it over?

The store was covered in a cloud of orange brick dust that was hard to see through. But it looked like just one wall remained standing.

I turned toward the howl.

One of Nergal's demons had broken through the debris. It was a mangy creature, half dog, half lizard, and the size of a calf. It barged past the panther lamassu, and its claws skittered on the cracked street as it charged straight for me.

"Belet!" cried Ishtar. She hurled Kasusu toward us in a high arc.

A lot happened simultaneously—I'll try to break it down. I grabbed a brick and swung. But I was too panicked and too early and missed the beast's snout by a second. The sword flashed in the corner of my eye, because the rest of my attention was on the demon as it opened its mouth to chomp off my head.

Belet leaped.

She grabbed Kasusu out of the air as the demon's putrid breath choked me. She spun like a ballerina and slashed downward.

The demon's eyes blazed scarlet with bloodlust. It stretched out its neck to reach a little bit farther. . . .

Kasusu did the rest.

The head spun onward as the body collapsed right by my feet. The hind legs scrabbled wildly in the air for a few seconds before the message got through: It was dead.

Syrup-thick green blood oozed from the stump.

"Nice," said Kasusu. "Right between the second and third vertebrae."

The last standing wall of the clothing store cracked and tumbled down with a dull rumble.

Nergal raised his rusty spear as Ishtar spun to face him.

Belet cried out even as she started sprinting toward her mom, but she didn't have the strength to throw Kasusu the necessary two hundred feet.

Nergal tightened both hands around the haft of his spear and roared as he thrust forward.

The deadly point went straight through the center of Ishtar's chest.

Belet screamed.

The tip tore out of Ishtar's back. The lamassus roared and abandoned their battles to sprint in to help their mistress, but it was too late. Nergal leaned back, hoisting Ishtar into the air.

Filled with blind fury, Belet and I charged him.

The lamassus struck first and Nergal pulled out the spear to defend himself, but he instantly vanished under a mass of frenzied big cats.

As Belet fought two more demons, I reached Ishtar first. She lay there, tears swelling in her eyes, but there was a smile on her face. "I'm glad Belet has you, Sikander. Defender of the World."

"But you're a goddess," I said, not knowing what to do. "You can't die."

She laughed, and winced. "I think this proves otherwise."

Belet joined us then, just in time to receive Ishtar's gaze. "Of all my children, I think I might have—"

We're told we're made of stars. That every atom in us originally came from a shining light at the heart of the solar system. With Ishtar it was obvious. She glowed brighter and brighter as she disintegrated back into the starlight she'd been created from.

Belet knelt down, staring at the empty space.

The lamassus were flagging. Now that their mistress was gone, they'd lost their will to fight. Nergal threw off the tiger and grabbed the panther around the throat, his massive hand easily encircling its neck.

I took Belet's hand. "I'm so sorry, Belet. But we have to get away from here."

"I have to fight!" she yelled, squirming in my grip.

"We've lost, Belet! We need to run!"

She stared at me, her face pale. "Lost?" She sagged as if all her spirit had bled out, and Kasusu dropped from her limp fingers. There was nothing left to keep her going. She'd never failed before, and she didn't know how to handle defeat.

I did. "Get up, Belet. You've done all you can for now. And don't forget your sword."

Belet looked over at Kasusu. "My sword?"

Nergal dropped the now-lifeless panther. The surviving lamassus began to retreat, and the remaining demons grew bolder. Nergal turned his gaze in our direction. "Get the boy. Alive. Belet can join her mother."

At last, Belet shook herself into action. Grabbing Kasusu, she jumped to her feet, glaring at the plague god.

"Leave him," I said, pushing her in the other direction. "This is not the time. Start running."

I was surprised when Belet obeyed. She sprinted ahead and vanished around the corner and into the darkness.

I might have been able to catch up. I could've pushed myself a little harder, and the two of us could have raced into Midtown. I wanted to run and run and not look back.

Then what?

Nergal's demons had our scent, and most had twice our number of legs. They'd capture us easily and tear Belet to pieces, just to get to me.

I couldn't let that happen to her.

I slowed down, stopped, and raised my hands. "I surrender."

The demons crowded around me. No longer the entire fourteen—the battle had taken its toll—but I was disappointed to see that Idiptu and Sidana were still alive. Sidana doffed his top hat. "The master wants a word, my dear." Then he grinned. "And it will hurt you much, I fear."

NINETEEN

———✦———

"END OF THE LINE," JOKED IDIPTU AS HE DROPPED me in the dirt. Demons were perched all around me on derelict equipment and abandoned train cars like the audience of a gladiatorial match. They watched me with hungry eyes and frothing mouths. I counted ten injured survivors out of the original fourteen. But four dead demons were nothing compared to one dead goddess. Nergal had come out way on top.

The ground shook as a distant rumble increased in volume and the wreckage around us vibrated. A moment later, a freight train thundered past on the other side of the broken fence that separated the tracks from this junkyard. The air was split by the shriek of the heavy iron wheels, which threw spinning sparks over the rails as one car after another rattled past.

Where was I? It was nighttime and Manhattan glistened

to the west not far away, so I was in Queens. That meant I was in Sunnyside Yard, the massive, sprawling labyrinth of tracks that led into different train routes and across the entire country.

The demons had dragged me underground after I'd surrendered. I'd been pushed and shoved through dark subway tunnels with the monsters howling and snapping at my heels the whole way. I'd heard trains and seen the flashing lights of engines on nearby tracks, but our tunnel had held only rusty tracks and broken cars. Nergal had secret access to the entire city. No wonder the transportation system was collapsing.

The plague god himself squatted on a throne made of old, stripped-down locomotives. He groaned as his demons licked his wounds. Flies nestled over patches of his dried blood, feeding happily. His eyes fluttered, the raging yellow now dimmed.

One of the demons, a mangled-looking mix of crow and man, crouched beside him and offered a dead rat. "You need to eat, my lord. Come, feed on this fresh—"

Nergal, ignoring the rat, grabbed the demon by the throat. "Yes . . . eat . . ." he muttered. He opened his mouth.

The crow demon thrashed his wings and squawked as the god's jaw cracked open wider and wider. Nergal's oily black tongue caressed his face.

I couldn't help but stare, even though I knew what was

about to happen. I recognized Nergal's look—I'd seen it before on the faces of a thousand famished customers. . . .

The other demons laughed and jeered as feathers flew and Nergal shoved the struggling crow man in. He still kicked his scaly feet even as Nergal's throat bulged to grotesque proportions.

"Bite, snap, slurp, and crunch!" chanted Sidana. "Here comes a bird for the master's lunch!"

Other demons ran up to help force the meal down. The crow demon wasn't giving up, and Idiptu had to beat him in with his fists until, with a puff of black feathers, he disappeared all the way into Nergal's belly.

My list of Most Disgusting Things Ever had a new number one.

The demons cheered. They replayed the devouring, mocking their companion's struggles with malicious delight. Pain and suffering were their amusements.

Now there were nine of them left.

I stood up and brushed the dirt off my clothes. "Well, here we are. What do you want?"

Nergal's cloak of flies buzzed with fury. Hornets circled me, and shiny bluebottles buzzed in my face. I tried to ignore them and not swallow any.

Nergal's mucus-filled eyes blinked slowly. "You know what I want, boy." Then he glanced down at his forefinger, crawling with flies, and popped it in his mouth and sucked the buzzing insects off. A few fled through the holes in his cheeks; the rest he mashed up and swallowed.

Yuck. "Need some bug repellent? Maybe a better diet?"

Nergal and the demons weren't the only inhabitants here. Stray dogs pawed at overturned trash cans and torn garbage bags, scrounging for leftovers. They were mangy, some with patchy fur, others bare, their pink bodies swollen with deformities. One had a fifth leg hanging uselessly from its hip, and another had no ears, just a pair of holes. One caught my gaze and snarled.

I froze. It wasn't a dog. It was a man wearing a torn fur coat. His eyes blazed with rabid anger.

Nergal followed my gaze and smiled. "My plague dogs. Are they not beautiful?"

"You turned people into . . . that?" I tried not to vomit. "Why?"

"Because I can." He furrowed his brow. "You do not see the beauty, do you? You have spent too long basking in Ishtar's light."

Nergal laughed, then erupted into a chest-racking coughing fit, bending over double in agony until it passed. He looked around, eyes wide with confusion, muttering in a language I didn't understand. Who was he talking to? He reached out for something, or someone, then seemed to wake. He shook his head.

Despite the fear infiltrating every atom of my body, I felt—very briefly—some pity for the ugly god. He was old, sick, and lonely, his mind wandering to long-faded days of glory and adoration.

"You should go home," I said.

"Home? When my business here is not yet finished?" He drew himself to his full height, and my pity now felt completely misplaced. He was still a god, and I was, as the phrase went, just a puny mortal. "Now that Ishtar is gone, there is no one left to oppose me."

"Someone will," I replied.

He laughed. "Oh, you have heroes in this day and age? Pray, name one."

A person who would dare go up against a giant, disease-ridden immortal? Okay, no one immediately sprang to mind. . . .

Nergal's laugh descended into a hacking cough. As he wiped the bloody spittle from his mouth, the god gazed at me. "Humans no longer have any heroes to protect them. None of the caliber of the legends of old, like Gilgamesh."

"Ishtar said you were glorious once, like him. What happened?"

Nergal slammed his fist into the iron. "I am glorious still! Do you not know who raised humanity out of the quagmire of the Dark Ages?"

"Let me guess. . . . You're gonna say it was you?"

He beat his chest. "Indeed! With my plague! Half of Europe was decimated by the Black Death, forcing society to evolve! If not for that, you would still be digging for roots, a serf forever bound to your master."

"Yeah, villains always think they're doing things for the greater good."

"I am the lord of decay, of plagues, of mental illness, and of rot. And it is from these things that we become greater than we were before. As we decay in the soil, do we not nourish it? As plants rot, does not the garden grow? And who can distinguish genius from madness? Boy, you do not see what is plain in front of you."

"I certainly see plenty of insanity." I'd been so terrified for so long, I'd come out on the other side. I was surrounded by demons and standing only a few feet away from a god of disease, and yet I could stare him in the eye without flinching. Had I gone insane, too?

As he clambered stiffly off his perch, his pain was obvious. Everything he touched corroded and flaked. The dense iron of the locomotive rusted from his mere presence, and the paltry patches of grass shriveled and died under his feet. Nergal corrupted everything. "So many people in this city . . . So much filth and pollution, just below the surface. All it needs is a little stirring to bring it bubbling out of every gutter and drain. The people are ripe, boy—ripe for squeezing. And then we shall let their foulest thoughts and deeds *pour* out. And from that a new world will blossom."

His gaze drifted to the glowing Manhattan skyline. Hunchbacked, he dragged himself over to me, and despite his size, we were eye-to-eye. "Where is it, boy? The treasure your brother stole?"

"Mo never stole anything. Not from anyone. He even shared his tips with me."

Nergal growled. "It is unwise to defy a god."

One of the demons cackled. "A plague, my lord. One that boils his spleen and rots his lungs."

"No, no, no," whispered another, one with a slimy reptilian face. "Infest him, sire, with maggots in his flesh and spider eggs in his eyes. Put larvae inside here"—it tapped its forehead—"so he can hear them buzzing as they grow."

"BZZZZ! BZZZZZZ!" said the fly-faced demon, rising a few feet on its stubby wings with excitement. "BZZZZZZZZ!"

The others clapped and hollered, "Yes, my lord! What Tirid said!"

Nergal smiled, wrapping his fingers around my collar. "Tell me, or I shall contaminate every cell in your body. Though I do think Tirid's suggestion is fine indeed."

"Let go of me!" I struggled hopelessly. "And Mo didn't steal anything!"

"Liar!" roared Nergal. "It is here! It has to be!" He dangled me like a rag doll. "My patience runs thin."

I wasn't getting anywhere, and he was ready to do . . . whatever Tirid was buzzing about. It took me a few seconds to appraise my situation. I was alone, surrounded by cannibal demons, at the mercy of a god, far from home, and without so much as a fork for a weapon. Against all this I had . . . what, exactly?

A lifetime of customer service experience?

Not just any customers, but the most impatient, demanding, and critical on the planet: New Yorkers.

And maybe that might be enough. . . .

I waved my hands in front of him. "Okay, okay, I'll tell you. You win."

Nergal's eyes narrowed, but he let me go.

I hit the ground hard. I got up slowly, taking a good look around. My chance of survival was bleak, verging on nonexistent. There was a hole in the chain-link fence that separated us from the rails and the long lines of empty cars. If I could get through it, I'd find a million hiding places and maybe, just maybe, get away. But the distance from here to the fence was blocked by a host of demons.

I needed their help if I was to escape.

You have to be a master psychologist to run a deli. Hundreds of people come through your door each day, each wanting something different and all demanding they get it first, believing their needs are the most important in the world. My job, day in and day out, was to make every one of them *believe* they would get exactly what they wanted. In short, I needed them to trust me.

If I got this wrong, it wasn't just a one-star review on Yelp; it was a fast trip down Nergal's feather-lined gullet.

I coughed and loosened my collar. "In . . . in a minute. I think I swallowed a fly." I looked over at Tirid. "Maybe a relative of yours?"

One of the other demons laughed. Tirid spun around. "BZZZZZZZ!"

Another demon, a pustule-covered man with waxy skin, snarled back at Tirid. "Come on, then, try it and I'll swat you."

This was my chance.

"It's no good." I coughed again and looked over at Idiptu, giving a helpless shrug. "Hand it over."

Idiptu frowned. "What?"

I faced Nergal, my face the perfect mask of openness and honesty. "He took it the night you attacked the deli. He said he'd kill me if I told anyone, but I guess I'm more afraid of you. Totally terrified, to be honest."

Rat-faced Sidana turned on his companion. "Idiptu, could these words be true? I thought there were no secrets between me and you!"

I laughed. "Secrets? He's got plenty. Ever since . . . er . . ."

Sidana stared. "How long do you plan to hold that against me? You said you didn't want dead Roman for tea!"

"Yeah, the Roman thing," I said hastily. "He and . . . Tirid are . . . you know."

Tirid joined in. "BZZZZZZZ!"

"Just hand it over!" I yelled at Idiptu.

Idiptu whirled this way and that. He didn't know who to face first: the stunned Sidana, the buzzing Tirid, or Nergal, who was slowly turning his massive frame toward the squat, bowler-hatted figure.

Idiptu threw himself to his knees. "It's not true, my lord! The mortal's lying."

I smirked. "If I'm lying, how did I know about the Roman?"

"BZZZZZ!"

Sidana snarled at the fly demon. "I have had it with your lies. And your many roving eyes."

They were demons. They fed on hate, jealousy, and betrayal. The cracks were all there—I had just widened them a bit more. Only their fear of Nergal held them together. But at this moment, with half of them mauled from the fight with Ishtar's lamassus, and Nergal bleeding from a dozen wounds, tempers were bubbling out of control. Under more normal circumstances, the god could have commanded them with a snap of his fingers, but not tonight.

I laughed loudly as I looked over at Idiptu. "You were right about Sidana. That rhyming does get irritating real quick."

Sidana screamed as he dived at Idiptu. Fly-faced Tirid joined in, his wings slapping another demon, who bit at them. Soon all nine demons were tearing and clawing at each other. Nergal stared in bewilderment, his shouts falling on deaf ears.

And I ran. Around them and through the hole in the fence.

Empty passenger cars, graffiti-covered boxcars, and lifeless engines packed the yard. I had dozens of tracks to cross before I'd hit a concrete barrier. Beyond that was freedom.

The tracks under my feet rattled as a stark white light suddenly bathed the darkness. I jumped just before the locomotive roared past, its wheels shrieking as one car after another rumbled by.

Nergal yelled out commands, and there was a sharp cry of pain from one of the demons. I hoped it was Sidana.

A light shone in the distance. Another train was approaching. I looked back and two of the demons appeared around the side of a car. They spotted me and gave chase.

I hopped and stumbled over the rails. They were half-hidden in the darkness, but I couldn't risk being careful.

The engine horn blared its warning.

The two demons dropped onto all fours to gallop.

"Stop him!" Nergal tore down the chain link near him. He knew that if I made it over the concrete wall, he'd lose me.

I ran, my eyes straight ahead, ignoring the train coming in from my left.

"Allahu Akbar, Allahu Akbar . . ." I repeated the takbir with every gasping breath.

The horn sounded again as I stepped on the active track.

I was just about to clear it when I heard Nergal roar behind me.

A god surge exploded from him. He threw out a wave of pestilence and decay. The air turned thick and foul, as if I'd been dipped into a cesspit. The vegetation, feeble as it was, died, and the earth cracked open.

Sparks flew as the rusty rails tore from their fixings. Metal screamed against metal.

The oncoming locomotive came off the twisting tracks.

The massive wheels tore deep trenches into the hard soil, the engine screamed, and my world contracted to noise and the stark, blinding headlight.

The momentum was unstoppable. The engine had to weigh at least twenty tons, and there were dozens of box-cars behind it, each one shoving it forward.

I managed to get to my feet, but I knew it was too late. The train swung around as it slid; then it began to roll, showering me with gravel and debris.

I wasn't afraid; I was sorry. My past didn't flash before my eyes—they were too blinded by the headlights—but the future

I'd never have did. Would Belet survive? What would happen to my parents? Who was going to stop Nergal?

And yet . . . and yet . . . there was one thing that made me smile.

"I'm coming, Mo."

The train hit. I didn't feel anything.

TWENTY

"POOR KID," SAID A TIRED-SOUNDING VOICE. "YOU CAN put up a thousand warning signs and still they jump the fence."

"They're young. Think they're gonna live forever," replied a gruff, second voice.

"This one ain't."

The second guy sighed. "They'll shut down the whole system after this."

"At least he didn't go under the wheels." The tired voice continued. "I've seen worse."

"Dead is dead," said the gruff voice.

What was going on? What had happened? I had a bad feeling about this. . . .

* * *

"Yes, I knew him. Sikander Aziz. He was my friend," said . . . a girl.

But who? It was hard to make sense of all this, and yet I recognized the voice.

"Aziz?" asked an older voice. "Do you know his parents?"

"They're in the hospital. You've heard about the recent outbreak? They're victims of that."

"Oh. I thought the name rang a bell. Patients zero, aren't they?"

"Something like that."

"Thank you, Miss . . . ?"

"Belet. Just Belet."

"No last name? Guess that's modern parents for you."

"Quite the opposite," said Belet. Then footsteps receded and a door opened and closed.

The older voice hummed. "Sikander Aziz. Tag him and let's break for lunch."

A really bad feeling . . .

I awoke and instantly banged my head as I tried to sit up.

Where was I? There was no light, and I could barely move. I was in some kind of freezing-cold metal box. I hit the ceiling a few inches above me. "Hey!"

What was I wrapped in? Definitely not Ishtar's silk sheets.

And why did I stink of antiseptic?

I realized I was in a clear plastic bag. I started to panic. "Hey!"

Someone shouted, and there was a crash.

I kicked hard even as I clawed at the bag. "Let me out!"

My tiny dark prison shook, and I was suddenly dragged out into the light. Someone fumbled for the bag zipper and pulled it down. I blinked, and when the blur gave way to clarity, I met the horrified gaze of a man wearing glasses and a white lab coat.

I sat up. "Is this some sort of prank? I could have suffocated in there!"

He stumbled backward and grabbed a chair for support. "I assure you it's not. We don't pull pranks down here."

I was in a surgical room of some sort. Two metal tables dominated the center of the space and one was . . . occupied.

By a body. That was opened up.

"Where am I?" Though I was beginning to have a pretty good idea.

"The fridge," the man mumbled, backing away from me. "I mean, the morgue."

"And . . . why?" Though I was beginning to have a pretty good idea about that, too.

"You were . . . You were brought here. There was . . . an accident at the . . . at the rail yard." He clutched his chest. "Oh, dear."

"And you are . . . ?" I turned around slowly. The wall behind me was made up of a dozen steel drawers.

"Dr. Brian Walker. I'm . . . I'm the city coroner," he said, turning a little pale. "I think I . . . I . . ."

"Did Daoud put you up to this?" I swung myself off the drawer. "And where are my clothes?"

"I'm feeling faint." He sank into his chair, his pallor turning gray. Which was not a good color on him.

And while on the subject of not-good colors, I caught my reflection in the shiny chrome drawers. I was a mess of multi-colored bruises and bore so many cuts it looked like I'd been tattooed in cuneiform. I turned my plastic shroud into a kilt and jumped from one foot to another on the chilly floor. The cold was the only thing stopping me from freaking out.

The old guy panted. "Oh, dear," he said again.

On the counter, I spotted a file with my name on the tab. I opened it to see the word *crushed* on the top line, so I decided not to read the rest. The lion ring Ishtar had given me sat in a tray along with my house keys and the broken pieces of my phone. I took the ring, and as I searched the rest of the counter, I found the guy's packed lunch. I helped myself to an apple and saw another smartphone nearby. "Can I borrow this?"

"Excuse me, young man," he murmured. "Could you get a nurse? My chest feels very . . . tight. I think I'm going into cardiac arrest."

𒀭𒌓𒌁𒈨 𒀭𒅀 𒁁𒅖𒌋 𒒐𒅕𒌋 𒁁𒅊𒈨 𒈜𒀊

I poked my head out the door and saw a nurse at the end of the corridor. She dropped her coffee cup when I said, "Hey! The guy in here's not feeling so good."

I ducked back into the lab and, trying hard to avoid looking at the body on the table, opened the cabinet doors under the counter instead. I found a bag of blue scrubs and a pair of black sneakers.

"She'll be right with you," I told the old guy.

But when I peeked outside the room again, the nurse hadn't moved. She just stared at me, agape. I smiled at her. "I'd hurry if I were you. And is there a restroom nearby?"

She gestured down the side corridor, her hands shaking. "Third door on the left." Then she backed away, giving me a wide berth, only turning to dash into the morgue at the last moment.

I scurried barefoot into the restroom. I checked to make sure it was empty, then punched a number into the phone. It rang twice.

"Who's this?" answered Belet. "How did you get this number?"

I never thought I'd say this, but I was genuinely happy to hear her voice. "Belet, it's me. Sik."

"Sik?" asked Belet. "Is this a joke?"

"Apparently not, according to the coroner."

"Who is this?" snapped Belet. "I don't find this remotely funny."

"Meet me at the masjid," I continued, ripping open the scrubs bag.

It went quiet on the other end.

"Belet?"

"Is it really you?" she whispered.

"It really is. How soon can you get to Dar al-Islam?" I picked up the pair of sneakers.

"No, not there. It might be confusing," she said. "Imam Khan is leading Salat al-Janazah prayers, for you."

I pressed the sneakers against my soles to size them up. "Why? You only say them when someone's . . ."

A tag dangled from my big toe.

SIKANDER AZIZ. AGE 13. DOA.

"Oh," I said. "Yeah, that could be awkward."

"You think?" replied Belet. "There's a Wendy's near the masjid. I'll be there in twenty minutes."

"Don't be late." I stared at the tag, rereading it over and over, hoping the words might magically change. "I've had a strange day."

TWENTY-ONE

"WILL YOU STOP THAT?" I SAID AS I SHOVELED IN MY
fourth helping of baklava.

"Stop what?" asked Belet.

"Staring at me like . . . like you've seen a ghost." Wow, the
fourth piece was as good as the first. I wondered how a fifth
might taste? Only one way to find out. . . .

There had been a hug, albeit a pretty awkward one. It
was hard to know what to say in this kind of situation. Then
Belet had taken me straight to a discreet boutique hotel called
Nineveh, whose manager had been great friends with Ishtar.
We went up to the penthouse suite, no questions asked. It
was decorated in the goddess's flawless style, with elegant
furniture, tables from Versailles, linens from Egypt, lac-
quered cabinets out of Beijing, and masterpieces covering
the lapis-lazuli-tiled walls, including a portrait of Ishtar by
a guy named Matisse. Kasusu had been thrust halfway into

the wall and Belet's jacket was hanging off the hilt. She had rustled up some clothes for me, so now I was less "off the slab" and more "off the runway" with a T-shirt from Dior that went on like a second skin, a sleek black quilted jacket, dark gray jeans, and the most comfy kicks I'd ever worn.

She passed me the whole plate. "Tell me again, what's the last thing you remember?"

I picked the top slice of the sticky treat. "Staring at a huge bright light."

Her eyes widened. "It wasn't . . . heaven?"

"Nope. The train's headlights." I licked the honey off my fingers. "These are really good. Are they from the Izmir Canteen?"

"Never mind that," said Belet. "And afterward?"

I shook my head. "Nothing. Not really. Not until I woke up in the morgue."

"You were dead, Sik."

"People get declared dead by accident all the time," I replied, helping myself to the last of the baklava.

"Not those flattened by trains."

Couldn't argue with that. Somehow, my body had not only survived but been *rejuvenated*. My cuts and bruises had almost disappeared. How? Had Ishtar put some kind of spell on me? It hurt my head to think about, so I concentrated on a more pressing concern. I looked at the empty plate. "Got anything else to eat? I'm starving."

Belet slid over a bowl of fruit. "Probably because you've not eaten in three days." She peered closer at me. "Are you sure you're not part—"

"Wait. I've been"—I couldn't bring myself to use the d-word—"*resting* for three days?!"

"A lot has happened. We've got poxies loose in the city."

"Poxies? What're those? They sound cute."

Belet shook her head. "They're anything but. Poxies is the nickname they're giving those who've come down with a new disease. The luckier ones ride it out. They get sick for just a short while. They'll be feverish, have terrible nightmares and hallucinations."

"They're the lucky ones?" I said.

"The worst cases cause mutation. Some might grow boils or develop black lumps, but others suffer from warped bones and muscles—even their skulls change shape, and new limbs grow where they shouldn't." Belet grimaced. "Eventually the buzzing begins. It sounds like a thousand flies are breeding in your ear canals. It drives the victim insane—insane and consumed with an unquenchable rage. Some can resist it, but not many."

I thought of the dockworkers, and Nergal's plague dogs. He'd promised something worse than them. The baklava roiled in my stomach. "My parents . . . Do you think they . . . ?"

Belet put her hand on mine. "Stable, but it's impossible to go see them. Manhattan General is overwhelmed, as is every hospital in the city. People are trying to get off the island before the mayor declares a lockdown tonight. After last time, he's not taking any chances."

I pushed aside the fruit. "I'm starting to wish I'd stayed in that drawer."

"That's not all." Belet grimaced. "You'll want to know about the swarms."

"I probably won't, but tell me anyway."

"Gigantic clouds of flies," she said, showing me a video clip on her phone. A shifting black mass hung low over Manhattan. "Wall Street is infested with them."

Just then one of the bedroom doors opened and Daoud came out, yawning and wearing a full cucumber face mask, so it had to be Thursday. "Will you keep it down? I'm trying to sleep. The nutrients need three solid hours to soak in."

Okay, I have to admit I was happy to see him. "Salaam, Daoud."

Cucumber slices fell off his eyes and rolled on the floor. "Alhamdulillah! Sik!" Daoud leaped over the sofa and attacked me. He got green paste all over my cheek and hair as he wrapped me in those big arms of his until I couldn't breathe. "I knew it wasn't you!"

"Knew . . . who . . . wasn't me?" I gasped for air in his embrace. Those muscles weren't just for show after all.

He let go eventually and shed a few real tears. "The police got my number from your school—I'm an emergency contact,

I guess. They called to say they'd found . . . a body. I met them at the morgue, but I couldn't bear to do the identification, so I called Belet. She did it instead."

Belet looked at me. "I guess I made a mistake. Seems you're hard to kill."

"You made Belet do that?" I asked Daoud. The warm and fuzzy effect of his hug had already worn off. "And then I suppose you wormed your way into this penthouse?"

Daoud started to protest. "She offered—"

Belet cut him off with a wave of her hand. "It's okay. He didn't have anywhere else to go."

"Somehow, Daoud, you always manage to avoid getting your hands dirty," I said. "You leave the hard work to everybody else, just like at the deli."

Daoud hung his head. "I'm sorry I left you back on Venus Street," he said. "I didn't know Ishtar was going to . . ."

"Die?" I blurted angrily. "Sorry, Belet," I added when I saw her wince. "But Daoud needs to face facts. She's gone, and now Nergal is stronger than ever."

"I'm not stupid!" he snapped. "I want to help. Help you, your parents, Ishtar, and—"

His phone rang.

I ignored it. "Nergal isn't just some steroid-pumped thug. He's much more. In fact, he's—"

"Can you hold that thought just a minute?" Daoud interrupted me, checking his screen. "It's my agent."

"Daoud, this is important!"

"So's this!" He waved the phone in front of me. "Look! That's a Hollywood area code!"

"So, what terrorist role do they have for you?" I snapped. Every time I hoped Daoud might finally rise to the challenge, something like this happened. "Iranian? Another Afghan? Or are Pakistanis the bad guys of the month?"

"I'm not taking any more of those roles," said Daoud. Then he took the call. "Claire! How's life on the West Coast? What have you got for me?"

Forget him, I thought. I turned back to Belet. We didn't need him.

"Oh," said Daoud. "Yes, I can do a Mexican accent. Why?" His shoulders slumped as he continued. "Okay. Audition at four. I'll be there. Bye."

He gazed sadly at the screen. For once he didn't seem to be checking his reflection in it. "I've got to go. New gig. Isn't that great?" He looked anything but excited.

"What is it?"

"Oh, drug dealer." He pushed his lips into a broad, fake smile. "But, hey, that's how Benicio del Toro started out, and now look at him!"

"Mabrook, I guess?" Despite my anger, I felt a twinge of pity for the guy. "Maybe you'll be the hero in the next one?"

"Heroes don't come in this shade, Sik." He retreated into his bedroom to get ready.

Sure, Daoud and I had history, but none of it had been great. He'd been closer to Mo in age, so they'd spent a lot of time together. In fact, everyone had assumed they were brothers. I'm not above admitting that had made me jealous sometimes. . . .

But that was my problem, not his. I couldn't blame Daoud for the mess we were in, especially as Ishtar had used him as bait. Though he could be incredibly annoying, he wasn't a bad person. It was just that everyone else came second to his dreams of fame and fortune.

I met Belet's gaze. "I'm sorry about your mom."

"She threw her sword away," said Belet. She stared somewhere beyond me, as if reliving the moment.

"To save me," I reminded her.

Belet's eyes snapped back to mine. "Let's hope it was worth it."

"Belet, you're in a low place—the lowest. I know how it feels, I really do."

"You really don't. My mother was an immortal goddess. You cannot compare her life to your brother's. No offense."

I took a deep, deep breath. "Okay, I'll give you a pass on that, but only this once. If you ever say anything about my brother again, you'll be left with absolutely zero friends in the universe."

Belet didn't know how to react to that. She didn't know how to process any of this. Ishtar had gone to great lengths to protect her adopted daughter. And Belet had grown up trying to be perfect for Ishtar. Belet had never had to learn how to pick herself up, because she'd never fallen down.

Somehow I needed to get her back on her feet, back to being badass, with her talent for extreme violence fully functioning. So I spoke to the one who knew her best. "Do you have anything to say, Kasusu?"

The steel hummed. Its edge reflected light, spraying the wall with a rainbow. "Yes, I do. Now listen to me, Belet. And sit up straight when I'm talking to you."

To my amazement, Belet did.

"That's better. Your mommy's gone, boo-hoo-hoo."

Belet blanched, and I was too stunned to say anything.

"So what?" the sword continued. "You want to stay a little girl all your life? Want her to hold your hand while you cross the street and tuck you in at beddy-byes? Ishtar, may Ea bless her, was not that kind of mother. She seized life by the throat and shook it until it rattled. Girl, she lived every moment like it was her last. That's the kind of goddess she was. And that's the kind of daughter she raised. Cry now, cry all you want. Then wipe your face and put on some war paint."

I grinned. "Thanks, Kasusu. Now—"

But the weapon wasn't finished, unfortunately. "Because let's be honest, Private Clown here hasn't got a chance against Nergal. Sik'll go down like the three hundred Spartans."

"Hey!" I said, offended. "You're looking at someone who

survived a train wreck." Though I still didn't know how. . . .

Belet reached over to grab Kasusu's hilt. "You were at Thermopylae?"

"Took Leonidas's head clean off myself," the sword boasted.

"Cool," said Belet. "But have you ever killed a god?"

Kasusu chuckled. "That's my girl."

They were genuinely fond of each other. It was genuinely weird.

Belet pulled the sword out of the wall and faced me. "All this talk isn't moving things forward. We need a plan, no matter how desperate."

I showed her the gold lion ring Ishtar had given me. "One desperate plan coming right up."

TWENTY-TWO

SHINING GOLDEN AND RUBY LEAVES CROWNED the trees. The branches echoed with birdsong, and the paths wound around lush flower beds and between heavy emerald bushes.

Everything beyond its borders may have been withering away, but Central Park was full of fall's royal beauty.

And tents. A few big family dwellings with multiple wings, others just big enough to crawl into, and everything in between. People had raised flags and put up clotheslines between them. They were clustered mainly around the park entrance at Columbus Circle and the busier paths, but some had been set up deeper in the undergrowth.

"It looks like a refugee camp," I said.

"It is." Belet had wrapped Kasusu in a white pillowcase and tied it across her back, disguising it as . . . a sword wrapped in a pillowcase. "Thankfully, the blight that's wiped out the other parks hasn't hit here. Yet."

"It's as if Central Park is under a protective dome," I said, still marveling at its lushness. "Unlike the rest of the city."

Manhattan was falling apart. The subway system had shut down, traffic had been reduced to a crawl, the skies were dark with massive swarms of insects, and the sidewalks were filled with people wearing surgical masks, hoping they could stay safe from whatever strange germs were contaminating the air. Most of the bridges had been closed due to cracks and fractures. The Lincoln Tunnel had sprung a leak. Times Square had been barricaded off and converted into a temporary CDC—Centers for Disease Control—compound, complete with portable labs. The doctors and scientists were trying to fight back, but unless we found a way to stop Nergal, the city would be his very soon. And if Manhattan fell, the rest of the country—and the world—would follow.

No pressure.

I held out the lion ring. "Now what?"

"It's a royal seal," said Belet. "It would have been worn by an official on an important mission, to grant them safe passage through the kingdom."

"Kinda like a free pass?"

Belet grimaced at my comparison. "Kind of."

Great. But a free pass to where, exactly? I was already lost. I'd never been able to find my way around Central Park. The paths lead this way and that through a labyrinth of foliage, and one tree looks pretty much like any other to me. I guess I was too urban even for a park.

"And who do you think the owner of the ring is?" I asked. "I wish Ishtar had told me. . . ."

"She said he was in Central Park, so we'll just have to keep looking until we find him."

This was as good a time as any to tell her. "Belet, Ishtar said something else, right before she gave me the ring. She wanted . . ." What? For me to be Belet's friend? Ishtar hadn't needed to ask me that, and I hoped Belet knew that already. "She wanted you to be happy."

"How can I be happy? My mother's dead." She shook her head. "It doesn't matter. I'm going to get her back."

"I know how you feel. When Mo died, I couldn't believe he was gone forever. I had this idea that—somehow—he could come back. But Ishtar's dead."

"As were you—laid out on a cold slab and everything—and yet here you stand. So don't tell me what can and cannot be done." Belet's eyes blazed. "Mother was in the Kurnugi before, and she got out. She can do it again, I know it. There are ways."

"Like what?" Maybe, when it came to gods, there *was* a chance. . . .

"Someone can swap places with her," said Belet. "Someone who loves her enough."

I did not like the way she said that. "Ishtar would want you to get on with your life."

Belet turned on me. "Like you have? I've heard you talking to 'Mo' at night. You can't let him go, either. Why should I be any different?"

"That's not the same. I'm not planning—"

"Shut up, Sik."

"Hey! I'm just—"

Belet grabbed my wrist and jerked me down into a crouch behind a bush.

The foliage ahead rustled. Someone, or something, sniffed nearby. It snarled, and the sound was neither human nor animal.

A twig snapped behind us.

Belet pulled Kasusu from the pillowcase.

More movement to our left. We were surrounded.

A man crept on all fours along the path. His gray suit was torn, and his bare feet were deformed, the long toes capped with talon-curved nails. His nose and mouth had mutated into a snout filled with yellow fangs. He lowered his face right into the dirt, snuffling and twitching.

One of Nergal's plague dogs. It didn't take a genius to know who he was tracking.

I turned as I heard voices arguing. Familiar voices.

"Though you may have once been my treasure, don't think this venture is a pleasure!"

"C'mon, mate! I told you that kid was lying! It's been you and me always!"

There was a pause, followed by a long sigh. "Perhaps you are indeed right. That boy has become a blight. We are best companions once more! Let's have celebrations galore!"

"That's more like it!" Idiptu said, then sniffed. "Now let's have a look at these tracks. . . ."

The disgusting duo of Idiptu and Sidana shoved their way into view.

Wow, they'd grown since I'd seen them last. Both topped six feet, and Idiptu was bloated like a blimp, waddling on his stumpy bowed legs. Sidana was more ratlike than ever, so hunched over that he scurried on all fours when he wasn't talking. They were cloaked in a haze of flies, and the stench coming off the demons made the nearby leaves curl.

Belet tightened her grip on Kasusu, her gaze narrowing into laser intensity.

I grabbed her wrist and shook my head. "There could be others around," I whispered.

Sidana jerked his head. "Be quiet, my dear. What did I just hear?"

Idiptu's belly rumbled. "Apologies. I'm famished."

Belet stiffened, resisting me. Her eyes gave away her intentions. She was filled with pain and wanted to pass it on to others. I gently pulled her back.

The plague dog bayed.

"He's caught a scent!" shouted Idiptu. "He wants us to go . . ." His head swiveled, and he spotted me. "It ain't possible."

"Time to run," I said to Belet. "Again." I barged deep into the undergrowth, pulling her along.

"By all the demons in hell," said Sidana. "How can the boy look so well?"

The park was filled with hideous, pitiful howls as more plague dogs raced after us through the trees. Their eyes shone with fevered madness, and each had a uniquely grotesque, disease-ridden shape. You saw the cruelty in Nergal's work; each plague dog suffered. But that wouldn't stop them from tearing us apart.

"Yallah, Belet!" I yelled when she looked back at our pursuers. "You can't fight them all!"

But she wanted to. I knew she craved a glorious final stand. To go out battling against massive odds before, inevitably, being killed, just like her mother had. I gave her a fierce yank. "Now come on!"

We stumbled on through the ever-thickening foliage, the howls echoing from all directions. My heart pounded so hard I thought it would burst, and I could barely see the path because of the sweat dripping into my eyes.

Belet came to a dead halt.

"What?" Then I stopped, too, as the vegetation opened up to reveal a greenhouse. I gasped, and not only because I was trying to catch my breath.

A glass ziggurat. I'd seen hundreds of photos of these ancient stepped pyramids, but how could there be one in

Central Park without anyone having noticed? Yet there it stood, seven tiers high, reaching far above the tallest trees. There were hundreds of sparkling windows, some panes over a dozen feet in height and width, shining like mirrors in the sunlight as they rose above the canopy. The wrought-iron frame mimicked the weave of vines, decorated with flowers and leaves of green copper. Beyond the glass structure stretched a vast misty jungle. I half expected to see monkeys swinging from the boughs of the massive trees.

"This is impossible," I said, craning my neck. I could just make out the summit.

Belet pointed over to the left. "There's a door, easier to defend. They can only come at us one at a time."

We sprinted over, and miraculously, the door was unlocked. Maybe the staff had already fled.

The moment we entered, I was smacked by a wave of humidity. Butterflies flitted through the moist air, bigger than any I'd ever seen, and there were flowering plants everywhere. The scent was overpowering, as if there'd been an explosion at a perfume factory.

The plague dogs arrived on the scene. Two hulking beasts tore through the bushes where we'd stood just seconds before. Then they stopped and looked around, bewildered. Another pack of four half-human beasts bounded along the outside of the ziggurat, barely five feet away from us, but they never even glanced in our direction. Sidana and Idiptu showed up, but instead of peering into the glass, they wandered around aimlessly.

"Where'd they go?" Idiptu asked. "We had 'em in our sights."

Sidana twitched furiously, pulling at his whiskers and grinding his crooked teeth. "How can he be alive, this boy named Sik? It must be magic; it must be a trick."

"They can't see us," whispered Belet.

It was more than that. "They can't see the ziggurat."

Apparently, they couldn't hear us, either.

"We gotta tell the boss." Idiptu licked his lips, leaving green slime over them. "But don't say we lost 'em."

The demons hurried off. Howling and snarling in frustration, the packs leaped back into the trees.

I pulled the royal seal out of my pocket. "Safe passage, just like you said."

We explored. The glass ziggurat was its own ecosystem. Hundreds of platforms filled the interior, some supporting no more than a few flower beds, others holding huge ferns and bushes. The thin wrought-iron supports were wrapped in climbing white roses and emerald ivy. Plants blossomed in the thick black earth, sprawling out in all directions while trees—palm, oak, ash, and fruit-bearing ones of every variety—reached up into the misty heights, their branches draped with vines. You couldn't see farther than fifteen feet before the mist became too thick.

But I could hear something: a man's voice.

"What are you doing here?"

The plants quivered at the depth of the sound.

I squinted into the distance but still didn't see anyone.

"Hello?" I asked. "Are you the caretaker?" That reminded me: I really did need to go to Mo's community garden at some point and water our beds.

"For now." He emerged from the haze. He towered over us, at least seven feet tall with biceps the size of cannonballs. He wore a pair of stained olive-green overalls without a shirt underneath, and he had a broad utility belt holding pruning shears, twine, a hand rake, and a trowel. A spade rested on his mud-splattered shoulder, and he spun it idly as he gazed down at us. Leaves and twigs were tangled in his thick, wiry black beard.

"We, uh . . . had an emergency," I faltered.

"There's no public restroom in here," the gardener said.

"Not that kind of emergency," I replied. Butterflies danced in the air between us as he looked us over, and I learned how an especially small ant must feel when facing a particularly large elephant.

Belet nudged me with her shoulder. "Ask him about the ring."

"Why don't you?"

𒀯𒈠𒌓𒅗 𒀭𒅀 𒂗𒉌𒈫𒊬𒈫 𒂍𒐊𒌅 𒈾𒀯

She glared at me, and I realized I was more frightened of Belet than this guy, so I held out the royal seal. "Do you know anything about this?"

The man picked it up for a closer look.

He smelled. Not bad, but strongly, of working in soil. There was a heavy earthiness about him, the smell of grass after it has just rained. It was a million miles away from the flat odor of damp city concrete. Maybe my eyes were deceiving me, but I swear the skin of his upper torso was covered with patches of green moss.

"I haven't seen this in a long time," the gardener finally said.

"Then you know who it belongs to?" I asked eagerly.

"Yes. Me," he said.

"You?" Okay, I was not expecting our emergency backup plan for saving the world to include a gardener, even one the size of a house.

Belet didn't care about being polite. "We were sent by Ishtar."

"And who might you be?" the man asked.

"I am Belet, daughter of Ishtar," she said.

"I'm Sikander Aziz, son of restaurant owners. Best falafel in town."

"Sik has a condition," Belet added. "He can't die. I think."

The man arched a bushy eyebrow. "Interesting condition."

"Can you help us?" I asked.

The guy pulled a rosy apple from a nearby tree and polished it on his dirty overalls. "I no longer meddle in the affairs of the gods, and they do me the same courtesy."

"But Nergal killed my mother!" snapped Belet. Tears swelled in her eyes as she confronted him. "We have to stop him! People are suffering!"

He offered her the apple. "People suffer when gods go to war."

Belet slapped the fruit out of his hand, and it spun into the undergrowth. She didn't say anything, but her glare was worth a few thousand words, all of them furious.

What was it with her? She had to pick a fight with everyone.

I decided to intervene before this giant swatted us with his shovel. "Ishtar was counting on you to help us, Mr. . . ."

"Gilgamesh," he said. "Just call me Gilgamesh."

TWENTY-THREE

"YOU?" I ASKED. "*THE* GILGAMESH?"

"Yes."

"The king of Uruk, demon-slaying, monster-wrestling, and questing-for-immortality Gilgamesh?"

"I suppose. In my younger days."

I felt as though a thousand tons had just been lifted from my shoulders. We had found the greatest hero in the world! The greatest hero *ever*! Everything was going to be okay.

Gilgamesh caught sight of Belet's sword. "I see you brought Kasusu. How's life, my old friend?"

Light rippled along the blade. I think that was its version of a joyful smile. "A constant battle, milord. Just how I like it. And I'm looking forward to working with you again."

Gilgamesh chewed the tip of his mustache, then gestured over his shoulder. "I was baking. Come and eat."

Now, that wasn't what I'd expected to hear from history's most legendary warrior, but I was still hungry from my time of being . . . not alive, so I followed him.

Belet did, too, grilling him along the way. "You were supposed to have died. Everyone knows the story."

Gilgamesh smirked. "Oh? And which story is that? Is that the one where I try but fail to gain immortality and die after many years a sadder, wiser man?"

"Er . . . yes." If you knew any story about Gilgamesh, that was the one.

"Good," replied Gilgamesh. "That's exactly what I wanted the world to think."

The middle of the ziggurat was more untamed jungle than greenhouse. There were weeds among the roses, and vegetables grew beside fruit trees planted so close together they'd become entangled. The smell was overwhelming, a mixture of sweet perfume and damp decay. Mo would have loved it.

"Stay on the path," warned Gilgamesh. "It's easy to get lost in here—it's bigger than it looks."

We arrived at a small clearing with palm trees arching overhead. A circular table with three stools around it was set with plates, glasses, napkins, and desserts. The centerpiece was a tall vase filled with exotic flowers of vivid, electric blue.

"You were expecting company?" I asked.

Gilgamesh smiled and offered us seats. "I may be retired,

but I'm not a hermit. Not quite yet." He picked up a platter with thick slices of cake on it. "Try this. Sugar-free and a hundred percent vegan."

"Bismillah . . ." I recited, looking over the choicest slices before picking a wedge plump with sweet dates and nuts. "Nice."

He poured out rose water as we sat down. We picked our way through the treats, each one more delicious than the last. Belet began reluctantly but was soon piling her plate high with cookies, tarts, and slices of cake.

Gilgamesh gazed around him. Now that I was sitting across from him, I could see that his eyes shone with starlight. How had I missed it before?

"All that time I spent in palaces, clad in silks and gold, not realizing that true riches come from the soil," he said. "All that time I wasted making war when I could have been growing beautiful things."

I finished off a small honey cake. "We could use a warrior now, Your Majesty."

"Just Gilgamesh," he replied. "I don't rule over anything anymore."

"I wish my brother were here. He was your biggest fan."

"Where is he?" When Gilgamesh saw my expression, he got it immediately. "I'm sorry. I lost someone dear to me, too. It was centuries ago, but I miss him as much now as I did then. All this"—he gestured at the lush trees and flitting butterflies—"is because of Enkidu. He loved nature."

"Centuries . . ." I said, my stomach sinking. "The pain never goes away?"

"It evolves into something else, Sikander. The emptiness in your heart is gradually filled with the joy of having known him."

I thought I heard Belet mumble, "That's not enough," but I could have misunderstood her. She glowered at her tower of treats as though it had insulted her.

"You're not how I imagined you'd be," I said to the demigod.

Gilgamesh shrugged. "A man changes, given time. And I've had plenty of that. But enough about me—tell me about your brother."

Belet banged her fist on the table. "What has this got to do—"

"Indulge me, Belet," said Gilgamesh. "Go on, Sikander."

I talked as we ate. I told him about Mo's fascination with botany, and how he recorded every flower he found. About the pressings he'd made since he was little, and the cuttings he collected. About how, since we only had an apartment, he'd spent all his spare time working at the local community garden, and how it had been named after him.

"Sounds like a man after my own heart," said Gilgamesh, brushing the crumbs off his beard. "Since you've come this far, I think I owe you some explanation. Right, Belet?"

"I'd rather have your help," she grumbled. Her lack of respect made me squirm in my seat, but a part of me respected her boldness. Between her and Gilgamesh, Nergal didn't stand a chance.

"Perhaps this story will shed some light." He sipped some rose water before asking, "You know the tale of how I found the flower of immortality in a cave at the bottom of the endless ocean?"

I nodded. And helped myself to another slice of cake. It fit my mouth perfectly.

"All that is true. And what's also true is that it was a long swim back to the shore."

I began circling a date tart. "And you fell asleep and a snake came along and ate the flower."

Gilgamesh smirked. "Sounds a bit convenient, don't you think?"

Belet hadn't touched anything on her plate; she was too agitated. "Then what really happened?"

"This." Gilgamesh plucked a flower out of a vase and popped a few petals in his mouth. "I ate part of the flower right there and then. Afterward, I fed the rest to a snake basking on a rock. It slithered off and that was the end of the matter, or so I thought."

Now I understood. "You didn't want humanity to learn the secret of immortality."

"I'd been around long enough to know that the wrong sort of people would be after it for all the wrong reasons. Best not to tempt them. I returned home to Uruk and told my scribes the snake had stolen it. A few years later, I faked my death, stepped aside from history, and took up gardening."

Gilgamesh *had* lied. And Nergal knew it.

"That's it?" Belet asked. "You've been pottering around for the last four thousand years just . . . gardening?"

"It's not easy. Still, I feel I've made some solid progress."

"That's all very sweet, and we'd love to hear about your vegetable patch later," continued Belet, "but right now we need the skills you're more famous for. You need to deal with Nergal. Right now."

"I put down my weapons a long time ago," said Gilgamesh.

This was not turning out as I'd hoped. "But you wielded the Sky Cutter itself, Abubu. What did you do with it?"

Gilgamesh pointed to the big shovel resting against the table.

I stared at it. "You turned the greatest weapon of all creation into a gardening tool?"

"I could hardly dig with a sword, Sikander."

Belet took a deep breath and, very reluctantly, held out Kasusu. "Here, then. Take mine."

The blade hummed with excitement. "Now this is more like it. It's an honor to be working with you again, lord.

Perhaps we should start with a few simple stretches, then—"

"No," said Gilgamesh. "I've renounced all weapons."

"What?" Kasusu shrieked, loud enough to crack a nearby glass pane.

I finally caught on. "You've become a pacifist."

He nodded. "It was the only choice. I was born and raised in the Middle East. It's my home and I love it, but has it ever enjoyed a time of peace? At first it was hard not to get involved. To fight the Babylonians, the Assyrians, the Judeans, the Romans, the Byzantines, the Saracens, the Crusaders, this group of people or that. All wrestling over a patch of land, most of it desert and uninhabitable. What should I have done? Killed them all?"

"So you gave up being a hero?" asked Belet.

"I gave up madness," said Gilgamesh.

"But you're the greatest warrior the world has ever seen!" I exclaimed. "You can't give up fighting!"

"I can, and I did. And if I can, so can everyone else," he said. "I plow. I seed. I grow. In this small way, I try to make amends for all the damage I caused. This dirt on my hands is there to cover the blood. I concern myself with creating life now, not ending it."

"Yeah, but you can make an exception, right?" I asked. "This is a jihad, Gilgamesh. A righteous cause. The classic good-versus-evil showdown."

Gilgamesh laughed. "There are always righteous causes."

How could I argue with him? Our family's history had sprung from war. Everyone we knew had a tale of homes destroyed, families torn apart, and heartbreaking loss. How many sacrifices had Gilgamesh witnessed before realizing how futile they all were? He was totally right. So why did it feel so utterly wrong?

"It's simpler than that," said Belet, glowering. "He's scared of Nergal. I don't believe it, but Gilgamesh is a coward."

"Belet . . ." I warned.

"What's he going to do? Throw a cookie at me? He's given up fighting—he said so himself."

But Gilgamesh didn't rise to her bait. He met Belet's gaze calmly. "Believe what you wish, daughter of Ishtar."

Then it came to me. . . .

I sighed, hoping I wasn't overdoing it. "Of course, there's a simple way to prove Belet wrong. I'm not saying you need to fight Nergal, but I bet just showing your face would make the god reconsider his recent life choices. His demons wet themselves when I merely mentioned your name, so imagine how they'd respond to a personal appearance. . . ." I looked over at his spade. "You could take that with you. It's big and heavy."

One corner of Gilgamesh's mouth lifted. "You know the quickest way to start a fight?"

"No . . ."

"Show up." Gilgamesh passed around another plate of cookies. "Though I appreciate your attempt to appeal to my ego, Sikander, I'm not going to start a war to prove a point, to you or Belet or anyone."

Belet slammed down the cookie plate. "Then what use are you? Mother was depending on you!"

"Your mother helped me go into hiding, Belet. She agreed with the path I'd chosen, despite being the goddess of war. In return, I gave her my ring, just in case she might need my help one day. I owed her that much at least."

So that was why she'd been so cagey when I'd asked her about the truth between her and Gilgamesh. She'd kept his secret until the very end.

Belet crossed her arms. "And she sent us to you so you could kill Nergal."

Gilgamesh gazed calmly back at her, and I saw pity in his eyes. "If you think the answer to everything is violence, then you truly are your mother's daughter."

I needed to get things under control. Belet was losing it, and I couldn't blame her. Here we had found the greatest hero of all time, and he'd decided to hang up his sword belt. "We do need your help, Gilgamesh."

"And I'll give it freely, Sikander. But I will not raise a weapon ever again." Gilgamesh stood up and walked over to his herb garden. "What's the problem you need solved?"

"Nergal? We just told you?"

"No. He's the *cause*, not the problem itself."

He seemed like a pretty big problem to me, but what was it I wanted, really? To cure my parents. "The problem is the diseases infecting the city."

Gilgamesh plucked a leaf and handed it over. "You know what this is?"

"Fenugreek. Mama uses the seeds to make aish merahrah flatbread."

"It can also manage diabetes." Gilgamesh pulled out a stinging nettle. "*Urtica dioica*. Effective in treating kidney disorders, hemorrhages, and gout." He gestured to his herb garden. "Every plant here has medicinal properties. Somewhere in the Amazon forest there's a plant that will cure cancer."

I wasn't convinced. "Nergal has brought on the apocalypse, and you're talking about herbal remedies. This isn't like treating a cold with a slice of lemon."

"Actually, it is," said Gilgamesh. "I'm living proof of that, and so are you."

Okay, now he'd lost me entirely.

He put his hand on my shoulder. "You know the beginning of my story, but what about after? Did you ever wonder what happened to the snake that ate the flower of immortality?"

"It lived forever?" guessed Belet.

𒀴𒈛𒂵𒉿 𒀴𒀉 𒂊𒋻𒄖𒊏𒀴𒉿 𒂖𒌓𒉿 𒈝𒀴

Gilgamesh rolled his wrist, prompting me. "And fertilized the earth . . . ?"

I knew what he was talking about, thanks to Mo. "It ate the plant and swallowed the seed. Then the seed worked its way through the digestive system and . . . out it came. Animal droppings often contain undigested seeds. . . ."

"It's the most natural thing in the world," Gilgamesh agreed. "So, this seed settles in the soil of Mesopotamia, and it grows and blossoms into a flower. The strain flourishes in some lonely place in the desert until, one day, thousands of years later, a keen botanist stumbles upon it."

An electric shiver shot up my spine. "Like Mo."

"He sent you a cutting. Somehow you accidentally digested part of it—perhaps a piece of the leaf. Or maybe a few drops of its sap entered your bloodstream through a cut. It happened so easily, you didn't even realize it. It's in your system, Sikander."

Belet stared at me like I'd grown a second nose. "The train."

Not just that. There was also the night at the deli, when I'd been bitten and stung by insects, and the day when I'd been beaten up at the docks. Each time, I was back to full health within twenty-four hours. It wasn't normal, but in all the chaos I'd ignored it.

"I'm immortal?" I asked, hardly able to say it out loud

because it sounded so ridiculous, so impossible.

"What did you do with the cutting?" asked Belet.

"I must have planted it. In Mo's community garden. That's what I did with all the cuttings he sent."

"It must have bloomed by now," Gilgamesh said. "The flower of immortality. The cure to every illness, even death itself."

Belet sprang up. "We need to get to that garden of yours right now."

She wasn't wrong.

𒀭𒈾𒆠𒂊 𒀭𒅀 𒄿𒁹𒀯𒅗 𒋫𒊹𒅆 𒂊𒅅𒂊 𒌨𒀭

TWENTY-FOUR

GILGAMESH FACED US BOTH, ARMS FOLDED ACROSS HIS massive pectorals, and for a moment, he was the man in charge once more—the king. "Nergal is being devoured by the very plagues he spreads. He is literally rotting away. He's dying."

"Okay, but so what?" I asked. "He'll end up back in the netherworld to try all over again?"

"No," said Gilgamesh firmly. "Nergal broke many sacred laws when he escaped Kurnugi—laws that govern even the gods. If he fails here, he fails forever and will be utterly annihilated. That's why he wants the flower. He needs to cure himself so he can go back to being the god he once was. He risked everything coming to New York, Sikander, and he'll risk everything to ensure he succeeds."

"So can't we just wait this out? How long has he got left?"

"Too long." Gilgamesh shook his head. "Look at how

much damage he's done in less than a week. How much of Manhattan will remain if he survives another month?"

Not much was the answer. Once again, it was up to just us.

Belet put Kasusu back in the pillowcase. "I'm ready."

It was all falling into place at last. Mo had always been on the lookout for new plants. I could picture his excitement at finding a flower he couldn't categorize, growing in some lonely, desolate part of Iraq. I didn't remember which cutting it was; he'd sent so many, some to be pressed when he got home, others to be potted, and some to be transplanted into his garden. Now that I thought of it, it could have been his final shipment. Little had I known then that it would attract the god of rot.

Gilgamesh wrapped up some cookies for us to take along. "Get the flower and bring it here. I should be able to use it to make a healing potion for the pox Nergal is spreading."

"A lot of people are already infected, including my parents," I replied. "How are we going to cure them all?"

"First things first, Sikander. Get the flower." He tucked the cookies into a net string shopping bag.

"These magical?"

Gilgamesh smiled. "The food? No."

"Do you need this back?" Belet asked, showing the ring to him again.

"Leave it here. I'd rather it not fall into less deserving hands."

Belet frowned, and I knew she wasn't happy about parting with any object her mom had once treasured. Still, she handed it to the demigod. "We won't need it to return?"

"Once you've been a guest in my house, you can always find me again."

I wasn't paying close attention to their conversation. I was still trying to get my head around the fact Mo had found the flower of immortality. I inspected my hands. No bruises or cuts at all. I didn't feel so much as a twinge of pain, despite having been flattened by a train three days ago. "So I'm gonna live forever?"

Gilgamesh paused. "How about you get through the next few days before worrying about the next hundred years."

"But . . . is it lonely?"

"That depends on you. The ones who manage it best are those who continually find fresh purpose."

"Like gardening?"

"Like nourishing others." He pulled two oranges off a branch and added them to the bag, then pulled it shut with a stone toggle. "My advice is to start off as you mean to go on."

"You mean spend the next thousand years running a deli?"

Gilgamesh stopped. "A deli?"

"Mo's. It's on the corner of Fifteenth and—"

"Siegel. I know it well. That Baghdad sauce of yours is a once-in-a-lifetime experience. Even an eternal lifetime."

𒀭𒈹𒂗𒆲 𒉌𒌓𒆤 𒀉𒅎𒂍𒈾𒌓𒐼𒐊𒌋 𒐊

He fanned his mouth. "Anyone who can eat a whole kebab covered in that will never have to prove their courage any other way."

Wow. Our first ever celebrity customer. I know the fate of Manhattan was at stake and all that, but the one and only Gilgamesh had eaten at our deli! I scratched the back of my neck, feeling a little awkward about making my next request. "Could you put that on Yelp?"

Belet looked around the small clearing, scowling as usual. "Cookies and fruit. Is that it? No magical weapons?"

"I'm a gardener, Belet," said Gilgamesh.

"You must have something useful," she persisted.

He held out the net bag. "Take this."

I took it and slung it over my shoulder. "Shukran," I said, throwing a glare at Belet. How was it that she had absolutely none of Ishtar's graciousness? Gilgamesh took us to the ziggurat entrance and then turned to me. "Be careful, Sikander. You've cheated death, and that has consequences. There will be an . . . urge within you, and around you, to redress the imbalance of being alive when you shouldn't be. It happened to me, and the next thing I knew, I was trapped in Kurnugi. I had to serve my time until opportunity presented itself to leave."

"You think the same thing will happen to me?"

"Just be prepared."

* * *

"Can I take a moment to fanboy? That was Gilgamesh," I said. We were back out on Fifth Avenue. "The actual in-the-flesh Gilgamesh!"

"A bit of a disappointment, if you ask me," said Belet. The subway was shut down, so we stalked the street, searching for an available cab. "I really don't know what Mother saw in him."

"Come on, Belet. The guy is *literally* a legend."

"And Ishtar was *literally* a goddess, so forgive me if I'm not impressed."

"He's trying to help us."

"With homeopathy!" she snapped. "He turned Abubu into a shovel!"

"I'm sure he knew what he was doing. A sword named Sky Cutter doesn't sound like such a big deal."

Kasusu screeched from inside the pillowcase. Belet just stared at me in horror. "That statement is so outrageous, I'm amazed you haven't been struck by lightning."

I ground my teeth, trying hard to keep my temper. "Why are you so angry about everything?"

"Why aren't you?"

"Because being angry won't bring Mo back," I said.

Belet sighed. "Where's the garden, Sik?"

"Downtown, not too far from the deli. Mo would head there once a week, right after Jummah prayers."

𒀭𒈾𒄴 𒉪𒇲𒁲 𒍝𒋾𒀭𒁉𒀀𒐕𒌋𒐊 𒀲

"And you?"

"I worked, of course. Fridays are our busiest time—all the clubbers need their carbs before pulling all-nighters. Mo asked me to look after the garden while he was away, but he was away too much. And then he . . . Anyway, gardening's not really my thing."

"So . . . the plants tended to die?"

"Not all of them. The weeds were doing great last time I checked." Drizzle started to fall, increasing the already cut-throat competition for a cab. Belet paced up and down the street, trying to hail one.

The package had arrived a week after Mo died. It had been freaky, seeing the box with our address in his handwriting. The cutting was in a small airtight box with some soil, still a little damp. He'd stuck a Post-it on the front with a simple message—*Plant this!*—and the initial *M* hastily scrawled in the corner. I'd almost thrown the cutting away, thinking that the garden didn't matter anymore. Mo would never see it again. But that had felt wrong, so I went ahead and fulfilled his last wish.

Had he known it was the flower of immortality? If only its sap had seeped into my system instead of mine!

"Why couldn't you have been more careful?" I asked him. "You never paid attention to what was happening right in front of you. Always had your head in the clouds."

What's that supposed to mean?

I stuffed the shopping bag under my jacket. It was just made of loose netting, so hardly waterproof. "Nothing. It's just . . ."

Just what?

"Why did I have to stay behind?" I snapped.

But you love the deli!

"Like I have a choice! But did it ever occur to you that I might have wanted to go with you? Even for a week? Even for just a few days?"

Why didn't you say something, Yakhi?

Belet stepped into the street, nearly getting hit by a cab, but it didn't stop for her. I hoped the cookies hadn't gotten wet. Gilgamesh made great cookies.

Sik?

"Fine, I guess we have to discuss this right now. Did you ever offer to stay and take care of the deli? Just once? Mama's and Baba's eyes were always filled with dreams of Iraq, and you fanned those dreams. They couldn't say no to you. All those evenings the three of you talked about home. Baghdad, Basra, Nineveh, and all the sites you'd visit here, there, everywhere."

A cab finally rolled up.

You could have joined in.

"How?" I hurried over. "Iraq wasn't my home."

Belet and I squeezed into the back, and I gave the cabbie

the address. He turned for the long, slow drive down the West Side Highway.

"I hope your mom left you enough money for this ride," I said to Belet. "It could end up costing hundreds by the time we get there."

"See this?" Belet held up a black credit card. "The stars will grow cold before it runs out of funds." She turned her attention to the news feed on the TV in the partition.

I stared at the raindrops as they slid down the window. It was weird to see so few lights on in the stores and restaurants.

Had it really been like that? Me an outsider in my own family, always lesser than my big brother, the apple of my parents' eyes? Mo must have had his own struggles, but it had seemed to me that everything had always come easily to him. I hadn't been around to witness the defeats, only his victories, while I ran behind on my little legs, trying to catch up, asking him to wait up as he sprinted off on his adventures.

"Look, you're famous." Belet pointed at the screen.

My old school photo gazed back at me. The one with all the zits.

The mayor was giving a press conference. I turned up the volume.

". . . can confirm that the disease spreading through Midtown did originate with an Iraqi family, the Azizes, who, until recently, ran a deli on Fifteenth and Siegel. The entire block has been quarantined, and the residents admitted to

Manhattan General. However, there is no word on the where-abouts of Sikander Aziz, thirteen years old and a potential patient zero. The health authorities have been searching for him since his disappearance from the hospital last week. If anyone has any information regarding his present where-abouts, please call the tip line at—"

I quickly turned down the volume, but it was too late. The cabbie was already looking at me in the rearview mirror. "You're him, aren't you?"

Uh-oh.

The driver's eyes went wide, and he put his hand over his nose and mouth. "I've seen you on TV! You're the plague boy!" He slammed on the brakes, almost throwing us from our seats. "Get out of my cab!"

"Hey, hang on a minute. I—"

"Out! Now!"

"I am not the plague boy!" I yelled back, but he had already jumped out and was on the street, shouting and pointing at my window.

"That's him! The plague boy! He's the one spreading all the pox! Get the cops!"

People started crowding around the taxi, peering in, snapping photos with their phones, making me feel I was something from a freak show.

Belet pulled the door handle. "We're leaving."

The crowd backed off the moment the door opened.

"It's him! He's all over the news! The plague boy!" shouted the cabbie. "They'll have to burn my cab! I just finished paying it off!"

"There is nothing wrong with me!" I shouted, but it was clear no one believed me or was willing to take the risk. The onlookers kept their distance but didn't leave, both afraid and curious. The trouble was, the crowd was getting thicker and we were trapped in the middle of it.

"The plague boy!" someone shouted. "He's got leprosy!"

"Look! You can see the black boils! He's gone bubonic!"

"It's Ebola for sure!"

Belet shoved someone aside, but it did no good; the crowd was five layers deep.

"All right!" I yelled. "Get out of the way before I cough all over you!"

Now *that* cleared a space.

We sprinted through, but everyone around me was yelling, "Plague boy!" until it felt as if it was coming from every direction and the city was placing me under a curse. The gawkers fell over themselves to get away, and some were trampled. A woman screamed as I brushed past her, and folks started fleeing from *her* as if she were infected with some fatal disease.

"This is insane," I said.

"Forget it," Belet said over her shoulder as she continued running.

Yeah, forget it. We'd get the flower, and by this time tomorrow, everything would be back to normal. Mama and Baba would be cured, and we could get back to reopening the deli.

We turned the last corner, and Belet glanced around. "Where's the garden?"

"Just a little farther," I said, taking the lead.

I'd come here a lot when Mo was around. Carting trays of plants, or gardening tools, or bags of topsoil for him. It was the only time I got in touch with nature. These days I avoided the place, because the memories hurt. I'd planted Mo's cutting two years ago and hardly visited after that.

We stopped in front of a high gate.

"This wasn't here last time." I peered through it, down the alley leading to the garden. A truck blocked my view.

We read the large sign on the fence:

SABAH CONSTRUCTION

LUXURY CONDOS IN THE HEART OF GREENWICH VILLAGE

COMING SOON!

The truck honked, then started reversing as a workman joined us. "Step aside, kids," he warned as he unchained the gate. "Come on, Bill! Straight back!"

"What's going on?" I asked.

"Can't you tell?" He motioned for the truck to keep going. "Tight schedule, too, and a fat bonus if we finish early."

"What about the garden? There was a community garden here."

"Yeah, a small one," he said. "We paved over it last month to make room for the parking lot."

The truck rolled past, clogging the narrow alleyway with its oily exhaust.

The guy waved the driver off, then shrugged. "It's not like anyone cared about it, right?"

TWENTY-FIVE

I COULDN'T BELIEVE IT. THE CITY WAS DOOMED BECAUSE of a parking lot. No! It couldn't end like this!

I turned away from the fence. "We need to go back to Gilgamesh and persuade him to fight. It's the only way."

"He won't. It's down to us," said Belet. Her disappointment had instantly turned to steely determination. "I'm off to kill Nergal."

"Are you that desperate to follow your mom to the netherworld?"

She clenched her fists. "We wouldn't be in this mess if you'd looked after the garden." Belet stood before me, our noses inches apart, so I could register the fury burning in her eyes. "You broke your promise to your brother, and now we're all going to pay for it."

"Guess what? I'm about to break another promise right

now." I stepped away. "Good-bye and have a great life."

"What do you mean?"

I was too mad to stop the words from coming out. "Ishtar made me promise to stick with you. But if you're going to be—"

"You're only my friend because you promised Mother?"

"No, it's not like that." Why did she always have to be so frustrating? "It's just . . ."

Belet gritted her teeth. "Just what? Tell me, Sik."

"She wanted to make sure you wouldn't be alone if anything happened to her."

"News to me," said Belet, crossing her arms over her chest.

"She was trying to protect you," I said. "That's why she kept it a secret."

"It wouldn't be the first time," said Belet. Then she drew something from her back pocket. "Mother always kept secrets."

It was the photo of her biological parents. The one thing she'd saved from Venus Street.

"No more," said Belet. Then she ripped the photo in half.

"Why'd you do that?" I watched, horrified, as she tore it into quarters, then eighths.

"They're not my parents. It's just a picture from an old magazine—two actors from a soap opera," Belet said, her tone cold and flat as she tossed the shreds into the air. "Mother thought I didn't know. I pretended to believe they were my real parents, to make her happy."

"Ishtar made it all up? Why?"

"Because she thought she wasn't a good enough parent. So she gave me two perfect ones. But how could anyone be more perfect than her?"

Up to this point, mostly all I'd seen from Belet was bickering and criticism. But now the wall she'd built to hide behind was crumbling and all her pain was pouring out.

She blinked, but that didn't hold back her tears. "She was supposed to have always been there for me, Sik. All those other children she adopted, over thousands of years . . . they got to have her until the end of their lives. And I'm the one to lose her. The only one."

"I know what it's like to lose the one person you love more than anything. Mo was my world. Everything I looked up to, everything I wanted to be. Then he was gone, and I was so angry. Angry at him for going, at my parents for letting him, at everyone and everything. Myself most of all, for not making more of every moment we'd shared."

Belet looked up, eyes wet, and I took her hand. I felt the calluses on her palm and fingers from all the time she'd spent weapons training with her mom.

"But don't let that anger eat you up," I said. "It'll destroy you."

"Sik . . ."

"Stick with me, Belet. We'll figure this out." I looked into her eyes as sincerely as I could. "I'm your friend, and not because Ishtar asked me to be."

"Do what you want." She pulled her hand free. "I'm going after Nergal."

"Belet!" I shouted as she sprinted across Broadway. "Belet!"

It was no use. A moment later, she ducked into another taxi and was gone.

I ran after her for a couple blocks before stumbling to a stop. Now what? With my face on every screen, I wouldn't be able to get a cab—not that I could afford one, anyway—and the subway was totally—

Hold that thought. I saw someone heading down the stairs into the Canal Street station.

At last, something was working in the city! If even just one of the lines was open, I could get to Manhattan General and try to learn the latest about my parents. Then I could go back uptown toward Central Park and try really hard to get Gilgamesh to join the fight.

A heavy rain was hitting the streets, making everything gray and slippery. I pulled my hood over my head and started down the steps, passing an old guy clutching the handrail.

I stopped and looked back at him. "Need some help?"

He smiled and held out a hand. Wow, it was just skin and

bone. "That's very kind of you, young man. But should you be here?"

"Not really, but here I am," I replied.

His cold fingers gripped mine tightly as he steadied himself.

"It's a tragedy, that's what it is," he said, shaking his head. "What's your name?"

"Everyone calls me Sik."

"I'm Harry. So, did you get a chance to say anything to your family? That would be something, at least."

"I'm off to see them now."

"They went before you? I see." He met my gaze, and his rheumy eyes sharpened. "I hope you didn't do anything . . . rash so you could be with them."

"Uh . . . nope?" Poor old guy was senile, I guessed.

"Good, good." He looked back up the stairs and raised his head, letting the raindrops splash on his pale, wrinkled skin. "It's time I went."

"Where are you headed?" I asked as we took the next step down.

"Same place we all go in the end."

"Okaaay." We reached the bottom of the steps and shuffled toward the turnstiles. "Do you have a MetroCard?" I asked the man. "If not, I can swipe mine for you."

"No need," said Harry. The turnstile allowed him in

without payment. Did senior citizens get some kind of special deal?

I swiped myself in, and we walked along the platform. It was crowded—with old folks, mainly. Was there an AARP convention happening nearby or something? As we slipped past, trying to find a good place to wait for the train, I caught snippets of their conversations.

"I was just crossing the street. Looked left when I shoulda looked right . . ."

"I knew there were nuts in that cake. . . ."

"I wish I could see their faces when they learn it's all been left to Mr. Whiskers . . ."

The air shifted, and a deep, distant roar traveled out of the dark tunnel mouth. The wheels screamed on the steel rails, and wind rushed through the narrow space, hurling dust and loose papers down the platform.

Harry smiled. "It'll be good to see Betty again."

The train slowed to a stop. Like some of the older trains in the city, this one was heavily decorated with graffiti. Unlike the rest, the graffiti was cuneiform.

I was getting that bad feeling again. . . .

A pair of boys pushed past us to get on the train, one shoving the other. "I told you the ice wasn't thick enough."

A middle-aged man adjusted his tie as he stepped inside. "Well, the life insurance should cover their tuition."

𒀭𒌝𒈨 𒀭𒁹 𒂗𒊏𒈨 𒊏𒂍𒉺 𒁁𒈨 𒈾𒀭

I turned slowly to Harry. "Can I ask you something?"

"Sure, Sik."

"No offense, but are . . . are you dead?"

"Of course." He looked surprised but not shocked, as if I'd asked something stupidly obvious. "Aren't you?"

Then I was pushed on board.

TWENTY-SIX

———————

"I HAVE TO GET OFF!" I ANNOUNCED TO ANYONE who would listen. But nobody batted an eye. I peered through the crowd of passengers, looking for the emergency brake, but there was none. "Hello! I'm not dead!" I yelled.

Harry checked his watch and gave it a shake. "Seems to have stopped."

Out the windows all I saw was darkness—deep, *deep* eternal darkness. "Okay, I am officially freaking out."

How had I ended up here? A few minutes ago, I'd been on the street, talking to Belet. As far as I knew, I hadn't been run over. Unless I'd blacked out . . .

Had I caught a disease from Nergal or one of his demons? But I felt fine. . . .

This had to be a big mistake. A *huge* mistake!

"I am not dead! Not anymore!" I kicked the train door hard. "Let me out!"

Equally alarming, the other passengers began to fade away, one after the other. The two boys who'd fallen through the ice disappeared together.

There were only a few of us left. "What's happening? Where is everyone going?"

Harry straightened his tie and adjusted his sleeve cuffs. "To their own personal afterlives, I suspect. Whatever was deepest in their hearts' desire, whether they knew it or not. What else could heaven be, Sik?"

"I thought being dead would be less complicated than this."

Harry started combing the few strands of his wispy white hair.

"You look great, Harry."

"I want to look my best for Betty."

More and more people faded away, silently, without care or worry. Eventually it was just me and Harry.

"So much for my so-called immortality," I said.

The train began to slow.

The darkness gradually gave way to light. Instead of an underground tunnel, we were moving through a desert landscape.

The train stopped, and the car door opened to scintillating colors. I squinted against the brightness. "I guess this is my stop."

Harry patted my shoulder. "It'll be fine."

"How do you know?"

"Do you know anybody who's ever come back?"

I faced the exit. Whatever else the afterlife might be, it was warm and breezy.

I stepped out.

The train didn't roll away—it dispersed into the air like smoke. I heard the distant rattle of wheels on rails, felt the air rush past, and then there was silence.

"Hello? Asalaamu alaikum? Namasté? Guten Tag?" I cast around for the welcoming committee. "Shalom?"

A vast, empty desert stretched out before me, all under a night sky filled with wild splashes of color. Great smears of orange, blue, red, and green covered the black canvas above, as though a divine painter had attacked it with wild fury. Even as I watched, a pinprick of light near the horizon erupted silently, pulsed with soft blue light, then spread outward.

The sand was grayish blue, though the weird illumination made it difficult to judge its true color. The landscape was dotted by mounds. At first I thought they were hills, but they were too uniform; nature wasn't so neat.

I realized they were tells. Mo had bored me stupid with a million photos of them. They covered Iraq like freckles. Ancient cities that had decayed, leaving massive sandy lumps over the flat desert.

𒀯𒈾𒀭𒂊𒈾𒄑𒈨𒊩𒀭𒍪𒈾 𒂖𒊩𒂊𒀯

"This is it?" If this was the afterlife, it was pretty disappointing. I remember someone at the masjid telling me there'd be seventy heavenly companions waiting. . . .

The train wasn't coming back, and standing there was achieving nothing, so I struck out toward the biggest mound. It seemed as good a plan as any.

The tell grew before me. Its steep slopes still bore the marks of humanity. Steps, sagging with the weight of countless centuries, crisscrossed the sides, and there were paths too straight and angular to be anything but the work of stonemasons. I followed one of the walkways and explored the skeletal remains of a forgotten civilization. The buildings sagged like molten candles. Statues lay broken on the ground—whether they were supposed to be beasts or gods I couldn't tell anymore. I saw a few tall stone slabs—steles—engraved with cuneiform and other unintelligible markings.

I stubbed my toe against something half-buried in the hard-packed sand. I hunched down and pulled it out. I brushed off the encrusted grit and ran my fingers over the smooth wooden shape of a lion. Someone had taken a lot of care in carving it. The mane had been delicately cut, as had the wide-open roaring mouth and the wrinkles in the folds of fur. The eyes were inlaid obsidian. I put it in my net shopping bag.

"Beauty must be preserved, eh?" someone said.

I spun at the voice, and a figure rose out of the shadows of the ruins. His face was hidden under a black-checkered keffiyeh, and his kaftan was dusty. Pebbles crunched under his heavy hiking boots as he climbed over a wall. The leather satchel he carried looked familiar, worn and oily dark with handling, the edges frayed and repaired with duct tape.

The way he looked at me made my heart ache. "Do I know you?"

He laughed.

It was a laugh I thought I'd never hear again.

"Alhamdulillah." He reached up and pulled his keffiyeh loose. "So, what brings you here, Yakhi?"

My heart surged as he revealed his face. I swallowed hard. "I've missed you so much."

"And I you," said Mo.

TWENTY-SEVEN

IT WAS MO. MO MAKING A FIRE. MO EATING ONE OF
Gilgamesh's cookies. Mo sitting cross-legged in the dust and
ruins, smiling. And laughing. At everything.

That's what I'd forgotten: how much Mo laughed.

Dying hadn't dented his spirits one bit.

There was nothing to say, and too much to say. So my
eyes just drank him in. Having him back was all I'd thought
about, all I'd dreamed about for two years. I watched how
he constantly fiddled with his keffiyeh and beat the dust off
his clothing while stealing glances at me, making sure I was
still there, that this wasn't a dream of *his*.

We sat in a shelter at the foot of the tell. It must have once
been part of a temple or sacred dwelling. The broken walls
were covered with friezes of men and women in strange outfits with bands of cuneiform running both above and below.
This may not have been my idea of the perfect afterlife, but

it was certainly Mo's. Notebooks lay scattered in all corners, and I saw his translations written on the open pages.

"So, am I dead?" was my first question.

"You tell me," he said as he nibbled. "Is there any reason you should be?"

"I don't think so . . ." I said. "Though I did have an incident with a train recently. That *should've* brought me here."

"Oh?" Mo's raised eyebrows disappeared under his keffiyeh.

"Do you remember finding any strange-looking flowers while you were in Iraq?"

"I saw lots of flowers." His eyes crinkled. "As botanists tend to do."

"Think, Mo! It would have been somewhere remote, an unlikely place for any flower to grow. You took a cutting and mailed it to me just before you . . . just before your accident."

Mo took a minute to ponder it. "Hmm. I did find a flower out in the desert south of Basra. . . . Like an orchid, but totally adapted to an arid environment. I was amazed that it could survive there." He looked up at me. "And yes, I did ship you a cutting. What about it?"

I took a deep breath. Might as well get this over with. "The last cutting you sent me was from the flower of immortality."

"Ya salam! That can't be! According to the stories, a snake ate the last one."

"And pooped out the seeds, continuing the circle of life."

I grinned at him. "You, Mohammed Aziz, rookie botanist, actually found the flower of eternal life and didn't know it. You coulda been rich and famous at a young age, if you hadn't . . ." I trailed off. It was all so ironic and unfair.

Mo was too mind-blown to speak, so I went on. "I planted the cutting, just like you told me to, and I must have inhaled its pollen or eaten a leaf or gotten some of its sap in my bloodstream. Somehow it entered my system, and things have gotten really complicated since then."

"What do you mean by 'complicated'?"

So I told him about Nergal and his demons, the destruction of the deli. Mo went pale when I told him about Mama and Baba being in intensive care. "But they're still alive, right?"

That sent a chill down my spine. "They aren't here, are they?"

"No, they're not," he said, relieved. Then he removed a flask from his satchel, opened it up, and dripped a thick, red liquid onto a cookie.

My eyes began to water. "Is that the Baghdad? How did you get it here?"

He held out the flask, and one sniff was all I needed to tell me, yes, it was our fabled shock-and-awe sauce.

"You gave it to me, Yakhi," said Mo. "Every time you pour it down the sink and say 'For you,' my flask is refilled.

The ancient Mesopotamians used to make offerings to the departed, and the system still works." He held out the dripping cookie. "Want a bite?"

"Seriously? On a cookie? No wonder Mama never wanted you on food prep." I shook my head. "Can we get on with the story? Nergal's in town, looking for the flower, and I teamed up with Ishtar and her daughter to stop him."

"Ishtar has a daughter?" he asked between chews. "What's she like?"

"Nothing like her mom," I said. "In fact, nothing like any girl I've ever known."

"That's not exactly a long list, is it?" said Mo, smirking.

I ignored that. "So we need to get back to the world of the living and save our parents."

Mo paused. "We?"

How could he not realize this? "Yeah, *we*. I figured you knew all this, and that's why I'm here. If I'm not dead, then you must have sent for me. There has to be a way to get you home."

He laughed suddenly. "Just think: If I'd taken a bite of that flower, I'd be immortal, too! I never would have died!"

"I don't know why you find that funny," I said sourly. "We were all really upset. We're *still* really upset. We take your death very seriously, and so should you."

"Me?" he asked. "Why?"

𒀭𒉌𒆷𒀭𒈹𒉿𒀭𒅆𒈨𒆠𒉿𒇲𒀭

"Because it destroyed our world! Nothing's been good since the night we got that call. Do you know what it's like, wading through the day when your heart's been shattered into a million pieces? It's impossible to care about anything, because the only thing that mattered is gone. Forever."

"And yet here I am, sitting beside you," he said simply.

"This doesn't count!" I kicked the dust. "And don't tell me I should be content with remembering the good times. I wanted more and didn't get them. Neither did Mama and Baba. You took all that from us. The night you became a shaheed."

That's what everyone called him now. He'd died trying to help the country he loved. But if the idea of Mo becoming a martyr was meant to make the reality of his passing easier to take, it had totally failed.

"They still have you, Sik."

"Yeah, the spare. Great," I muttered. "You were the one they pinned all their hopes on."

"That's not true—"

I wasn't listening. Too many memories were fighting it out. "'Oh, look at these grades. Mohammed's got a scholarship! There he goes, off on another great adventure! Why, Mr. and Mrs. Aziz, you must be sooo proud of him. Sik? He's in the kitchen, washing the dishes.'"

"I always thought you liked working in the deli."

𒀭𒈾𒁺 𒄿𒈾𒂊 𒐊𒀭𒌋𒂍𒈨𒀀 𒅆𒐊𒐊 𒐊

"*Someone* had to help Mama and Baba. You were never—"

He held up a hand, cutting me off. "Let me get this straight. You miss me, but you resent me. Because I went on trips?"

"No," I said, feeling weary. "Because you never took me."

"But you were too young, Sik. The places I went were hard."

"So? I would have had my big brother to protect me."

He spread out his arms. "Here you go, then! We're camping under the extinction of galaxies!"

I gazed up at the wild, exploding colors in the night sky. "Is that what they are?"

"A billion stars going supernova, death on a cosmic scale. This is Kurnugi, Sik. This is where you go when it all ends."

"Well, it hasn't ended for me yet." I stood up. "I have to get back, and you're coming with me."

He just shrugged, as if his death wasn't that big a deal. "Just pluck a flower from the community garden and take it to—"

Oh, boy. This was a conversation I didn't think I was ever going to have. "The garden is gone, Mo. They paved over it."

He stared at me, aghast. "Paved over the garden? To make what?"

"Uh, a parking lot."

"You didn't save *any*thing?!"

I wished I were dead. For real. "I . . . I didn't visit the garden as often as I should have."

𒀭𒈾𒁲𒂗 𒀸𒁲 𒄿𒋾𒐊 𒈾𒐊𒈪 𒂍𒌨𒁲 𒈝𒀸

"One thing, Sik. I asked you to do one thing for me. That garden was supposed to be my legacy. . . ."

Now I was angry. "Like I didn't have enough to do helping Mama and Baba? Daoud's completely useless. He—"

"Ah, Daoud. How is he? Still playing terrorists on TV?"

Mo's constant easygoing nature made it impossible for me to stay mad. "Yeah. I don't know why he doesn't just give it up. I kinda feel sorry for him, wasting his life, dreaming of being a hero."

"Ah, Daoud will save the day. You just wait." Then Mo turned back to our small camp. "So, Ishtar and Nergal in New York City? Tell me more. I want to know everything."

I gazed across the tells dotting the landscape as far as the horizon. I peered harder. "There's a dust cloud out there."

Then the quiet night rumbled with roars. Far away, but getting closer.

Mo sprang up and dug binoculars from his satchel. "Ugallus on the hunt."

I snapped my fingers. "Lion-men, right?"

He laughed. "Glad all my stories sunk into that dense head of yours."

The roars grew louder as they headed straight for our mound.

"Uh, what are they hunting, exactly?" I asked nervously. "Should we run?"

"Nowhere to run to," Mo answered matter-of-factly. I wished I could be as fearless.

Now that they were closer, I could see that in addition to the sprinting lion-men were a pack of actual lions, including a pair harnessed to a chariot carrying two people.

"Erishkigal," muttered Mo. "It has to be."

"The goddess of death," I remembered. "*Now* should we run?"

Mo lowered his binoculars. "No point. This is her queendom."

The lions and ugallus reached the tell long before the chariot and its occupants did.

An ugallu leaped to the top of a boulder, panting hard. He was twice the height of a normal human and muscled like a sprinter, and from the shoulders up he bore a thick-maned lion's head. His body was covered in scars; some of them looked fresh, like the big one across his face that had taken out an eye. "On your knees before the Queen of the Night," he ordered.

The lions and other ugallus gathered around us, sniffing and growling softly. The un-subtle threat made the hairs on the back of my neck rise straight up. The ugallus smelled musty. Their long embroidered kilts had seen better days: The colors were faded and the tassels frayed or missing entirely. Despite their hulking, muscular physiques, the guardians looked ill, with mangy pelts and fangs yellow and blunt. Still long enough to put deep holes through a skull, though.

"On your knees!" roared the one-eyed ugallu.

Mo took my arm and hauled me down beside him. He looked over at me. "Let me do the talking."

I couldn't help it . . . when the chariot rolled out of the dust cloud, I had to look up. The wood creaked as the passenger stepped off, leaving the charioteer to park the vehicle.

Erishkigal bore an aloof, regal beauty. Her hair was midnight dark and spun with strands of cold moonlight, and her skin was pale, covered by a plain black robe and a cloak that she shook off and tossed to one of her ugallus.

"Face in the dirt," snarled One-Eye.

A chill descended as Erishkigal stopped in front of us. "Mortals are not permitted in my realm."

Mo said, "I can explain, Your Majesty. This is my brother and—"

A deep, threatening growl from One-Eye shut him up.

Erishkigal crouched to my level and gazed into my face. Her eyes were colder and emptier than the edge of the universe. "We have punishments for those who violate my domain. Exquisite sufferings that last—"

The charioteer coughed loudly as she joined the queen. "'Exquisite sufferings'? Really, Erish? Are you still doing that whole 'torture trespassers' routine?"

Wait a minute. . . .

Erishkigal's jaw tightened. "This is none of your business, Sister."

Wait another minute. . . .

I raised my eyes to get a better view of the charioteer.

Ishtar waved at me. "Hi, Sikander. Nice handbag."

TWENTY-EIGHT

"SHUKRAN," I SAID, HOLDING UP GILGAMESH'S NET shopping bag. "They're all the rage nowadays."

She smiled widely. "It suits you." Her bare toes played in the sand. For someone who'd recently died a horrible death, she seemed surprisingly cheerful.

Ishtar shone, literally. It wasn't just her ivory-white breastplate or silvery kirtle—she glowed softly from within, radiating a warm, comforting light that elevated her physical perfection to something on a higher plane. Here in Kurnugi, she didn't need to hide her true nature. "How is my darling Belet?"

"Angry, as usual." Then I added, "And upset. She blames herself for what happened."

"Of course she does. But she has you around to give her a reality check from time to time." Ishtar flicked her loose hair from her face, and starlight sparkled within her locks.

"We would have been here much earlier, but Erish insisted on taking her chariot, rather than mine."

Erishkigal scowled. "You know I get airsick."

"You have a flying chariot?" I asked, seriously impressed.

"Several," said Ishtar casually. "They were all the rage in the third millennium BCE."

Mo cleared his throat.

"Oh, yeah. This is my brother, Mohammed. The one I told you about."

Ishtar laughed. "The expert in all things Mesopotamian! You have done your brother proud, sweet Mohammed."

Mo blushed. "Just want to say I'm a big fan, Your Highness. Big fan."

Erishkigal huffed. "What man isn't?"

Ishtar took Mo's hand. "Oh, do get off your knees. We're all friends here."

"Of . . . of course, Your Highness."

Ishtar looked at us standing side by side. "Family reunions . . . Aren't they beautiful? Your dashing friend Daoud isn't lurking about, is he?"

Why was she going on about him, the coward who'd fled during her last stand? "No. He's only interested in himself."

Ishtar shrugged. "You are far too harsh on him, Sikander."

"Yeah! Daoud's a great guy!" added Mo. "We used to spend all summer in the garden."

"Yeah, I remember," I said. "Without me."

𒀸𒊏𒉌𒌋 𒀸𒅗 𒁹𒂊𒀭 𒂍𒌋𒌋 𒊏𒈠𒂊𒉼 𒁁𒅆𒂊 𒈨𒀸

Mo scowled. "You were never interested in flowers. Daoud taught me how to press them."

"Daoud? Why?"

"He wanted to create fragrances. We Arabs invented the perfume-making technology, you know. Distillation, steam extraction from flower petals. He kept a kit back at the deli."

"Oh, I wondered what those smells were. So is that why you two were always hanging out?"

"One of the reasons."

"See? Your friend has hidden talents." Ishtar rested her chin on her thumb as she inspected me. "And speaking of flowers, you've gained certain benefits from one, haven't you?"

"You knew?" I asked.

"I suspected, especially after your fight at the dockyard. Your skull was cracked and your arm broken, yet within a matter of hours your injuries were less than bruises."

Our reminiscences were interrupted by an irritated cluck.

Ishtar rolled her eyes. "Oh, and may I introduce my *much* older sister, Lady Erishkigal, Mistress of the Everlasting Palace, Queen of Night, and Goddess of Death."

That was the problem with Ishtar: She stole all the attention. Even from other gods. Erishkigal stood there with her arms folded and a scowl on her face. "If you've quite finished?"

Ishtar gave an offhand shrug. "All yours, dear sister."

Ouch. Ishtar was everything Erishkigal wasn't. And they both knew it.

You cannot escape sibling rivalry. Ask Cain and Abel. Ashurbanipal and Shamash-shumukin. Heck, ask Fredo and Michael Corleone. If the firstborn does better, then perhaps it feels more . . . acceptable? Primogeniture and all that. Mo had taught me how to ride a bike. He'd had a seven-year head start. But it doesn't feel great when your younger sibling surpasses you.

Erishkigal was as beautiful as Ishtar, but she held herself stiffly, while her sister always looked ready to dance. Erishkigal's eyes were narrow and her lips thin. Ishtar smiled with her entire face.

There was no joy in Erishkigal. Ishtar had taken it all.

If that sounds like I felt a little sorry for the goddess of death, I did. I bowed to her. "Your Majesty."

She gazed down at us. "My dear sister has told me your tale, Sikander Aziz, and that of your brother. It's unfortunate that he discovered the flower of immortality. It will bring great suffering to the human world."

"Because of your husband," Ishtar muttered.

Erishkigal's jaw stiffened. "When a person dies, their life is written on a tablet and stored in my great library. My husband, idle as he seems to be nowadays, came across Mohammed's story and realized the significance of the flower immediately." She sighed. "Nergal became agitated. He's not been well for a while, and when he summoned his demons, I thought he was just craving familiar company. He and his monsters often gather to reminisce about the great slaughters. Good times."

"But he was planning a breakout, wasn't he?" Ishtar said.

Erishkigal's gaze chilled by about a hundred degrees. "When he told me he planned to leave, we . . . argued. He unleashed his demons in open warfare against my ugallus. He demolished the seven gates between here and the world of the living." One-Eye scowled as he touched his empty eye socket. "Even now there are monsters roaming loose around the netherworld and beyond. They're causing a lot of trouble."

Ishtar tapped her breastplate. "So it's fortunate that I'm here to clean up your mess."

Erishkigal's hand tightened into a fist. "Lucky me."

Whatever else, Erishkigal gave good sarcasm.

I approached the goddess of death. "Your husband's infecting New York City with his plagues. I'm trying to stop him."

"And how do you intend to do that, young man?"

"I'm open to suggestions."

Erishkigal's laugh was sharp-edged. "Only the greatest of heroes could hope to defeat my husband. And then only on their very best day."

"You must have a few heroes down here I could, uh, borrow?"

Ishtar nodded thoughtfully. "I'm sure we could find someone. I saw Alexander the Great in the beer hall earlier. He's
good when he's sober." She snapped her fingers. "Wait. Cyrus
the Great is at my shrine right now. I could command him to
battle Nergal. He's the best charioteer in the netherworld."

"I'm not sure how useful a chariot would be in
Manhattan," I said. "Cops wouldn't allow it, no matter how
great you were."

Ishtar huffed. "You can't call yourself a hero until you've
fought from a chariot."

"Surely there's another—" started Mo.

Erishkigal whirled on her sister. "Who's queen here?
Ah, that would be me. And I have made my decision." Her
lips widened into a skeletal smile as she said to me, "You,
Sikander, have broken the most sacred law of Kurnugi. The
living are not permitted in the netherworld."

"But I came here by accident!" I protested. "I don't
even know how I—" I cut myself off when I remembered
Gilgamesh's warning: *You've cheated death, and that has consequences.* Would I be stuck here, like he once was?

Ishtar took her sister's hand. "Could I have a word with
you in private, Erish?"

"If you must. But Sikander has to be punished for—"

Ishtar pulled her sister away from us.

I looked over at One-Eye. "They always like this?"

"Sisters, right?" He looked around to make sure no one

was listening. "Last time Ishtar came down here, Erishkigal had her hung from a pair of bronze hooks. Goddess or not, that had to hurt."

One of the other ugallus growled. "Hush. They're coming back."

Ishtar was smiling, which was a good sign. So was Erishkigal, which wasn't.

"I'll start," said Ishtar. "We've decided to help you. There is a way to stop Nergal and save your city. You will need the flower of immortality."

I winced as I saw Mo frowning at me. "But they've paved over it. Which was not my fault. Mostly."

"No. What Mohammed found was a *descendant* of the original. His had grown in the deserts of Iraq and, after four and a half millennia, evolved to suit its new environment. Its properties would have differed from the first one."

"Differed how?" I was stunned. "Does that mean I might not be as immortal as I think I am?"

"Who is? Otherwise, I wouldn't have ended up here." Ishtar glanced over at Erishkigal. "Though it's always a pleasure to visit my dear sister, of course."

Mo caught on first. "There's another flower from the original strain still growing, somewhere else."

Ishtar clapped. "Exactly! In the Sea of Tiamat. A place we gods cannot venture."

"Why not?" I asked. "You're gods."

"We were formed out of Tiamat. If we went in again, we'd dissolve back into it. Our existence would end."

Mo nodded. "Otherwise Nergal could have retrieved the flower himself."

I pointed at Mo and me. "But we can go there?"

Ishtar nodded. "You, Sikander, aren't a god, but you have the benefit of being more or less immortal, so the sea's properties won't affect you. And Mo's already dead. The worst is over for him."

"I'm glad being dead has its benefits," said Mo.

Ishtar clapped. "Go get the flower. Save Manhattan. It's really very simple."

Somehow I doubted that. "And where is this Sea of Tiamat? How big is it?"

"It encompasses all that is made, unmade, and yet to be made." Erishkigal spread out her hands, and the sand around us became animated, showing a storm-racked sea with a pinnacle of rock rising out of it. "The flower of immortality lies in a cave at the base of the Rock of Nisir, the only feature within the endless ocean. Wherever you might be, you will be able to see it."

"And how do we get to this sea?"

"It will come to you," she replied enigmatically. "But you will need a boat. Only one vessel could hope to survive the

Sea of Tiamat, and that's the very same one Gilgamesh used when he sought the flower himself."

"Great. So where's this boat?"

Erishkigal grinned. "In the Cedar Forest."

Ishtar was worryingly silent. Mo looked like he was about to be sick. Even the ugallu shifted uneasily. None of this was encouraging. "I'm guessing this Cedar Forest is a dangerous place?"

Erishkigal shrugged. "Consider it more a place of heroes."

"And I assume the boat is guarded?" I'd played enough computer games in my time to recognize a quest when I saw one.

"Clever boy. I see why you like him, Ishtar." Erishkigal nodded, but her eyes shone with malevolent amusement. She was enjoying this way too much. *This* was my punishment for entering Kurnugi. "It's guarded by a creature that is invulnerable to attack."

Mo whispered despairingly, "Humbaba of the Seven Auras of Awesomeness."

I turned to Mo. "How awesome?"

"Very." He counted on his fingers as he listed Humbaba's traits. "Immune to earth, wind, fire, air, and metal, and all things living and dead. Only one person in all history has ever defeated him."

"Let me guess. Gilgamesh," I said. "How'd he do it?"

Mo looked surprised. "Why are you asking me? You're the one who had tea with him."

"We didn't have time to review his top-ten kills."

Ishtar suddenly threw her arms around us both. "Oh, this will be so exciting."

Not exactly the word I'd use.

"What else can you tell me about Humbaba?" I asked Ishtar while the others set up our camp. Erishkigal's ugallus had erected a palatial tent of shimmering midnight blue. The goddess and I stood outside its entrance while Mo prepared a cooking fire a few feet away.

"He's a big, grotesquely ugly giant with the strength of a thousand elephants and a gigantic appetite, for human flesh especially. The usual."

"He must have some weak spot. Every monster does."

"Only here." She tapped her forehead. "He's remarkably stupid."

"How did Gilgamesh beat him?"

"He tricked Humbaba into lowering his auras, then cut his head off with Kasusu. Thus the giant ended up in the netherworld."

"Okay, say we do fight him. What's the worst that can happen? Mo's already dead and I'm immortal. Well, kind of, at least. We might get bashed around some, but we'll be back to normal sooner or later, right?"

"I'm not sure how much fun being immortal will be if he tears your head off," said Ishtar, as coolly as if she were giving me the weather report. "And with regard to your brother, there are places darker and more terrible than Kurnugi. Those are the risks you'll be taking."

"Thanks for the 'heads-up.'" Being dead was pretty complicated. Who knew? But I had no choice, with my parents, my friends, and all of New York City at stake. "Do you have any weapons I could borrow?"

"I'm the goddess of war—I have them all. But did Belet teach you how to fight?"

"Not exactly . . ."

"You could end up chopping off your brother's arm in the middle of a battle. Trust me, I've seen it happen. Better to rely on your other skills."

"Like dishwashing?"

"Tell me more about Belet."

There was so much to tell, but time was a-wasting, so I just focused on the highlights. "She wants you back. She said you'd escaped Kurnugi once before. That you swapped places with someone from the world of the living."

"It can only happen under special circumstances, between two people who truly and completely love each other."

"Like you and Belet," I said.

Ishtar frowned. "She shouldn't be thinking along those

lines. She has her whole life in front of her. . . ."

"Not if we don't win against Nergal," I said.

I looked over at Mo, squatting by the fire, stirring a pot. He met my gaze and smiled. He was so carefree. My heart raced with the . . . possibility. I'd been there the night Mama and Baba's world was destroyed. I'd seen how they'd changed under the heavy sorrow that weighed on their shoulders every single day. I could bring Mo back, make them happy again. "Would it work with me and him?" I asked.

Ishtar took my hand. "Do you think your parents would miss you any less than they do him?"

"Everyone misses Mo so much," I replied.

"But he lives on in their hearts. Love always remains. Believe me, I know all about that." She gazed up wistfully at the supernovas. Then her demeanor became serious. "I need you to be careful with the flower of immortality when you find it. If you get contaminated by it—if its pollen or sap enters your system—there could be adverse side effects."

"Like what?" None of this conversation was making me feel any better.

"The properties of one flower could cancel the properties of the other." Then she shrugged. "Or not. Who's to say? No one's ever been in your position, so all the more reason to be wary."

"But—"

"Get some rest, Sikander. You and your brother have a

big day ahead." She entered the tent, where her sister waited. "Good night."

Mo was finishing off some hot chocolate as I joined him. "What were you two discussing?"

"Just catching up on the latest gossip." He didn't have to worry about anything anymore, while I carried the burden of the world on my shoulders.

"It seemed pretty intense."

"What part about her being the goddess of love and war don't you get?"

"All right, Sik. You win." He lay down on his sleeping bag, hands behind his head as he gazed up at the supernova night. "Ya salam, it's beautiful here, isn't it?"

Sure, it was. But my mind was on a small corner deli downtown. Mom was chopping lettuce while Baba ground the lamb. The sun was shining through our big sidewalk windows, and there was a line at the counter.

We all had our own idea of paradise.

The moment I woke, I knew something was wrong.

The tent was gone. The ugallus were gone. Erishkigal and Ishtar were gone.

I punched the dirt. "They said they would help. . . ."

Mo yawned. "What are you muttering about?"

A roar shook the trees. We'd gone to sleep in the desert

and woken up in a forest. We stumbled to our feet as a great, hot wind ripped through the area, burning our skin and stinging our eyes. Branches creaked as something big—huge—pushed its way toward us. The ground trembled with each footfall. The roar still echoed around us and was joined by a cruel, deep, and hungry growling. Trunks snapped and were ripped aside.

"Guess we'll qualify as heroes after this, eh?" I said.

The thicket of cedar trees buckled as Humbaba strode into the clearing.

𒀭𒈹𒂊 𒀭𒅀 𒂊𒀹𒌍𒅕𒈫 𒉺𒁉𒀹 𒂍𒈫 𒈠𒀭

TWENTY-NINE

HUMBABA HAD GUTS. SLIMY PINK INTESTINES COILED over his wide face and draped around his neck; sagging sacks of stomachs and bloated bags of bowels dangled from his torso. As he walked, they sloshed and swayed and dripped, leaving a shiny trail of greenish digestive fluids in his wake. His eyes sat deep within puckered flesh, and he blinked slowly. "Shhtrangersh."

"Got any weapons, Yakhi?" Mo whispered. "Ishtar must have left something."

"What difference would they make? He's got those seven awesome auras to protect him."

"Gilgamesh beat him," said Mo. "He tricked him into removing them."

"Think he'll fall for the same trick twice?" I patted Mo on the shoulder. "If not, now would be the perfect time to impress me with all the fighting skills you've learned since being here."

"I'm sorry, but Muhammad Ali isn't in Kurnugi," Mo replied. "He got an express pass straight to Jannah."

Humbaba pulled a tree out of the ground as easily as I would have plucked a daisy. He began chewing it, branches, leaves, and all. "Tresshpasshers."

As I looked around for something, anything, we could use against him, I spotted a long, moss-covered object half-hidden in the foliage. I nudged Mo. "What do you think?"

"Looks like a boat to me."

I waved my hands at Humbaba. "Hey, salaam! Sorry about intruding in your lovely forest, but I was wondering if we might borrow that canoe?" I strolled over to it, keeping my eyes on the gut monster. "Just for a short while. I promise we'll bring it right back."

Humbaba's eyes narrowed. "Gilgamessh's boat."

"It is? Fancy that."

"I hate Gilgamessh." Humbaba towered over us now, and the stench coming off him was poisonous. "Boyssh. I like boyssh."

Now that was good news.

"Shoft and not too crunchy."

Aaand that wasn't.

Now that he was up close, I could appreciate his full

disgustingness. How many miles of guts were wrapped around him? They dangled from every limb and trailed on the ground. Many were infected; ugly sores dotted the lining, and the stomachs had lacerations and bleeding patches. Florid scarlet ulcers everywhere. He groaned and belched—at both ends, if you know what I mean. If I hadn't been immortal, the stench would have killed me then and there. Even Mo, who was dead, turned green. "That's some serious IBS," my brother said.

Yep. Humbaba had the worst case of irritable bowel syndrome known to medical science. "Remember Mr. Erwin?" I asked Mo.

He nodded, though he kept his eyes on the monster. "Extra yogurt on everything?"

Mr. Erwin, a sweet old guy, came in most Mondays. He'd lived in the neighborhood since forever and remembered our place from back when it was a Jewish deli. He had a delicate stomach, so he needed to eat yogurt with whatever we served to prevent it from blowing up in his belly. One time I accidentally dropped a spoonful of our mid-grade Cairo sauce in his breakfast pita, and . . . I glanced over at Mo. "You thinking what I'm thinking?"

He smirked and took out his flask. "Yeah, I think I am."

I looked up at the monster as it licked its lips. "So you're gonna eat us?"

Humbaba slurped.

I sighed. "I guess this is it, Mo."

"I guess it is, Sik." Mo held up the flask. "One final toast to our gruesome and imminent deaths?"

I nodded. "At least we'll die happy, eh?"

Humbaba jerked forward. "What'sh that? Shhow me!"

I clutched the flask close. "Hey! Eat us if you want, but this is ours! The finest drink in all Manhattan and thus the whole world. Me and my brother deserve this at least."

"Give it!" roared Humbaba. He leaned over me, and I got a good look at his boulder-size teeth and, unfortunately, a powerful whiff of his breath. He really needed to diversify his diet.

"Don't give it to him!" yelled Mo. "It's too delicious!"

Humbaba roared. The hurricane that blasted from his mouth knocked us off our feet and obliterated the leaves from the trees.

Mo lay on the dirt, sobbing. "No, Sik. Don't give it to him. . . ."

I held out the flask to the giant, my hand trembling. "You win. Best swallow it in one big gulp so it doesn't touch the sides."

I was lucky he didn't tear off my arm in his eagerness. A tongue the length of a stair carpet encircled the flask as he popped off the lid and tossed the whole contents down.

I took a step back. "This could get messy."

We watched it dribble down his digestive tract. The deep-red sauce coated the rough patches, the worst ulcers. Humbaba winced. "Hot. It'sh hot."

"Shock and awe, Humbaba," I said, taking another step back. "Pure shock and awe."

A few drops splashed into the first stomach. The reaction was instant. Every ulcer blossomed like a firework, deep red, yellow, green, and blue hues pulsing with Humbaba's cries. He clutched one stomach, then another. He even tried to tie a knot in one coil to stop the sauce from spreading further, but it was to no avail. The Baghdad was unstoppable.

Humbaba crumpled to his knees and clawed the earth in agony, tearing great ragged trenches with his claws. His eyes rained rivers, and long ribbons of snot dangled from his wheezing nostrils. "Water . . . water . . ."

I pointed into the distance. "I think we passed a river a ways back there."

Still on his knees, weeping, Humbaba trembled as another series of explosions rocked his innermost world. "I hate boyssh." Then, holding his biggest coil of guts, he scurried off into the forest, knocking down trees in his path as he wailed, "I hate boyssh!"

Mo dropped his arm over my shoulders. "Now, that was pretty good."

"Pretty . . . awesome?"

He grinned and gave me a squeeze.

With Mo at my side, I could take on anyone and anything. Next we just had to make a short paddle across the Sea of Tiamat, and the flower was as good as plucked.

We both walked over to Gilgamesh's boat. I tried to lift one end. It didn't budge. I wiped off some of the moss so I could look at it more closely.

The boat was made out of stone. Even the two paddles lying within it were marble. Just great. How was a thing this heavy supposed to float? We couldn't even move it. I pushed while Mo pulled. I pulled while he pushed. We both pulled and then we both pushed.

Not. One. Inch.

I sank down beside it. "This must weigh a couple of tons. It's not going anywhere."

"Does it need to? Erishkigal said something about the sea coming to us, remember?"

Hands on hips, sweating, I scanned the forest in all directions. "That doesn't make sense. There's no shore anywhere near here."

Mo took a seat on the bench in the boat. "You've just got to have faith."

"This is stupid," I declared. It felt like we'd been sitting in the boat for hours. "Nothing's happening."

Mo picked up one of the paddles. "Sea of Tiamat, eh?"

𒀭𒌷𒈾𒄿 𒀭𒅀 𒂖𒌫 𒑊𒅖 𒊺𒊑𒈨𒈠 𒂖𒌫𒂊 𒈾𒀭

"Yeah."

"The primordial ocean from which all existence arose. Bottomless trenches, gigantic whirlpools, tempests ravaging the surface, and who-knows-what kind of leviathans patrolling its depths. Waves so high they could drown continents. This is going to be an adventure."

"If you say so," I replied glumly.

He cast his gaze at my bag. "Got any more of those cookies?"

I handed one over and took another for myself. Each bite sent a sugary tingle along my tongue. Gilgamesh really knew how to bake.

He laughed. "Do you remember that time we went rowboating in Central Park?"

"Right after you made me watch *Jaws*?"

Mo nodded. "Baba had to wade in to carry you out on his back. Made it halfway before he slipped, and then those screams!"

"Something *did* bite me!"

Mo wiped the tears from his eyes. "Have you ever taken a bath since? Filled the tub deeper than your ankles?"

"Showers save water. I'm doing it for the environment."

"Riiiight, Sik. Of course you are."

I couldn't believe I had missed this guy.

We waited some more. The moss was staining my pants. "This is stupid," I said again.

Mo nudged me with his big toe. "Weren't you given a magical incantation or something?"

I sighed. "No, I forgot to go see Professor Dumbledore."

"You know what the most amazing part of all this is?" Mo idly tapped the bottom of the canoe with his paddle. "You actually got out of Manhattan."

I lifted the other paddle and added a little beat of my own. "'When a man is tired of Manhattan, he is tired of life.' I read that somewhere." I looked out at the still-waterless surroundings. "Why did you always want to leave?"

"All those stories Mama and Baba used to tell, about their old home, the world they used to live in . . . Didn't you ever want to see it for yourself?"

"Nope."

"What about your heritage?" asked Mo. "Isn't it important to know where you come from?"

"I'm more worried about where I'm headed." The canoe rocked from a slight tremor under us. The branches of the trees swayed in a rising breeze. A stronger gust blew, carrying with it a faint roar.

Mo gripped his paddle. "Is Humbaba coming back?"

The wind picked up and the ground trembled as the horizon began to rise above the treetops.

And that roar . . . "It's a tidal wave, Mo."

I stared as water rushed toward us, growing higher and higher, closer and closer.

The Sea of Tiamat was coming to us. The trees were torn from their roots as it crashed through the forest. How high was it now? Hundreds of feet for sure, and still rising, until it blocked out the sky.

"Hang on!" yelled Mo.

I grabbed the sides of the boat and bent over, wedging the paddle across my lap and chest. I took a deep breath—

And the wave struck.

THIRTY

———◆———

IT WAS WORSE THAN BEING CRUSHED UNDER A
train. That had been bright light and—*smash!*—all over in
an instant. Here, gigantic waves pounded us over and over
again, never giving us a moment to recover.

The noise of the crashing waves reached into my bones,
shaking me so hard I felt like a tomato in a blender. The
canoe, and us clinging on with every ounce of strength, spun
in the barrage of churning water. We rolled without letup as
we were dragged into the lightless ocean depths. With eyes
squeezed shut, teeth locked together, and lungs screaming
for air, I absorbed every wave, each one loosening my grip
just a little bit more. But I knew that if I let go, I'd be lost forever. The canoe, pathetic as it was, was our only hope. Mo
knocked against me with each churn.

We were forced deeper and deeper underwater, the

devastating roaring receding into a dull, faraway drone. The viselike pressure of countless tons of water above compressed me from every direction, and my lungs were full of agonizing fire. Just one gasp of air, that's all I wanted.

Then, just when I thought I couldn't take any more and felt my hands slip, we shot up. The pressure lessened as, instant by instant, the colossal weight lifted. I renewed my grip on the canoe as it accelerated up from the depths.

We sprang out of the water, grabbing a moment of hang time before smacking down onto the sea's surface. I gasped and released my aching fingers.

A storm raged. Heavy black clouds battled lightning in the churning sky and pelted us with leaden raindrops.

Wave after wave broke over our ancient stone boat, and yet it—somehow—stayed buoyant.

I jumped as Mo slapped my back. "You okay, Sik?"

I twisted around. "Not at—"

"Ya salam!" He laughed. He turned his face to the sky, his eyes closed, and let the rain hit it. "Can you believe we're here? The Sea of Tiamat!"

Guess what? I started laughing, too. That was the thing about Mo—his joy just carried you along. I was freezing, my stomach was doing double flips, and each fresh wave felt like it was going to drown me, but so what? I was with my brother, the guy who'd been my hero since the day I was born.

"Watch this, Sik!" shouted Mo. He began to stand up.

I grabbed him. "Sit back—"

Mo raised the paddle aloft. "Come on, gods! Is that the best you've got? We'll take you on! My brother and I against you all!"

How could you not love him?

Mo pointed ahead with the paddle and cried, "Look!"

The rain and sea spray stung my eyes, reducing everything to a blur, but as the lightning flashed, it lit—for a second—something jutting out of the sea. Oily black, slick, and sharp.

Wobbling, I stood up for a better look.

An ugly rock stood defiantly against the sea with five jagged spires projecting from it, as though a hand were clawing its way out. Waves crashed against it, swamping it for a moment before surging away, leaving it bold and grimly reaching upward. The surface was covered with razor-sharp edges and spikes, seemingly impervious to the smoothing effects of the seawater barrage.

Mo dropped back into the canoe and grabbed his paddle. "What do you think?"

"It has to be."

Without another word, we started paddling toward the Rock of Nisir.

For every wave we conquered, another rose up in front of us, higher than the last. Wind skimmed the crests of the waves, throwing thick spray straight into our faces. I could barely feel my fingers—they'd gone numb.

"Are we there yet?" shouted Mo.

I didn't have enough spare breath to answer. Instead, I heaved the paddle through the black water, eyes glued to the rock still achingly far ahead of us.

But then, when I stopped to swipe dripping hair out of my face, the Rock of Nisir suddenly rose before us. One minute, it had looked like an arm sticking out of the waves; now it was an ominous black-granite mountain surrounded by half-submerged clawlike reefs.

The canoe rose up on the crest of a wave, and the next thing I knew we were roller-coastering down the slope, faster and faster, headed straight for the rocky protrusions.

"Abandon ship!" I yelled, and dived over the side.

I went straight down, briefly sensing the second splash as Mo came in after me. Blinking against the stinging seawater, I watched as the spikes of rock shattered the stone hull.

I came up for a second, took a deep breath, and swam for the rock, timing my strokes so I wouldn't be thrown onto the lethal surface.

My arms ached from the paddling, but I managed to get them on a low, horizontal ledge and hoist myself up onto it.

"Sik!"

Mo battled the sea. The tide had him and was pulling him

away. Even as I leaned out, stretching my hand as far as it would go, I knew I couldn't reach him.

I whipped off my string bag. I swung it over my head, my frozen fingers curled around the stone toggle. I hoped the bag would give us the extra length we needed. "Catch!"

Before my eyes, the bag grew.

Its ordinary dull strings transformed into a glowing gold net, and as I cast it, it spread wider and wider, wrapping itself around Mo. I drew him up onto the shelf without effort, as though the net itself were doing all the work. Warmth radiated from it, making Mo's wet clothes hiss with steam as he clambered onto the narrow ledge and collapsed next to me. The net shrank back into its bag shape, the glow dimming.

He panted hard, his head tilted back. "That . . . that . . . that was exciting."

"I guess you could say that."

Mo sat up beside me and leaned over to get a better look at the bag. "Handy little item. Where'd you get it?"

"Gilgamesh gave it to me."

"Let's have a look." Mo held it up, and then peered closely at the toggle. "See this?"

I squinted at it. I hadn't paid any attention to the toggle before, but now I could see it was engraved with a four-pointed star. "And . . . that means what, exactly?"

𒀀𒈾𒆠𒂊 𒀀𒁲 𒂍𒋫𒈨𒂊 𒅖𒁲 𒈨𒂊

"Symbol of Shamash, the patron god of kings, and the guy who had a magical net capable of trapping all sorts of terrible evils. You're very lucky to have such a powerful gift."

"If you say so." The string bag, soaked through, sagged and looked really pretty lame as powerful gifts went. And of course I'd lost the remaining cookies.

The sea surged around us, crashing against the rock. The black water had leeched all warmth out of me, and my teeth chattered, but that may also have been because I was petrified out of my mind.

Mo, however, was raring to go. He grinned and said, "According to Erishkigal, the flower's in a cave down below. Let's go find it."

"Just like that, huh? How do you know we won't drown?"

"Hey, I'm dead and you're immortal. What could possibly go wrong?"

I hate it when someone says that. But I didn't have much choice. "Okay, let's do this thing."

We slid off the nice, safe shelf and back into the sea. Mo and I put our hands on each other's shoulders, and we bobbed together in the rising waves. The sea spray hit my eyes, but I locked my attention on him.

"Stay close to the rock, Sik. We'll use it to push ourselves downward. Side by side, okay?"

I admit I was too frightened to speak, so I gave him the

okay sign instead. He smiled. "I'll be right beside you, Yakhi."

Sometimes that's all you need.

"Don't fight it," said Mo, before sinking under the waves.

I gulped down as much air as I could, hoping it would last long enough.

And down I went.

THIRTY-ONE

I IMMEDIATELY PANICKED.

I needed to go back up! I had to breathe!

But I forced my hands against my sides, locked my legs together, and descended. The sea was murky.

I pursed my lips, trying to hold in oxygen, but the pain in my chest was increasing. I could just make out Mo, waiting a dozen feet below. He beckoned to me. I accidentally opened my mouth, and water rushed in.

I reacted instinctively, coughing violently, trying to vomit out the seawater, but each gasp just dragged more in. I stared at the surface, desperate to beat my way up to the glorious air, but . . . but . . .

I stopped trying to breathe. I . . . didn't need to.

Weird. Very weird.

I started sinking. Now that there was no air left in my lungs, all my buoyancy was gone. I kicked toward Mo.

Okay? he signaled.

I answered with the same.

He stuck his thumb down. *Descend.*

The current wasn't as powerful. It was calm down here, peaceful. We'd left the raging storm above us.

We entered a school of fish, their scales patterned with scintillating colors as they investigated us. Even as they swam, they evolved. Second by second, their fins altered, their bodies grew longer or shorter, and they mutated from species to species. Then, with a flick of their tails, they darted away into the great void. Other creatures lurked just on the edge of sight. Massive shapes made their leisurely way through Tiamat's world, our presence too insignificant for them to notice.

In contrast to its all-black surface, the submarine section of the Rock of Nisir was vividly bright, clad in rosy coral and coated in plant life. Vast clumps of seaweed swayed in the current, forests of red and blue and green and all hues in between, home to creatures that had never existed in the natural world. We explored a universe of beautiful monsters.

There was other treasure to be discovered as well. We swam near a long, curved section of wall to watch a family of giant crabs picking among five pillars. One of the pillars wore a ring. The coral had grown over it and it was covered with barnacles, but huge gems—rubies the size of my head and diamonds even bigger—glowed within the darkness. The gold band peeked out from algae patches.

Then I saw something that made me quickly paddle backward.

A gigantic skeleton was embedded in the coral. The skull was the size of a house, with its jaw hanging loosely open, easily wide enough to swim inside—not that I wanted to. The jaw still held teeth: fangs the length and thickness of an elephant's tusks. Bright red and orange plants sprouted within one of its eye sockets. I could make out the spine and ribs—wearing a breastplate of eroded greenish bronze—but the rest of the skeleton was too deep within the coral now.

Mo pressed his palms together and bowed as if praying. Then he waved his arm as though . . . fencing?

I gazed back at the ancient giant. There had been a battle between gods once. This was one of the losers.

I gestured to my brother. We had to go deeper.

We pushed against the rock to propel ourselves downward, the eerie glow of the plants lighting the way. Greater sea creatures glided past, their bodies decorated with pulsating, magical designs. I was so awestruck I was no longer frightened.

But there was a yawning abyss below us. A dark patch with no glowing plants. We swam toward it, and I realized it was a hole in the rock. A cave.

The cave?

You could have driven a jumbo jet through the opening, maybe even two. It was pitch-black, except for a small, shimmering pale light coming from deep within. We swam in side by side, our strokes evenly matched. The golden light shone brighter as we approached, and the current felt warmer. The glow was coming from an opening above us—a small chimney was allowing light to shine down to the water beneath. My heart started racing as I kicked upward and broke the surface of the air pocket.

I coughed out water as oxygen rushed into my lungs to replace it. My chest spasmed, and it hurt more than drowning had. But the viselike grip against my ribs eventually lifted, and then, fingers clasping a sloping ledge, I pulled myself out into a small grotto.

"Make way, Yakhi," Mo said behind me.

I grabbed his sleeve and helped him out.

We were on our hands and knees, aching all over, exhausted. I could barely keep myself from collapsing facedown. All I wanted to do was sleep right there for a hundred days.

When we had caught our breath, we looked around the space. Unbelievably, green vines wove their way through the coral. Thick, sinuous branches hung over our heads, sagging with immense age. They all fed to an alcove in the back. I stumbled to my feet so I could trace them.

"Ya salam. . . ." A tree rose out of the uneven floor. Within its trunk was a hollow holding a single white flower, its petals shining softly. As I got closer, a gentle warmth engulfed me, lifting the tiredness away. I felt a fresh, raw energy surging through me. I tingled from head to toe.

"Good job, Sik," whispered Mo as he came up from behind to gaze at the flower.

We had done it. Our parents could be cured. Nergal could be defeated and New York would be saved.

We'd found the flower of immortality.

THIRTY-TWO

"IT'S DIFFERENT FROM THE ONE I FOUND. MORE beautiful by far," whispered Mo. "All those centuries in the Iraqi desert changed the other one."

"Great. Let's grab it and get going." Curved thorns coated the stem. I had a feeling they'd be painfully sharp.

"Sik! This isn't a dandelion littering the lawn. This is a sacred artifact. A holy object. You need to treat it with—"

I went up to the flower and, using my sleeve, plucked it off its stalk. "You were saying?"

"You have no soul. No poetry of the spirit."

It still glowed, and I felt a gentle pulse of something warm and powerful radiating from the shimmering petals. "I have plenty of poetry."

"Ha!"

I wasn't exactly an expert on flowers, but this one looked more like an old rose than an orchid, small and cupped by petals as soft as dreams. It was difficult to look at it too closely—there seemed to be too many petals, all spiraling inward forever. Its perfume was delicate, changing from moment to moment, sometimes light and fresh, then heavy and cloying. I shook my head to clear it. "There once was a boy named Sik, who needed a flower real quick. So he went into a cave and, being quite brave, snatched it without getting pricked." I tucked the flower carefully in my jacket.

Mo scratched his chin. "I wouldn't quit the day job."

The cave shook, echoing with a dull thud.

"Uh-oh," Mo said. "There's something outside."

"Maybe it's a cute little turtle?" I suggested.

The next impact brought pieces of coral raining down on us.

"Probably not." Mo stepped away from the long tree branches that seemed to reach out for us. "Someone's not too happy about us being here."

The first person I thought of was Erishkigal. "Was this all a setup, do you think?"

Bigger chunks of coral broke after another tremor. Shards cut through the air like bullets.

Mo slipped back into the watery hole. "Let's not wait here to find out."

"What if it's worse out there?" But I was talking to myself. I buttoned up my jacket and jumped into the water.

Drowning was easier the second time. Still achingly

horrible, but less panic-inducing. Mo took the lead, and I paddled after him through the cave. The walls shook, and I tried hard not to think about being trapped in cold seawater for eternity. I put a few extra kicks in to get out a little faster.

When we reached the cave mouth, Mo turned around to check on me. I patted the flower that was firmly in place and warming my heart and gave him a double okay.

A huge shoal of fish circled the opening, barely acknowledging our presence. They mingled peacefully, searching and nibbling at the plants growing out of the immense mountain of coral.

But something else was out there.

Mo felt it, too. We floated, peering into the water ahead, but beyond the first fifty feet, it was only darkness. I gestured to Mo, mimicking a crawl close to the rock face. He nodded, and we drifted out and up.

It bolted out of nowhere. One second, there was nothing, and the next, a huge mouth opened before us, revealing the skeletal remains of whales and sea creatures even larger hanging within its mast-long teeth.

We pushed away as the creature smashed into the rock. The shock wave sent me spinning in one direction and Mo in the other. The coral splintered, and massive sections sheared off in an avalanche of color.

The Basmu serpent, it had to be. One of the children of Tiamat. Which Erishkigal had somehow neglected to mention. As more and more of its body appeared out of the darkness, it seemed endless. Its scales were glossy and dark, each one the size of a barn and encrusted with shells from a millennium of living underwater. The torso still bore the marks of battle. Some of the scales were dented, pitted, and cracked; others were missing entirely, revealing long, crooked scars in the bare skin beneath. Great spines ran along its back, and as it turned, I saw that each one was comprised of hundreds of smaller spikes, jutting out in all directions.

Something clamped my shoulder. My heart almost burst before I saw Mo. He signed, *Okay?*

The serpent circled above us, blocking any way up to the surface. Its great eyes searched the depths, but we were well hidden among the debris. For now.

Mo had picked up a long, jagged spear of coral. He gestured that I stay put. He was going to swim up.

I did a finger-twirl beside my forehead and pointed at him. *You're crazy.*

He made a stabbing motion with the spear. *I am a mighty hunter of the deep! I'll take care of the serpent!*

I clutched my stomach and opened and closed my mouth. *That's the funniest thing I've ever heard!*

He shook his fist at me. *Do as I say or else!*

I rolled my eyes. *As if.*

He folded his arms. *Got a better idea?*

I grinned. *Yup.*

I removed the bag from my shoulder.

Considering it was a gift from a demigod, it didn't look like much. The holes were big and uneven, and the rope was frayed. One good pull and it would probably fall apart. But even Kasusu didn't exactly have that out-of-the-armory shine to it. The sword was old, spotted with rust, and its blade was chipped. Were all supernatural gifts disguised as junk?

Using my hand, I mimicked a fish swimming into it. *We'll trap it in this net.*

Mo frowned. *That's the stupidest thing I've ever heard.*

I pressed my palms together. *What do you mean? It's a magical treasure!*

We both looked up. The monster wasn't going to leave. It was the net or nothing.

With a resigned expression, Mo took hold of one handle. I gripped the other.

I gave him a thumbs-up. *Let's go.*

We kicked upward slowly, eyes on the serpent, a vast black silhouette circling around and around the rock. Sharks, far bigger than any great white from my world, trailed behind it, looking like tadpoles in comparison. You know you're swimming in weird waters when giant sharks are the *least* of your worries.

The serpent was more than a creature; it seemed like a living monument, as eternal and elemental as a mountain range.

Mo let go of the net and kicked ahead of me.

What was he doing?

𒀮𒉿𒆷𒀀𒈾 𒀮𒈨𒌋𒍣𒊓𒅗𒁍 𒅖𒐓

Oh no.

He was going to distract it to let me reach the surface. He didn't think my plan would work. Typical! Why is it that older siblings *always* think they know best?

The sharks sensed him first. They broke off in ones and twos to follow him. Mo was going to get ripped to shreds. I paddled furiously after him, the bag dangling from my arm. I was in open water, away from the relative safety of the rock. There was no hiding place, and the sharks at the back of the line had turned their attention to me.

My heart raced. Life, in the end, is about survival. When everything else has been stripped away, the only options remaining are fight or flight. And once you make the choice, you have to put your all into it. There's no point in half measures. I clenched my fist. I couldn't fight like Belet, but before I got gobbled up, one shark was going to have to deal with a fierce punch to its nose.

A gigantic black shadow passed over us—the sharks and me—and the Basmu serpent opened its maw.

The sharks didn't stand a chance. The serpent could have swallowed the Empire State Building sideways. One massive gulp and they were all gone.

Now it was my turn.

As it widened its mouth, I saw other heads writhing within. That's right—the serpent had five other heads *inside* the main one, and they came forward now, all snapping and biting eagerly. Their eyes glowed a malevolent green-ish yellow, and their fangs still had bloody chunks of shark meat skewered on them. Their necks stretched out from the serpent's throat as the heads shoved each other aside, fighting over which would be the one to swallow me. They extended farther and farther out of the main body, as if the Basmu serpent was vomiting fresh, slimy offspring.

It looked like I was going to spend an eternity in the belly of that thing. I'd have plenty of time to review all the stupid life choices that had brought me here.

The Basmu flinched. It shook itself, twisting its head at a tiny figure hanging from its face.

Mo!

He had jabbed the spear into its huge eye. The Basmu jerked again. I doubted the pinprick had hurt it, but no one likes being stabbed in the eyeball. Mo dangled off one of the spines running along the serpent's snout, and he was now being tossed from side to side.

The inner heads were working their way around to him.

Mo's coral spear snapped. He'd tried to screw it through the serpent's pupil, but the lens was too tough and the coral too brittle. The serpent flicked its head, and Mo lost his grip and spiraled through the water. Two of the inner heads darted toward him.

My bag began to glow. Heat tingled through my fingertips as it pulsed with golden light.

𒀀𒈾𒉿𒄑𒅗𒀀𒅀𒂗𒍝𒌍𒐊𒂊𒊑𒀭𒋫𒈾

And that got the Basmu's attention. Its whole, mile-long body arced around. The displacement of so much water sent me rolling back toward the rock.

The five inner snakes forgot my brother. The glow of the net sparkled upon their scales. It was almost hypnotic.

I let go of one handle, and the bag unraveled quickly, reaching the size of a soccer net and then doubling every second. Soon I could have cast it over a house. I pulled the other handle off my shoulder. The rope still seemed ridiculously feeble.

As best I could in water, I threw it.

The net spun slowly, still expanding as it rotated. The snake heads snapped at it from different angles. I was sure it would tear with no effort.

But it didn't. The net caught on the spines, the rough scales, and the mane of horns surrounding the main head of the Basmu. The serpent curled around, thinking it would snag the net with its tail and use its whole body to rip it asunder. That was a mistake. The net got snared on the array of spikes jutting out at all angles from the tail, and now it was tangled front and back.

The Basmu serpent thrashed desperately as more and more golden threads wove over its body, locking it down segment by segment.

It began sinking. Bound up from head to tail, it couldn't swim anymore and was now a twenty-mile-long deadweight, looped in over itself like a ring of impotent fury. It never quit fighting, but the more effort it put in, the tighter it trapped itself. Only the web of golden light glowed up from the fathomless depths, growing fainter and fainter until it was finally swallowed by the darkness. I wondered if the Basmu would continue to sink for all eternity.

Totally not my problem.

I twisted until I was pointing straight up and then began kicking.

I broke the surface and found Mo had already climbed onto a small rock, barely breaking the water's surface. He pumped his fists at the sky. "Allahu Akbar!"

The storm had passed. The sea barely rippled, and a dense fog hung over it. Mo helped me onto the small boulder and hugged me.

He held me in front of him. "The flower! You still have it?"

I opened up my jacket, and there it was, glowing softly.

"Mashallah!" Mo laughed. "You did it!"

"*We* did it." I shivered as I looked around. I couldn't see more than a few yards.

Then I noticed movement in the sky—a small shadow. With a sharp cry, a bird circled above us. I frowned. "What's a pigeon doing here?"

"It's a raven," said Mo. "It's going to lead you home."

"That mangy bird? How do you know?"

"Just swim after it."

"Swim? I'm never going anywhere wet ever again!"

"Listen to me, Yakhi." There was an intensity in his voice now. "I'll tell Mama and Baba you're on your way to save them. I'll ask them to hang on, stay out of Kurnugi as long as they can, but we're all counting on you."

I grabbed his arms, fear accelerating through me. "No. *We'll* save them. Both of us. I can't do this without you, Mo."

"I don't belong in your world anymore."

"You do, Mo. You *do*! I can't lose you again."

"Sik, you have to let me go." He kissed the top of my head. "You're the best. You always have been. I just wish I'd told you that every day."

"I wasn't. I wasn't. I was jealous of you, Mo. I hated the way everyone was more interested in you than me. How you were the hero, and I just worked in the back. I . . . I wanted you to fail. That way you'd have had to stay home." How can a heart break twice? "I'm sorry. I'm so sorry."

"Me? The hero?" Mo grinned, despite the tears trailing down his cheeks. "I think Gilgamesh himself would have a hard time beating what you just did. Just be a hero for a little while longer, okay?"

I tightened my hold, digging my fingers deep into his flesh. I hugged him with all my might. "I'm not letting you go." I couldn't survive losing him again, not when he was right here. "I'm never letting you go."

"It's not meant to be . . ." he said.

𒀭𒈫𒌋 𒈦𒌋𒌋 𒂊 𒁕𒈫𒂖𒈦𒊏 𒉺𒀭𒈫 𒂗

"Then let me take your place in Kurnugi."

Anything, anything to have him live again. If that's what it would take to bring my brother back, that was fine by me.

"We'll see each other again, one day." Mo kissed my forehead. "Inshallah."

"Please, Mo . . . Don't leave me."

He laughed. "We had our one great adventure, didn't we?"

I felt him go. His warmth first. Then the beating of his heart against mine. His soft breath lifted, no longer disturbing the air. Finally, he faded from my embrace.

"No, no, no . . ." I gazed, bewildered, at my empty arms. I'd lost him again. I bowed my head. I just wanted to fade away, too. I couldn't keep going. Not without my brother. I could just give up.

Then something floated over the quiet water.

His laughter. Full of joy, full of fun, and so full of . . . life.

It echoed from all directions, as if Mo's spirit surrounded me. I wiped my face and forced myself up. He wasn't really gone, just out of sight.

The raven took off. It beat its wings above me, waiting.

I zipped up my jacket. The raven called for me to follow.

"We'll see each other again, Mo!" I shouted. "Inshallah!"

I slipped back into the water and started swimming.

THIRTY-THREE

I SWAM AFTER THE RAVEN AS IT DARTED BACK AND forth through the mist. Each stroke got harder and harder. I was exhausted—fighting undersea monsters had used up what little reserves I had left.

Litter bobbed on the surface: empty plastic bottles, sodden burger containers, soda cans, and pieces of Styrofoam. I wasn't in Kurnugi anymore, but where?

Then my hands met a concrete bottom. I stumbled to my feet and waded toward the cawing raven, which had landed on the bank a few yards away. Running alongside the water was a waist-high iron fence.

I knew this place. . . .

The sun was up, but it was struggling to pierce a thick gray curtain. I could just make out two stocky towers rising over the trees in the distance.

The Eldorado apartment building.

I was back in Central Park, emerging from the Jackie O. Reservoir.

Soaking wet, I clambered over the fence and looked up and down the running path. Where was everyone? The route was usually packed with people.

Trees creaked, and their fall leaves whispered as I left puddles on the dark asphalt. The emptiness was eerie. I hugged myself to try to control the shivering. I barely felt a warm tingle from the flower under my jacket and thought of Ishtar's warning about how its properties might affect my . . . condition. It was probably best that the bloom was separated by my T-shirt and not against my skin.

The bush ahead rustled. A pair of bright yellow eyes gazed through the foliage at me, and there was a dull, wary growl. Plague dogs? I crouched, preparing to run, but I knew my muscles were too tired to get me very far.

A snow leopard padded out of the brush, sleek and covered with speckled smoky-gray fur. Its white whiskers twitched as it sniffed the air between us. It sneered, revealing a full set of ivory canines. The cat kept a wary distance.

For some reason, I wasn't afraid of it. I held out my palm. "You're not one of Ishtar's, are you?"

"She's not. But I am." A girl stepped out from behind a tree. From her boots to her olive-green camo pants and black body armor, Belet was ready for all levels of badassery. The only bright color in her ensemble was a scarlet sash where she'd tucked

Kasusu's scabbard. Her hand rested easily on its pommel.

"Salaamu alaikum," I said. And then I hugged her. I know, but I'd had an emotional day. Surprisingly, she didn't kick me in the head, so I guess we were good.

We stepped apart, and she even smiled. "Wa-alaikum as salaam."

"How did you know I was going to be here?"

Belet looked up at the raven perched on a branch overhead. "A little bird told me. It's been circling all morning; I knew something was up."

"An omen?"

"Yes, an omen," Belet replied. "And here you are."

"I like your outfit. Chanel?"

She tapped her Kevlar vest. "Pentagon. This season's must-have.

"It's okay, girl," Belet told the snow leopard. "Sik's a friend."

A friend? Wow.

The cat flicked her long tail, paused to get a scratch behind the ears, then waded back into the mist.

"If that's not one of Ishtar's lamassus, then how . . . ?"

"Cats like me," Belet said with a shrug. "In all the chaos, some of the animals escaped from the Central Park Zoo. That one found me, and we've been looking out for each other ever since. I call her Qareen."

"Constant companion, eh? I like it." I looked around the eerily quiet park. "What have I missed? Last time I saw you, you were going off to kill Nergal. . . ."

She crossed her arms. "Yeah, well, that didn't go quite as planned. I couldn't get close enough to him on my own. I came back looking for you, but you'd disappeared. And over the last two weeks I've been preoccupied by other things."

"Two weeks?!" I exclaimed.

The park was suddenly filled with screams. Hellish, tear-out-the-back-of-your-throat bellows that almost made my ears bleed.

Belet scowled. "They're up early. C'mon, we need to get to the ziggurat."

The shrieks cracked, breaking into howls and bloodthirsty cries. It was as if the whole park was in torment. "It's horrible," I said, covering my ears. "What is it?"

"Nergal's legions." She turned back toward the mist. "It's his city now."

As we crept along a path carpeted with oily black leaves, I stared at the trees covered in fungi, and the withered grass and bushes that had turned to mulch. The tents we'd seen previously had been torn apart, and their ragged canvas flapped limply in the fetid breeze.

"All this happened while I was gone?" I asked.

"It's much worse outside the park," replied Belet. "That's why I came back here."

Flies feasted on dead animals. Birds and squirrels mainly,

but also rotten cats and dogs—pets that had wandered into the park looking for shelter when there was none left anywhere in Manhattan.

Not even in the ziggurat.

Many of the greenhouse's windows had been shattered, and its iron frame was spotted with rust. Plants spilled out of the broken glass. The tall trees still stood inside, but their leaves were shriveled and their bark was turning moldy and corrupt.

"Welcome back, Sikander." Gilgamesh clambered over the wreckage, untangling himself from thick ropes of vine and brushing dead foliage off his shoulders. He shook himself like a big bear, hurling off great chunks of mud. He flipped his shovel in his hand as he inspected the carnage around him. "A few demons got in, but they've been dealt with."

Dealt with? I liked the sound of that. "You joined the fight?"

"No need." Gilgamesh sat down on a tree stump. "They wandered into my bed of Venus flytraps. Big mistake."

"My guess is your plants are bigger than most?"

"Quite a bit." He rested his chin on the shovel and gazed over at me. "How was Kurnugi?"

Belet's head jerked up. "You were in Kurnugi?"

"Yeah, I was." I stared at Gilgamesh. "You warned me that would happen. I just didn't expect it to happen within the same hour."

He nodded. "Same thing happened to me centuries ago. I served my time but met some old friends while I was there. How about you?"

I turned to Belet. "I saw your mom. She's doing great. She's keeping her sister company."

"What? She and Erishkigal hate each other! The last time Mother visited, Erish had her—"

I stopped Belet right there. "It's not like that. They're fine— just the usual sibling stuff. She asked how you were doing. She wants you to be happy, that's all."

"I'll be happy when I get her back." Belet fidgeted with Kasusu, as if she were ready to charge through the seven gates to Kurnugi right then. Which I guess she was. She just didn't know the way.

"Uh-huh," I said, humoring her. If I couldn't bring Mo back, then she . . . But we had more pressing concerns at the moment. "First we've got to save Manhattan." I opened my jacket and carefully drew out the flower. "With this."

Despite having been squashed against me, the flower unfurled, its petals first shimmering, then glowing with the soft light you get just as the sun's coming up on a clear day. The light that's full of promise and hope.

Gilgamesh's eyes shone as he gazed at it. "Exactly as I remember it." He pulled a pair of gardener's gloves from his overalls pocket. "These are a little big for you, but you should put them on. That's powerful stuff you've got right there."

I did as he said, and even as I held out the flower, the plants around us began to recover. The patches of mold disappeared from the tree trunks, and the drooping plants rose upright, their leaves turning bright emerald as they basked in the blossom's light.

"It's fighting the disease already," said Belet, awed. "So what are we going to do with it? Shine it all over the city? Just like that?"

Gilgamesh shook his head. "There's too much ground to cover, Belet. I'll set up the distillation plant out back and turn the flower into a liquid. Then we'll put it into the water supply."

"That sounds great," I said, grinning at the miraculous plant. Our salvation.

As I looked, its light began to fade. The petals, one moment unfurled and bright, retreated into the center, curling up as an oily stench suddenly wafted through the greenhouse.

Flakes of rust fell from the creaking iron frame. More windows cracked, and the trees shook as if afraid.

Gilgamesh stood up, spinning the shovel in his hand. "Hide the flower, Sikander."

Flies clustered over the roof—millions of them, covering every remaining panel and plunging us into twilight.

Belet drew her sword. "Kasusu?"

The sword screeched. "I smell them! Twelve o'clock."

"This gonna be a last stand?" I asked. "I've only just come back from being dead. Again."

"Last stand?" Gilgamesh smiled to himself. "That depends on us, doesn't it?"

THIRTY-FOUR

"NOW WOULD BE A GREAT TIME FOR YOU TO BREAK YOUR vow of nonviolence," I said to Gilgamesh. "Just for an hour or so."

He shook his head.

"Half an hour? Ten minutes?"

The flies began a strange, repetitive drone, which rose and dropped with a harsh, military rhythm.

I admit I was terrified. Who wouldn't be? I wanted to go home and hide under the covers until it was all over. Let someone else take care of it.

Home? I didn't have one anymore.

And that was what this was all about.

I'd seen the pain in my parents' eyes when they remembered Iraq. They'd talk about the bakery on the corner, the schools they'd gone to, how they'd met at the University of Baghdad. . . . Then, inevitably, they'd fall quiet and the sadness would creep in. They hadn't been able to save their original home, and they'd struggled and suffered to build a new one here, in Manhattan. I wasn't about to let them lose it.

Belet didn't have a home. She didn't even have any family. So what was she fighting for? She looked at me sharply, as if she'd sensed my thoughts. It was what she did, simple as that. Ishtar had taught her war like other moms taught their kids cooking or soccer.

The bushes to our left shook, and my heart jumped. Gilgamesh gestured with his shovel. "They're here." He walked outside, and we followed.

This was it. I grabbed a garden pick.

We climbed through the broken panes and twisted metal and out into the park itself. The ziggurat wasn't a haven anymore. We stood among the decaying, rotting vegetation and faced our enemies. Old enemies.

"Well, lookie here, my friends. Our waiting paid off. I told you they'd be back, but all you did was scoff."

Sidana scurried toward us through the wilted foliage. He'd swollen to grotesque proportions since I'd last seen him, and he was now bigger than a horse. Sharp, venom-coated barbs covered his tail. Other demons bounded alongside him: Idiptu, Tirid, and some I didn't recognize—all bigger, uglier, more diseased. Behind them came the poxies, row after row, going back as far as I could see.

I glanced at Belet. "Looks like everyone's here."

"Except Nergal. The coward just sent his minions." Belet gave Kasusu a sharp flick. "Well?"

The sword muttered. "Let's swat some flies."

But Gilgamesh had other plans. He strode out ahead of us, armed with nothing but his shovel. Even so, all the monsters took a step back. "Leave now, demon! And take your disease-ridden mob with you!"

"Or what, O Gilgamesh the Great?" Sidana said with a sneer. "Step aside before it's too late."

"This place, these people, are under my protection." Gilgamesh flipped the shovel from one hand to another.

The clouds above darkened, and not with flies but a swelling storm. Lightning flashed within the broiling mass, and the sky rumbled. The air filled with static, making my hairs stand on end. The monsters shifted uneasily, snarling and tearing at the trees in frustration. A few edged closer, but none wanted to be first in line. Idiptu pointed an accusing claw at us. "Lord Nergal demands your allegiance!"

Gilgamesh's shovel crackled. The earth around him shook, and sparks jumped across his skin. "Then tell him to come here and demand it himself. I will not bow to his sniveling lackeys."

Under the stench of rotting vegetation, I smelled burning ozone as the air filled with ions. The rumbling turned into a tree-shaking thunder.

Gilgamesh twirled the shovel like a baton.

𒀭𒈾𒆳 𒀭𒉌 𒂊𒌋𒈫 𒊏𒂍𒈫 𒂍𒅎𒂊 𒈾𒀭

"You try my patience, demon."

I tightened my grip on my pick. It was vibrating as strange energy radiated from Gilgamesh's shovel. Yes, really.

Sidana gnashed his crooked teeth. "You laid down your arms to grow plant and flower. Begone, Gilgamesh, for you have no power!"

"Power?" Gilgamesh furrowed his brow, but in the depths of his eyes, something *glowed*. "I may have relinquished weapons, demon, but do not be foolish enough to think I've given up an ounce of my power."

He slammed his shovel into the earth.

The shock wave hurled us off our feet. As the energy rippled out from the epicenter, it magnified in strength. The demons tumbled and poxies were sent into the air as trees were torn from the earth and the buildings around Central Park lost their windows in a single devastating sonic explosion.

The sky shook with endless thunder and erupted with lightning, the clouds bursting with a billion joules of energy. Jagged bolts struck all around us, trees burst into flames, and deep crevasses appeared in the earth. The ziggurat's iron frame became supercharged as the bolts hit it again and again.

I grabbed hold of Belet before she was swept away by the hurricane-force wind and pulled her back inside the greenhouse. "Are you okay?" I shouted.

She nodded as the gust whipped loose soil and leaves all around us. "I think my ears popped!"

Gilgamesh stood on the first tier of the ziggurat, surrounded by a crackling cage of electricity. The entire greenhouse hummed with power, amplifying his until he was a one-man climate-change phenomenon. His shovel smoked as he raised it above his head like a lightning rod and used it to direct the bolts. They zigzagged across the park in blinding flashes, illuminating the terrified faces of poxies and demons alike. Some began to flee.

But for every one that ran away, a dozen more poured forward. A few tried to climb the frame of the structure and got electrocuted and fell, stunned and twitching uncontrollably. The whole greenhouse came to life as vines tangled poxies, gigantic Venus flytraps gulped down demons, and trees swatted the waves of flies filling the air.

Even with the help of the weather and vegetation, though, Gilgamesh was struggling to hold the enemy back. The blight was spreading thick and fast; the greenery was withering, and trees fell as their roots died.

I zipped my jacket to my chin and told Belet, "We need to get out of here. Save the you-know-what."

"I want to fight!" she said, swinging Kasusu overhead.

"Why?" I pointed up to our luminescent demigod. "We've got him!"

The storm continued to rage inside and outside the

ziggurat. The huge trees trembled and swayed as the park echoed with thunderous booms.

Sidana charged me. He bounded over a fallen oak tree, his long claws churning up the dirt. His beady red eyes were ablaze with rabid fury as he rammed his head into my chest.

I spun a dozen feet through the air and crashed into a tree trunk. I had just enough time to wrap my hands around his snout before he tried to fit my head into his jaws. He clawed the air furiously, trying to gut me.

And then he screamed. He jerked backward, thrashing. His tail flicked uncontrollably as he scuttled away, staring down at an oozing gash across his belly.

Belet rose to her feet and flicked blood off Kasusu. The sword spoke. "One skewered rat coming right up."

But even in his death throes the rat was lethal. His tail whipped through the air. . . .

"Belet, watch out!"

She slashed the hideous appendage, and Sidana howled as it flew off. Then he was silent and still.

But Belet stumbled and dropped to her knees.

"Belet!" I was beside her in an instant.

The rat's barbs had ripped her Kevlar as if it were tissue paper. She winced as I unbuckled the vest and gently spread it open. I could see the venom turning her belly black even as her face turned pale.

𒀭𒂗𒋛 𒈦𒂊 𒄀𒋾𒉌𒈨 𒆠𒀀𒋾 𒀀

"You'll be okay, you'll be okay. . . ." I fumbled with my jacket zipper. "You'll be okay. . . ."

"Inshallah?" she hissed through gritted teeth.

While still wearing the big gardening gloves, I pulled out the flower. A single petal would heal everything. We'd still have several left for our magical antidote. The flower's light spread over Belet, and I watched her sigh, the pain already lifting.

Sidana was dead, but I should have remembered Idiptu.

His tongue wrapped around my arm, from elbow to wrist. One tug and I was whipped across the ground. I plowed through the dirt, rolling over and over. Dazed and gasping for breath, I stared up and there he was, towering over me, grinning.

He ripped the flower out of my hand.

THIRTY-FIVE

"WE'LL STOP HERE, JUST FOR A MINUTE," I SAID, gently lowering Belet off my shoulder and onto the hood of an abandoned car. "I don't think anyone's coming after us. Let me have a look at—"

She slapped my hand away. "Will you stop fussing? I'm fine!"

She was anything but. Her skin was jaundiced, and when she checked her belly wound, I saw that it was lined with bubbling black sores. She caught my worried expression and scowled. "I'm *fine*."

"I'm just trying to help, though I don't know why I'm bothering."

"What you should have done was stayed and fought on! You practically handed Idiptu the flower! The only thing missing was a ribbon and a little card. How many fights have you run away from now?"

"All of them," I said simply. I checked behind us. I couldn't see any movement, but you never knew. Poxies could be hiding anywhere.

We'd managed to flee the park, and in all the chaos, no one had pursued us. Why should they? They had what they wanted. The demons' cries of victory had been louder than the thunder.

Gilgamesh? I didn't know. When I'd looked back, he was disappearing under a horde of poxies, too many for even him to shake off.

We were heading south down Seventh Avenue, hiding from the monsters on the streets. The city had no power. No streetlights, no traffic signals, no flashing billboards over Times Square. Cars sat abandoned, sprinkled in rust. It was eerily quiet without any traffic moving through.

"We should have fought," mumbled Belet, her eyelids closing. Then she jerked back awake and looked at me, embarrassed that I'd seen her weak.

I just smiled. "It's okay, Belet."

"Can you face the other way?" she asked.

"Why?"

"Because I want to cry!" she snapped. "And I can't with you watching!"

"Mind if I join you? I could use a good cry myself."

She laughed. She cried, too, but she laughed as well. Thunder rumbled above and there was the distant whine of the vast clouds of flies, but this little patch of Manhattan echoed with Belet's laughter. I couldn't help but think of Mo. They both laughed when things were at their worst. Belet curled up as the laughter gave way to a groan. "Ow. I think I pulled something."

"You need to be more careful."

"Or what? I'll die laughing? There are worse ways to go, Sik."

"No one's dying—it's no fun at all," I said. She wasn't going to be able to make it much farther, even with the help of my shoulder. Her breath was getting shallower by the minute. "We need transportation."

"Pick a car, then." She pointed to one. "That Mercedes will do."

"Uh-huh," I said, looking at the rusty heap stuck behind all the others.

Then my eye caught sight of something lying outside a Target. "Now, I know you're not gonna like this, but wait here. I'll be right back."

A minute later, I was back with my "transportation." Belet took one look. "I'd rather die in a gutter."

"That can easily be arranged." I hoisted her up and dropped her into the shopping cart. I laid Kasusu across her lap. "Better?"

"I'm the daughter of a goddess, you know." But then she

slumped over, her eyes closing and her breath whispering through her pale lips.

I'd failed everyone. I should have fought Idiptu. I should have grabbed Kasusu and chased after him as he bounded away. I should have cut a path through the hundreds of poxies and rescued Gilgamesh and not let anything stop me. Like a real hero.

Hero. The word was bitter. The only hero here was lying semiconscious in a rattling shopping cart.

I'd lost the flower. After all the trouble we'd gone to, I'd let it slip away, just like that.

I wasn't going to lose Belet, too.

We needed to get to Manhattan General. Someone there might be able to help Belet, and if it all went sour, at least I'd be with Mama and Baba at the end.

My route to the hospital took us by way of the deli. I wasn't exactly surprised by what I saw when we reached the corner of Siegel, but that didn't make it any easier to take.

"Ya Allah. . . ." Graffiti covered the exterior. The windows had all been smashed. One corner of the brick was stained with smoke. Someone had set fire to my home.

I started to read the words scrawled on the outside but stopped myself. The hatred made me sick. As things had gone from bad to worse, people had taken out their anger on the easiest scapegoats: my family. They blamed us for having brought the plague to Manhattan.

I'd wanted to return home, but it was gone. All that remained was this . . . defiled shell.

I dragged the cart to the curb and sat down on the bench outside Georgiou's. Someone had smashed up his pizzeria. Almost a century of family love and dedication had been poured into the place, and now it was gone, just like that, torn down by a city's rage.

"Don't cry, Sik."

Belet rested her head on her shoulder, one arm dangling over the side of the cart. She made an exaggerated frown. "Being sad doesn't suit you."

"I'm sorry, Belet." I sneezed. My clothes were still damp from my long swim, but what did it matter? It's not like I could die of pneumonia. "I should have stopped Idiptu."

"He would have torn off your arms, and you know it."

I looked over at her. "I don't like you like this, Belet. All reasonable and considerate. It's freaking me out."

"I've got no more fight left in me, Sik." She leaned back to look at the night sky. Clouds of flies drifted over us, their buzzing a faint background droning. "For the first time in a long while, I feel peaceful. . . ."

Her serene expression reminded me of Mo's back in Kurnugi.

Wait a minute. . . .

Belet wanted to see her mother, trade places with her. . . .

𒀭𒈦𒁲 𒑱𒐊𒂷 𒐋𒌍𒉿𒍣𒀀𒌍 𒐊𒍟

"Oh, no you don't," I said, standing up.

The sky rumbled, and there was an oppressive weight to the air, a sullen, foreboding pressure, as if it were waiting for something. A cat that had been sitting on the roof of a pickup truck across the street sprang onto the window ledge of our apartment and disappeared into the shadows.

I walked up to Mo's. There used to be a first-aid kit under the counter. It probably wouldn't do much good, but it was worth trying, if only to reduce Belet's pain. Wooden boards had been hammered haphazardly across the front, but there were gaps I could peer through.

I saw the countertop. The register. The big tin range hood. The framed flowers . . .

Mo's pressed flowers were hanging on the wall.

How could that be? Nergal had torn them all down.

There was more. The broken tables had been replaced, even if they were just wooden pallets resting on the tops of plastic barrels. I spotted a camp stove in the corner, and rows of cans neatly stacked along the wall. Another cat watched me from within, its big green eyes shining in the gloom.

I put my mouth to the biggest gap. "Hello? I'd like to order some takeout, please."

The security door to the upstairs apartment creaked open, and a shadowy figure stepped out.

"Sik?"

I couldn't believe it. "Daoud?"

𒀀𒈦𒄀𒆠 𒀀𒉌 𒂍𒋾𒈨 𒊺𒅕𒉺 𒂍𒆠𒌈 𒈾𒉿

He waved frantically to the back. "Come around! I'll open up!"

I slung a now-unconscious Belet over my shoulder—she seemed too light—and with Kasusu in my hand, ran around to the rear, finding Ishtar's gleaming black Jaguar parked in the alley. Its frame was rust-free, and no dust had dared to settle on the hood. Daoud unlocked the back door to the deli and waved me in.

"I thought I'd lost you, cuz," he said as he locked up behind us.

"It doesn't matter now, I'm just happy to—"

Daoud turned around.

"—see you?" I nearly dropped Kasusu.

Handsome, ridiculously beautiful Daoud . . . wasn't. Not anymore. His frame had withered, wrinkled skin hung off his face, his hair stuck out in brittle clumps, and he'd lost his top front teeth. The ones that remained sat, yellowed and crooked, in a too-large jaw supported by a scrawny neck. The dreamy brown eyes that used to make mothers sigh and the girls giggle were bloodshot and rheumy.

"It happened at the audition." He tapped his chin with bony fingers. "I was sitting in the corridor, waiting for my turn, when two of my teeth came loose. I was on camera, in front of the casting agent and director, when half my hair just fell out. Awkward."

"I'm sorry, Daoud, I really am. I got you into this mess."

"But there's a silver lining. My agent thinks I'll get more villain parts now." Then he noticed Belet for the first time. "What's wrong with her?"

"The usual. Run-in with a demon. That's bad enough"—my chin trembled as I spoke—"but she's also lost her fighting spirit."

It may have been my imagination, but it felt like Kasusu was drooping in my hand.

"Come on," Daoud said. "We can put her in your parents' room."

I shook my head. "No. We can't stay. I just want to clean her wound and then take her to Manhattan General. See Mama and Baba."

"Not happening." His face sagged even more in pity. "Poxies have the hospital under siege. No one can get in or out."

That's when the last of my hope evaporated. I trudged up the stairs behind Daoud.

He'd cleaned up the place. Even redecorated. There were fresh flowers on the nightstand, and candles on all the shelves. The windows were covered with blackout blinds, but the blinds themselves were plastered with travel posters.

I gently put Belet on the bed, and Daoud washed her wound with water from one of the big plastic containers lined up on the floor along the wall.

"You learn a thing or two when you're born in a refugee camp," he said. "Water's top priority."

I collected the first-aid kit, cleaned her wound as best I could, and secured a large patch of gauze over it with surgical tape. There was nothing more we could do for Belet. Her breath was a mere trickle.

When we were done, Daoud grimaced as he searched the back of his mouth. He gave a sharp tug and held out one of his molars. "I've never had a filling my whole life, and now I'll be wearing dentures by the time I'm twenty-five."

How could he be so nonchalant? Our world was collapsing all around us. I would have guessed that it was all too much and he'd lost his mind, but he seemed to be doing a good job of taking care of everything.

He tutted. "Go put on some fresh clothes. I'll cook up some rice. We can eat up here, beside Belet."

How long had it been since I'd seen my room? Mere weeks? It felt like a million years. Nothing had changed, except everything. My science homework was still spread out on the small desk by the window. I hadn't made my bed; the quilt was shoved up against the wall, and the pillow lay on the floor. The blinds were half-raised, and outside, I watched pieces of trash blowing down the street. Lightning flashed somewhere far away. I didn't see any poxies out there, but I imagined them scavenging among the debris of a fallen city.

Taking a cue from Daoud, I started to make my bed. But

after a few tugs on the sheet, I figured, why bother? I fell onto the mattress and pulled the quilt over my head.

"Dinner!"

Despite everything, I was hungry. I followed the smell of cooked rice to Daoud's room.

He gave me an awkward smile as I reached the open door. "I don't think you've been in here since . . ."

Daoud had taken over Mo's room when he moved in two years ago. In all that time, I'd seen no reason to visit.

Looking around now, I saw that it was still Mo's, but with a dash of Daoud. There were maps on the walls, and shelves of travel guides and history books, but they were sharing space with posters of Clint, Brad, and Keanu, as well as stacks of *Vanity Fair* and the *Hollywood Reporter*. More pressed flowers were strewn across the desk.

"Do you mind me using his room?"

I shook my head. "He wanted it that way. He thought you were a great guy."

"He was the best." Daoud handed me a bowl and fork. "Rice, with canned vegetables and sardines. And . . ." He waved a small jar.

"The Baghdad?"

"One spoonful, or two?"

"What's more danger at this point? Let's go for two." I sat down on the bed and stirred in the sauce. "You've been busy."

He looked over at the pressed flowers. "Yeah. Beauty's got

to be preserved. Now more than ever." He rubbed his flaccid cheek absentmindedly.

"I didn't know you taught Mo."

Daoud laughed. "We learned together! You know the fashion industry makes more from perfumes than it does from clothes? I figured it would be a good fallback skill. Here." He rummaged along the shelves and found a shoebox. "Have a sniff."

Inside were half a dozen tiny bottles, each filled with liquid and petals. Daoud picked up one and shook it before popping the cork. "I've been experimenting. It's not that different from cooking. You just distill something over and over until you get the richest scent you can."

I took a whiff. "Roses?"

A cat meowed out in the hallway and scratched at the door. A pair of mismatched eyes peered through the gap.

"Sargon?" I asked.

The tabby cat purred as he walked in and brushed against Daoud's leg.

"Okay, okay, I'll feed you." Daoud sighed as he lifted the scarred creature in his arms. "I don't know how, but they followed me here. I have half of Ishtar's kitties living downstairs. Never met such demanding beasts."

"Need any help?" I asked.

"La, shukran. You keep an eye on Belet." Before he left

the room, he turned back and said, "It's good to have you home, cuz."

I finished the bowl. I could smell the flowers across the room, even from their pressed petals. Daoud's portfolio was leaning against the desk, still dusty from the battle of Venus Street. Why had he risked his life for a few headshots and clippings? I picked it up, opened it out of curiosity. To find . . .

A photo of Mo.

He was laughing, his head thrown back, kneeling in the mud as he planted some bulbs. The sun sparkled in his eyes, and there were splotches of dirt on his cheeks.

The next one showed him frowning in concentration, hunched over the flower press, not even aware of the photo being taken. The room was dark except for the lamplight over the equipment, catching only half of Mo's face.

I'd never seen my brother like this. It was more than just good composition and a great eye for detail. Much more.

Daoud returned just then. He joined me at the desk and gazed down at the photos. "I've tried to take other pictures, but none have turned out as good as these."

How could they? These were taken through the eyes of love.

I flicked through page after page. I'd never seen Mo so . . . beautiful. There was no other word for it. The lighting was just right, the shadows perfectly cast, the location spot-on.

But most of all, it was how Mo gazed at the camera, and the guy behind it.

"Why haven't you ever shown these to us?"

"I tried, Sik. Remember?"

Oh. Yeah. He'd always offered up his portfolio, and I'd studiously avoided it. Life would have been so much better if I'd just given him a chance.

Why? Because of what was stuck inside the last cellophane sleeve. It wasn't a photo.

It was a flower.

Perfectly pressed, each petal carefully displayed on the ivory paper, their radiant colors dancing even in the weak candlelight. It wasn't quite an orchid, and not a rose, either, but something utterly unique.

I trembled. Could it be?

"I dug that one up the day before the bulldozers rolled." Daoud drew his finger lightly around the outline. "I'd never seen anything like it."

It had been a mere cutting when I'd planted it. A stalk with a few flowering buds. But the unusual colors were unmistakable.

"And with the other blossoms I made this." Daoud rummaged around in the shoebox and lifted out a bottle filled with a silvery, almost-mercurial fluid.

The jar had a neat, handwritten label on it: MO'S PROMISE.

𒀭𒅖𒆠 𒁹𒂊 𒀊𒈾𒁉 𒌓𒁲𒄿𒀉

I had to lick my lips—my mouth had suddenly gone dry. "Mo's Promise? That he'd come back?"

"No, nothing like that. I used to tell him about my auditions, all the times I got cast as the bad guy. I really wanted to quit, but he insisted I keep trying. He promised that sooner or later I'd get to play a hero. Y'know, save the day."

"He was right, Daoud." I took the bottle for a closer look. The liquid sparkled. "I think you just have."

𒀭𒆠𒅆𒄴 𒀭𒈨𒍑𒊏𒀭𒊏𒉺 𒂍𒈨𒁾 𒅇𒀭

THIRTY-SIX

———◆———

"WHAT ARE WE DOING?" ASKED DAOUD AS WE WENT into my parents' room.

Belet had gotten worse in the last thirty minutes. She looked a hundred years old. With a trembling hand, I gave the bottle a vicious shake and removed the cork. I sniffed. "It doesn't smell like anything."

"I know. You need hundreds of petals to make a scent, ideally thousands, but I had to try, for Mo."

"It'll have to do." I took a deep breath to calm my nerves, dipped the eyedropper into the liquid, and suctioned up a few drops.

I let a single one fall on Belet's cracked, blistered lips.

"That's not really how perfume works," Daoud whispered.

"Come on, Belet. Kurnugi can wait a while longer."

Was I too late? Was she already on the train to the netherworld to see her mother? Maybe a few more drops would do

𒀭𒈾𒂗𒆠 𒊏𒈫 𒂍 𒅗𒌓𒁁𒌷𒈨 𒊑 𒄑𒐋 𒋫 𒊑

the trick. That was it. But if that didn't work . . .

"Ya salam . . ." whispered Daoud, gazing at Belet.

It happened slowly. The stark pallor gave way to soft blossoms of color as her yellowed, paper-thin skin warmed. We stared as her flesh returned, swelling upon her bones and tightening her skin with muscles. Her lackluster, brittle hair rippled with life and shine. Belet licked her lips and gradually opened her eyes. "That was an unusual taste. What was it?"

Daoud stared. "How . . . ?"

Belet sat up and swung her feet to the floor. Then she paused and grimaced. I grabbed her as she swayed unsteadily. "Take it easy, Belet. You were practically dead a second ago. Lie back down for a while."

"We don't have time, Sik." She gritted her teeth, forcing herself to stand. "Where's Kasusu?"

The sword hummed from the top of my parents' dresser, where I'd put it. Even in the dim room it glinted with joy. She picked it up and slid it into her sash. "We've got to find Idiptu and get the flower back."

"No need. We have this." I held up the tiny jar.

And felt ridiculous. How much was left? Less than an ounce. Gilgamesh's plan had sounded good, but how could we cure an entire city with only a thimbleful of Mo's Promise?

"What's going on, exactly?" asked Daoud.

"This is what Nergal's been after all this time," I said. "The flower you pressed grants immortality."

"There was another flower?" Belet asked, her eyes wide. Then she pressed her fingers to her lips. "You gave me some of that?"

"Yeah," I said, my head swiveling between the two of them. "See what it can do?"

"Could it make me handsome again?" Daoud asked.

Why hadn't he developed any immunity? I wondered. Between all the gardening, perfume-making, and pressing, he'd handled the flower much more than I had. "Did you ever touch it—the flower, I mean?"

Daoud shook his head. "I always wore gloves. You got to understand—gardening ages your skin faster than a month of sunbathing. Not that that matters now," he said wryly, studying his wrinkled hands. "And when it comes to making perfume, you have to work in sterile conditions so you don't contaminate the product."

Poor Daoud. If not for his vanity and meticulousness, he would've been immortal like me.

Daoud wet his cracked lips. He didn't reach for the bottle, not exactly, but I could see the eager desperation in his eyes.

He wanted it. And it was his. It was horrible. What would I do if he asked for it? What reason did I have to deny him the cure?

Actually, I had eight million reasons. "We have a lot of people to save."

To his credit, Daoud nodded with understanding and took a step back. "It's not much, cuz."

"Tell me about it." I doubted there was enough for a city block, let alone the whole island. "We could take it to the hospital, at least."

Daoud rubbed his chin. "There *is* a way of making it go a little further. . . ."

"Really?" I asked.

"It's a concentrated perfume extract. I could dilute it into an eau de toilette."

"Dilute it? By how much?"

"One part in twenty, or thereabouts. You never know until you try, but the risk is"—his face dropped—"if you dilute it too much, it's basically just scented water."

There was so little! We could cure Daoud right now, or we could try to save more people—like my parents—by conserving every drop and diluting it. . . . But in doing so, we might end up with nothing.

Regardless, it wasn't my choice. I handed him the bottle. "It's your call, Daoud."

He didn't even hesitate. "I'll dilute it. The kit's in the basement."

That Daoud. Full of surprises. "Hurry up, then."

"I'll meet you out back."

Daoud exited, and Belet went over to the mirror. She raised her shirt over her abdomen and peeked under the bandage. Then she pulled the wrapping completely off. There was still an ugly scar across her stomach, but it had sealed into a thin, jagged line. She traced it with her finger, looking astounded. "You don't think . . . ?"

Yeah, I did think. Was she now the same as me? "Let's just get through the next few hours, eh?"

Belet nodded. "Do you really believe we can save the day with a bottle of perfume?"

"Inshallah."

What else could I say? There were too many things that weren't up to us.

THIRTY-SEVEN

THE CLOUDS CHURNED VIOLENTLY OVERHEAD, THEIR bellies rumbling with thunder, and lightning jumped across the sky. Wind howled through the alley, banging the trash cans against one another and sending newspapers fluttering through the air.

"This is Gilgamesh's doing!" Belet shouted over the wind, pointing at the black clouds. "It started when he unleashed Abubu, the Sky Cutter. It'll be a full-blown hurricane soon."

Good ole Gilgamesh. He'd come through for us in his own climate-changing way. I just hoped he hadn't fallen victim to those poxies. . . .

Four cats had followed us out of the deli—Sargon, another tawny feline, an orange tabby, and an all-black. They hissed and swished their tails like they knew something was up.

"Hello, my loves!" said Belet, bending down to pet them. "Good to see you again."

"They got names?" I asked.

"Sargon you know, and these are his friends: Simba, Shere Khan, and Bagheera," said Belet. Then she blushed. "I'm a big Disney fan."

"Who isn't?" I jangled the keys to her mom's Jaguar. "Let's get out of the wind, at least."

Though our future prospects were worse than bleak, I was still hoping we could save my parents and at least some of the other patients. Then we could all escape the city—maybe even grab Gilgamesh on the way out—and make a new life somewhere. My mom and dad had started over before.

Nergal had what he wanted now; maybe he would leave humanity alone. . . .

Yeah, right. Keep dreaming, Sik.

I sat in the driver's seat, Belet riding shotgun, or, in her case, riding scimitar with Kasusu. With the car doors closed, we settled into a cozy cocoon of black leather and wood trim. The engine growled to a start, and even though we weren't moving, I could feel the power of the vehicle. I ran my hands over the steering wheel, wishing I knew how to drive. Now, how to turn on the heat?

"Mother loved this car," said Belet.

"She called it her chariot," I said, my eyes sweeping the dashboard. So many lights and buttons.

"I think she was talking metaphorically," said Belet.

"'When I really need to fly,'" I said, repeating her words

from the day I'd met her. "Metaphorically, for anyone but a goddess." I began scanning the dashboard. "Where was it . . . ?"

There. The button covered with a warning.

DNT.

I ripped off the tape.

Outside the car, Sargon climbed up onto the hood and peered at me.

Belet put her hand against the windshield. "He's expecting something."

"Yeah, I think he is." I pressed the button.

There was a humming sound. Lightning crackled along the dashboard. Sparks jumped through the air around us.

Ishtar's Jaguar went full Chitty Chitty Bang Bang.

Belet gasped. The steering wheel melted in my hands. The seats re-sculpted under our bodies, and the chassis screamed as it warped. The windshield dribbled away like wax under a blowtorch.

The car was having a god surge. The whine of the engine was earsplitting, and the static charge inside was making everything, including us, glow a neon blue. The car shook until our bones bounced.

"Sik!" Belet grabbed me just as there was an intense flash of white light.

Then all went silent and still.

Eyes squeezed shut, teeth clenched, I stayed curled up in

my seat, waiting for my heart to stop racing. Then my seat disappeared, and I was sitting on the floor.

I opened one eye. Then the other.

I stood up and grinned. "Ya salam!"

The Jaguar was gone. In its place was a four-wheeled chariot. Not some rickety wooden contraption you'd see in some museum, but the weird, outrageous vehicle of a god, built of sleek, otherworldly metal and shimmering with starlight.

And in the harness were four majestic lamassus. Sargon, the biggest by far, twitched his wings. Next to him was Simba, rubbing his snout against the feathers. Shere Khan, a huge tiger, had feathers decorated with stripes. Bagheera's wings were as pure black as a raven's.

Belet stood up beside me, her eyes wide with wonder. "Oh, Mother . . ."

The reins were made of crackling electricity. I touched one carefully, wishing I had on Gilgamesh's gardening gloves. Getting electrocuted would end this adventure real quick. But instead of being incinerated by ten thousand volts, all I felt was a warm tingle.

Kasusu hummed happily. "Nice ride. This reminds me of the time—"

"I'm sure it does," said Belet, white-knuckling the side of the chariot and yelling in the wind.

"Well? You just going to admire the interior?" asked Kasusu.

"We're waiting for Daoud," said Belet.

"No harm in giving it a little test drive," I said, holding the reins loosely and giving them a light flick.

The lamassus growled and tugged and twisted under the yoke. The wheels clattered over the cracked concrete. I winced as one front wheel scraped the wall, tearing out some bricks before I was able to steer in the other direction.

"Do you have any idea what you're doing?" snapped Belet.

"Actually, no. But what's new about that?" I yanked on the reins. "Guys! Help me out here!"

Sargon glanced over his shoulder and growled.

I looped the reins around my forearms for a better grip. Energy tingled up my skin, connecting me through the reins to the power of the four lamassus, as if we were all part of a single circuit. Through the chariot I could practically sense the cats' thoughts and predict their reactions as they prowled along. We made it out to the street.

"Sik, look." Belet pointed Kasusu to the right. "We have an audience."

Poxies crept toward us, mutated to the point they barely resembled anything human. Their clothes were ragged and covered in filth, their bodies had warped into hideous designs. Insectile limbs stuck out from a few of the jackets, and mandibles clicked from grossly wide mouths. Others were human-headed slugs, trailing silvery slime.

The lamassus snarled and revealed their long claws.

I jumped when a scream came from our left. A poxie launched himself at us, mouth frothing and a wicked meat cleaver raised high for some skull splitting.

Sargon roared and swatted the guy out of the air with a casual swipe. The guy crashed into an abandoned pile of trash bags, and before he could get back up, Sargon was on him, jaws wide. . . .

"NO!" I yelled, pulling the reins as hard as I could.

Sargon yowled, keeping one massive paw on the poxie who'd once been someone I knew. Mr. Georgiou was covered in weeping sores and black bile dribbled from his nostrils, but he was still the person who'd helped us ever since we'd opened the deli.

"Bad kitty!" I said, straining to hold Sargon back. "Do not eat my neighbor!"

Sargon raised his paw and cuffed Mr. Georgiou lightly, like he was playing with a mouse, knocking the poor guy out cold. The big cat frowned at me.

"We can't kill them," I said, looking at the bloodthirsty mob approaching, leaning into the wind. "They live around here. Look, that's Charlie Yen. I'm in math club with him."

"They want to tear us limb from limb, Sik." But even as she spoke, Belet lowered Kasusu.

Before there could be any further debate, the ground

shook. The chariot lurched, and the poxies stumbled as a tremor rippled along Siegel. Then something came bouncing over the block. Something like a colossal toad.

"Murderers!" Idiptu cried as he descended out of the swirling black sky. He crashed through the roof of Georgiou's, shattering all the windows as it buckled under the impact. A moment later he rose out of the dust and shook off broken roof tiles. "You're gonna pay for what you did to my sweet Sidana."

When we'd first met, the toad demon hadn't even come up to my shoulder. But pestilence had been good for him. Now he had to be twenty feet tall at least, and just as wide. He unrolled his tongue down the whole length of the pizzeria, flicking it side to side and splashing stinking saliva over the walls.

Daoud rushed toward us from down the back alley. He was cradling one of Mom's tubs of tzatziki in one hand and waving a frying pan in the other. "I've done it! A whole pint! This should . . ." His gaze rose up to Idiptu. "Ya Allah. That's not good."

I gave the reins a sharp flick. The lamassus took up the strain. "Climb aboard, Daoud!"

Idiptu stood to his full height and extended his arms. He could almost reach our side of the street. "I'm gonna swallow you whole."

That wasn't an idle threat. His mouth had to be ten feet wide.

Daoud jumped onto the chariot and waved the pan over his head. "Allahu Akbar!"

Belet looked over at us and shrugged. "This has to be the most peculiar jihad ever."

With Daoud on my left, Belet on my right, and me holding the reins, we charged.

THIRTY-EIGHT

THE POXIES TRIED TO STOP US. THEY FORMED A SNARLING mob, armed with branches, rocks, even shopping carts, and tried to encircle the chariot. But it was like trying to corral a hurricane. The lamassus smashed through them, sending them tumbling like rag dolls.

"Good kitties," said Belet.

The strength of the lamassus and the power of the chariot passed through the reins into me, making us an unstoppable juggernaut.

The cats were just fast enough to dodge Idiptu's darting tongue and just nimble enough to stay out of reach of his sweeping arms. As we raced up Fifteenth, in the direction of Manhattan General, he bounded after us in huge, ground-cracking jumps, leaving craters in his wake.

"Faster!" cried Daoud.

I glanced back. Idiptu and the poxies were falling farther and farther behind. I pulled the reins hard left, and we swept onto Broadway. Then I saw what lay ahead: a gruesome parade of pestilence.

"More poxies," said Belet. "Looks like the entire city has turned out for us. Lovely."

I glanced at the plastic tub in Daoud's hand. Suddenly it didn't seem so big, certainly not large enough to cure a hospital full of people. We needed a tanker of it.

"Did you try any?" I asked Daoud. "You know, just as an experiment?"

He bit his cracked lip. "I was tempted, I admit," he said. "But I didn't want to waste a drop."

"It isn't too late, you know," I said. "I could sprinkle some on you now, and we could see if it—"

Sargon roared. The other lamassus joined him, rising onto their hind legs to slice the air with their forepaws. The poxies in front of us, rabid with bloodlust, paused. There were thousands of them, but no one wanted to be the first to take us on.

Daoud gazed at the huge crowd and tightened his hand on the frying pan. "I guess we get to be heroes, after all, eh, cuz?"

"About time!" I flicked the reins, and the lamassus pounced forward. They flapped their wings as they ran straight at the horde of frenzied poxies that surged at us as one. Their wings beat harder and harder.

𒀭𒈨𒌋𒊏 𒂗𒈨𒌍 𒀀𒈾𒆠𒈹𒅕 𒉺𒉌 𒀊

There were a hundred yards between us, then fifty. The chariot wheels bounced over the uneven asphalt, each time hanging in the air a little longer.

Twenty yards. I could see the raging madness in the poxies' bloodred eyes.

Ten.

The four lamassus roared simultaneously, and Sargon, taking the lead, leaped. I mean *leaped*. My guts dropped to my ankles as the chariot shot skyward. The lamassus, freed from the ground, lowered their heads to direct all their power to flight. With each beat of their wings, we climbed higher between the canyon of skyscrapers.

I shouted over the howling wind. I don't remember what I said exactly—I was too caught up in the moment—but if you can't have fun flying over Manhattan in a magical chariot drawn by four massive winged cats, then when can you?

Belet, her jaw fixed, nodded even as she clutched the side of the chariot all the tighter. Kasusu was cheering, shouting about some great chariot battle in Kadesh. The sword was loving this, while I struggled to keep down my rice dinner as the chariot rocked and spun in the hurricane. Daoud was praying really hard.

We never saw Idiptu coming. He must have been waiting down one of the side streets. He catapulted himself straight onto the back of the chariot, propelling us right into—and through—the glazed windows of a building.

Belet tried her best to cover me as glass shards sliced through the air.

The chariot hit the floor of an open-plan office and limped around, the left front wheel trembling unevenly. Two of the lamassus, Shere Khan and Simba, had been torn free of the harness and were lying on the floor, mewling pitifully as they shrank back into their cat forms.

Idiptu, who had jumped off one second before impact, swung himself through the shattered windows. "There's no escape for you now," he said, saliva dripping from his immense mouth.

Belet grimaced as she plucked a thin triangle of glass from her arm. "We need to end this, Sik."

She was right. I tugged the reins, struggling to keep the chariot upright as I turned it to face Idiptu. We'd been so close to reaching the hospital. . . . "Do you think you and Kasusu could . . . ? Hey, where's Daoud?"

We both scanned the room.

He lay to the right of the demon, his face bleeding from a dozen cuts. The tub had slipped from his hands and was rolling toward the broken window.

Idiptu smacked his lips as he zeroed in on Daoud. He flicked out his tongue and wrapped it around our friend like a boa constrictor. The demon opened his mouth wide. . . .

The tub began picking up speed.

"Mine!" yelled Belet. She leaped off the chariot platform and dashed toward the plastic container.

I slapped the reins hard over the two remaining lamassus, Sargon and Bagheera. They didn't need any encouraging— they had a reviled demon in their sights. Their claws shot out, long and sharp.

Idiptu's eyes widened as the chariot sped toward him. He dropped Daoud, but not fast enough.

When we slammed into the giant toad, it was like crashing into a brick wall. The impact jarred me all the way through to my toes and punched the air from my lungs. Sargon and the black panther tore at Idiptu, ripping great, ragged chunks of slimy flesh off his bones. The demon's scream is a sound I'll remember till the end of my days. I had no doubt it was the first time in a looong time he'd ever felt terror. Sargon buried his fangs into the disgusting creature's shoulder, and a fountain of green blood sprayed the ceiling.

Belet slid across the floor and clasped the tub as it tottered on the ledge.

As the lamassus jumped out of the way of Idiptu's slime, I left a pair of deep chariot grooves across the toad's head. Maggots spewed from the wounds across his body as he took a few rasping breaths. I pulled the chariot to a halt to make sure they were his last.

"Shukran," said Daoud as we helped him to his feet. Despite having been torn up by glass and nearly squeezed to death, he was smiling . . . until he saw the chariot. "Your chariot looks almost as bad as I do."

"We left half the team back there." I jerked my head toward the cats.

"Be careful with this," said Belet, handing me the tub before going to check on Shere Khan and Simba. "They're only dazed, but their god surge is spent," she reported, stroking them. "You were both so brave."

I wasn't sure how to say the next part, but I had to. "Without four lamassus pulling it," I started, "I don't know if the chariot can carry—"

Daoud interrupted. "Do what you need to do."

"Are you sure?"

"Daoud's right," said Belet, wrapping her bleeding arm with her sash. "Sargon and Bagheera will get the job done."

I started to lift the lid of the precious container of serum. "First, Daoud, let's fix you up with a little—"

"Don't waste any more time," said Daoud, waving me off. "Go save your folks already!"

He was amazing me more with every passing minute.

"There might be more demons out there," Belet warned me. "And we don't know where Nergal has gone off to. Be careful."

"'Be careful'?" I said, looking shocked. "I hope you're not going all mushy on me, Belet."

She made a sour face and a gesture that was probably rude back in ancient Mesopotamia.

"I won't be long." I sealed the tub of Mo's Promise and put it securely between my feet on the chariot platform. "I'd tell you to stay up here, out of trouble, but, hey, who am I kidding?"

I tugged the lamassus into a sharp right. Then I ducked behind the front panel as they leaped out the shattered window. More glass rained down, but then we were out in the raw gusts howling down Broadway.

I looked back to see Belet standing at the opening. She raised Kasusu and shouted, but the wind stole her words.

It was time to pay Mama and Baba a visit.

I flicked the reins and drove into the heart of the storm.

THIRTY-NINE

THE CHARIOT STRUGGLED AGAINST THE ELEMENTAL battering. Rain, driven horizontal by the winds, blinded me, and I was drenched and bruised. I couldn't see to steer, so I just gripped the frame for dear life as we smashed against gust after gust.

I smelled the raw ozone in the electricity-charged air around me. As we sprinted into the clouds themselves, the odor grew stronger.

The sky was lit up by gigantic sheets of brilliant lightning. Thunder erupted around us, and shock waves of sound sent us spinning. The two lamassus strained for all they were worth to keep us moving forward, but I knew they were tiring.

Where was the hospital? I couldn't see it below. There were no streetlights to navigate by. The only feature was the dark green block of Washington Square Park, sporadically lit by lightning flashes.

Masses seethed along the streets below—the countless poxies on a rampage of mindless destruction, driven beyond insanity by Nergal's diseases. Even if I could reach the hospital, would I be too late? What if Mama and Baba were poxies now?

I couldn't think like that. The two people I loved most in the world were down there somewhere. Not to mention my friends, teachers, neighbors, customers . . .

The tub contained every single one of my hopes, everyone's hopes. I picked it up from between my feet and hugged it tightly to my chest.

Sargon growled, but he sounded weak. Then his ears twitched nervously. I heard a distant roaring. . . .

A golden thunderbolt burst out of the clouds.

I got a glimpse of wings, of shining armor, and a crown as the thunderbolt crashed into the chariot, dragging us down hundreds of feet, the lamassus beating their paws uselessly in the air, unable to resist the impact that hurled us toward the ground.

We tumbled, me dangling from the chariot front with one hand, the other still clutching the tub as we spun over ourselves. I just managed to get one foot hooked on the spoke of a wheel as we performed a series of world-class corkscrews. When we finally leveled out, I struggled back into the carriage and re-looped both reins around one forearm. We pushed through another great wall of

𒐣𒌍𒆠𒂊 𒐣𒀉 𒂊𒌍 𒂷𒈬 𒅆𒌍𒂯 𒂍𒌍𒅗 𒈾𒐣

wind, into a cloud, and then out the other side . . .

To find Nergal waiting.

He circled us, soaring on two pairs of wings that shimmered with the colors of the rainbow. His skin, unmarked and smooth, radiated golden light, and his black hair flowed from under a helmet crowned with three pairs of horns. He carried a spear of gold and silver, long enough to skewer a bus sideways.

I fell to my knees, my head still spinning from our aerial acrobatics. Every muscle, every bone, ached. Was he making me feel this way, or had I just gone beyond utter exhaustion? "So . . . new makeover?"

Yup, my mouth muscles were still working even when everything else was on shutdown.

He orbited the chariot, gliding smoothly over the buffeting winds, spear raised. "Why do you still fight, mortal?"

"I was wondering the same thing." I stood up, but I had to lean my elbows on the chariot rim. Wow, he actually glowed—I had to squint to gaze at him. "But we don't have to. I'm happy to accept your surrender anytime."

"This attempt at wit . . . has it ever worked for you?"

"There's always a first time." I glanced around. I was just above the spires of the taller buildings on the Upper East Side, nowhere near the hospital. I shielded my eyes as I turned to Nergal. "Now I have a question for you."

"Yes?"

"Why are you doing this? You got what you wanted."

Nergal gazed down at the city. "Because it is beautiful."

"Uh, yeah. I mean, it used to be. . . ."

"There is nothing more captivating than chaos," Nergal continued.

"You're destroying us because you're bored?"

He laughed. "That is the way of gods."

"Not the one I believe in." I tightened my hold on the reins. The lamassus tensed, sensing my mood. They, too, wanted to fight.

Nergal drifted over his city, gazing down proudly at it. "It is rife with plagues, sicknesses no medicine can cure. Your people will tear themselves apart with tooth and nail. I promise you a bloodbath from which the city will never recover. And then it will spread across the land, and beyond."

"What about Gilgamesh? And Belet? You haven't defeated either of them." At least I hoped not.

He peered toward Central Park. "Gilgamesh will see reason eventually."

"Belet won't. She'll fight you for the rest of her life."

"The life of a mortal is short."

"You'd be surprised. I'm still here, aren't I?"

"I will remedy that here and now." He lowered his spear, pointing it straight at my chest.

I pulled hard to the right, forcing a sudden lurch as Nergal shot past me, his spear tip shredding the side of the chariot.

He roared louder than the thunder and arced high and back toward us.

Straight ahead, lightning flashed within an enormous storm cloud. Black and swollen with rain, enough water to wash the city clean.

That was it.

Gilgamesh had talked about using the water supply to spread the cure. As the raindrops pelted my face, I realized I had a better, faster alternative.

I needed to get higher. "Come on, guys." The lamassus didn't need to be told twice, and as we got closer to the cloud, their bodies began to glow with a soft blue aura.

I looked over my shoulder.

Nergal thrust his spear at me, and I twisted right before it went through my shoulder blades. Instead, it splintered the front of the carriage. I jerked the reins left. Nergal beat all four of his wings to change direction. I only had seconds before he would be upon me again, and the chariot wouldn't be able to take another hit like that.

"Come on!" I flicked the reins, and the two weary, battered lamassus gave everything they still had.

The chariot bounced violently as Nergal landed on the rim in front of me.

One hand on the reins, the other clutching the tub, I stepped backward and ducked as he jabbed forward with the spear, but not quick enough to avoid it ripping through my shoulder. He glared at me with wild delight. "Now we'll test the limits of your immortality, boy!"

His next stab went into my upper thigh, and I buckled. How could you escape a god standing only a few feet away? The winds that had been assaulting us suddenly disappeared. The pandemonium of thunder and lightning vanished behind us as, for just a few seconds, we were bathed in the cold, clean light of the full moon. But the enormous storm cloud was still in my sights, just a few yards ahead.

Nergal smiled as he steadied his grip on his weapon. He could finish me easily but was having too much fun and wanted to play his cruel little games even now. Then he noticed the tub in my hand, and his smile faded. "What's that? A magic potion?"

Uh-oh.

"This?" I said. "It's my lunch. A boy's gotta eat when he's saving the world. Would you like some?"

He didn't fall for my bluff. I guess he was smarter than Humbaba. Instead, he pointed the spear tip straight at my heart. "Why do you insist on interfering? Your people hate you now."

"That was your doing. You changed everyone into monsters."

Nergal shook his head. "I changed the outside, but what was within—that was always there. Deep in their hearts, human beings are monsters. You will save nothing. Hand over the potion to me, and . . . I will cure your parents. You have the word of a god."

"And I should trust you because . . . ?"

He tightened his grip, and the metal spear shrieked. "Because you have no choice."

I grinned. "Yeah, I think I do."

I jumped out of the chariot. Directly into the thunderhead.

And pulled off the tub lid as I tumbled.

Glowing droplets of eau de toilette streamed out behind me, instantly vaporizing into a silver mist that caught the eddies and spread, seeding the cloud.

Then I closed my eyes and let the storm carry me.

FORTY

"GET UP, SIK." THAT SOUNDED LIKE BELET. "IT'S NOT OVER."

A boot nudged my ribs. *Definitely* Belet.

"Leave me alone. This cold, wet pavement is sooo cozy. I am just going to lie here for a while longer."

"Sik . . ."

"Okay, fine. I'm getting up." I groaned as I slowly moved into a sitting position. "But this had better be worth it."

Rain poured down, my clothes were in shreds, and my flesh was one big purple bruise, clear signs that I was still in the real world. I winced as I got up. "How far did I fall?"

"About six thousand feet." Then she pointed to the adjacent tower. "But you did bounce off that a couple of times on the way down."

That explained the big crack in the asphalt under me and why my skeletal structure felt . . . rearranged.

"Well, you know what they say," I said. "Any landing you

can walk away from is a good one."

She helped me up, but Belet looked grim, cradling the arm she'd torn when we'd crashed through the windows. "Get ready to fight."

I looked around. "Everybody?"

Poxies filled Seventh Avenue as far as the eye could see, and more were spilling out from the side streets. They were beyond monstrous now, some unable to retain a single shape but melting and re-forming with every step. Through sheets of rain, I saw the suffering in their pain-crazed eyes.

Yes, it was clear now: Mo's Promise hadn't worked. Daoud had diluted it too much. So much for all my hopes.

I stepped next to Belet, wishing I had my wok. "What are they waiting for?"

The reply came from above. "Me."

Nergal beat his wings to land on the roof of a parked van. It sagged as he settled his weight on it.

Now that he was closer, I could see that his wings smoldered. One was torn, and the feathers were singed. Parts of his body smoked, too, the skin black and peeling under his molten golden armor. But none of that mattered. He still topped ten feet and radiated supernatural strength. The poxies were not here to fight but to witness his ultimate victory.

Belet readied Kasusu.

"Be joyful, Niece," he said. "I am about to send you to your mother."

"Those you kill with words live longest," said Belet.

Nergal shrugged. He spread out his wings and stepped off the van.

Only to fall flat on his face. Hard.

Even I winced. "God or not, that had to hurt."

He stood up and wiped his bleeding nose. "That's impossible. Gods cannot bleed."

His feathers wilted and started to molt. They dropped in sodden clumps as he flapped his wings, trying to rise. Nergal beat his metal breastplate. "I ate the flower of immortality! Why am I not healing?" He gasped as he gazed at his hands.

The skin began wrinkling. It was weird to watch his smooth, muscular flesh age, turn a jaundiced yellow, and start shriveling on the bone. His muscle faded, and Nergal bowed as his bones weakened. He sank to his knees as the last of his feathers fell and the wing structures sagged.

The poxies changed before our eyes, too. Their deformities shrank away. The boils, the sores, the putrid growths just melted back into healthy full flesh. Crooked bones straightened. Yellow fangs retreated into gums, leaving straight, normal-size white teeth. The monsters growing out of their bodies were washed away by the rain.

We both turned at the loud *clang*. Nergal sat in a puddle, breathing weakly, his breastplate discarded in front of him. His chest was concave, and mere skin sagged over a bony rib cage. "I'm . . . I'm dying. But how?"

I realized the truth as I said it. "Immortality is a sickness." I gazed up at the clouds, and the raindrops infused with Mo's Promise. "You've been cured."

Belet walked up to Nergal and pressed the tip of Kasusu under his chin. The withered god looked up at her with pleading eyes. "Help me, Niece. Help me, and together we'll rescue Ishtar."

"No, Uncle. I can do that by myself."

He laughed. It wasn't much of a noise, just a brittle croaking. "Please, sweet girl. Let me have just one more minute. A few seconds more."

All those thousands upon thousands of years he'd had, and it still wasn't enough. He'd never had to contemplate death before, and fear was overwhelming him.

Belet drew back Kasusu, but she didn't strike. She didn't have to.

Nergal opened his mouth and sighed. A fly crept out from the depths of his throat as his eyes glazed over. Another fly buzzed out. And another, and more. The swarm enveloped the body of the plague god in an opaque cloud, its buzzing reaching an ear-piercing whine. Then it flew away, dispersing over the crowd and into the sky. No trace of Nergal remained except for a few scattered feathers.

FORTY-ONE

BABA PUT THE PAINT CAN DOWN ON THE SIDEWALK. "I had the strangest dreams when I was in a coma. It was probably just the drugs, but sometimes I wonder."

"Oh?" I dipped in my brush and started applying the second coat of Overtly Olive to the window frame. Mama and Daoud were inside, arranging the flowers on each table, careful to avoid Sargon, who was having a nap. We'd been at it all day and were finishing off just as the streetlights were coming on, bathing our deli in soft gold.

Baba worked alongside me. "You and Mohammed, sitting in a rowboat in the middle of the sea. The waves were so high, Sik! And there was lightning and the blackest storm clouds. I was terrified for you, but you were both laughing. As if defying the chaos, the very elements that were trying to destroy you."

"Funny dream." I tried to avoid splashing the window frame—that was especially tricky.

"Mama had the exact same dream," said Baba. "Strange, eh?"

"I don't think it's strange for parents to dream about their kids."

Baba stopped painting and looked over at me with a thoughtful frown. He'd been out of the hospital for a month but still hadn't yet filled out to his normal size. His eyes sat deeper than they used to. "Then Mohammed came to me. He knew I was sick, and he told me to hang on, hang on and wait, because you were coming to save us."

I tried to keep my expression blank. "How was he?"

"Happy." Baba shook his head. "And carrying a string bag."

"Mama have that same dream, too?"

Baba nodded. "You were the reason we fought on, Sik. You know that, right?"

"I . . ." I blushed. It seemed so long ago already. With Nergal's destruction, his hold on the city was broken. His curse was lifted, and healing began immediately. I'd made my way to the hospital, past thousands of poxies, bewildered as their diseases receded and their health was restored. There were barricades around Manhattan General, but in all the confusion, I got past them easily. I raced up the stairs to find Mama and Baba waking from their long comas. I'd thought my heart would burst with relief.

We'd been so close to tragedy, and yet here we were, reclaiming our lives. All because of a flower. Mo's Promise.

Baba squeezed my shoulders. "Don't know what we'd do without you."

"Likewise, Baba."

He laughed, and it was the first time I realized how much it sounded like Mo's. Then Baba sighed as he spotted a guy setting up across the street. "Ya Allah. Not another one."

"Get your genuine Manhattan rainwater here! Guaranteed to cure anything! Just a hundred bucks and you'll live forever!"

I watched the guy line up a dozen plastic bottles on a card table outside Mr. Georgiou's wrecked pizzeria. He held up a bottle as a woman passed by. "Ma'am! Want to get rid of those wrinkles? Better than Botox, and gluten-free!"

Daoud came out and joined us. "Another hawker?"

"Third this morning," Baba replied. He took off his painting gloves and tossed them onto a table. "Your shift now, Daoud. I've got to make up the sauces for tomorrow's grand reopening."

"Hey, Baldilocks! Just fifty bucks and you can grow an Afro overnight!"

I sighed as I continued painting, all the while listening to the guy's increasingly extravagant—and desperate—sales pitches.

"Collected on the actual night of the Big Rain! These are

my last bottles! Once they're gone, they're gone! One gulp will mend a broken heart! Two will deliver you the man of your dreams! You, sir! Want to lose that gut of yours? Here's a six-pack in a bottle!"

Mama waved at me through the glass. She had the counters polished like mirrors, and the new wall tiles gleamed. We'd gotten them from a Turkish wholesaler: blue branches spreading across a shiny white background, a design called the tree of life.

"You serving yet?" The street vendor strolled over and perched on a fire hydrant. "I could use a Coke."

I gestured at the bottles he'd left behind on his table. "Your magic rainwater not good enough?"

"That, kid, is for purely medicinal purposes." He gazed around and sighed. "Thought I might have better luck selling on this corner. Y'know, because of all the tourists. This is where Sikander Aziz used to live, isn't it?"

"What?" I asked, bewildered. "And what?"

"The Hero of Manhattan," said the guy. "Shame he's dead. An endorsement from him would have made me rich."

"He's not dead. I mean, *I'm* not dead." I pointed the paint roller at myself, splashing speckles of green on my T-shirt. "I'm Sikander Aziz."

The guy laughed. "And I thought *I* was a con artist. Nice try, kid. Nice try." Then he pointed at Daoud's face. "Hey, how about I give you one of my bottles in exchange for the Coke? The water'll fix that up no problem."

Daoud touched the scar on his cheek. "How 'bout you just give me two bucks?"

Reluctantly, the guy handed over the money, and Daoud passed him the soda. I watched the hawker head back across the street.

"So, I'm the Hero of Manhattan?"

"Couple of weeks ago you were." Daoud chuckled. "Fame's a fickle thing. It's gone before you know it."

"It was gone before I even knew it arrived!" I complained. "I *did* save the city."

"There's been a Kardashian baby since then. The world's moved on, Sik."

Maybe it was for the best. At least people wouldn't be turning up to test my immortality. Some guy, convinced the Big Rain had made him invincible, had dived off the Brooklyn Bridge to prove it. He'd ended up in critical condition, with forty-three bones broken.

Me? Mo's Promise had affected me after all. When it came to Nergal, the desert hybrid had neutralized the effects of the original flower I'd brought back from the Sea of Tiamat, as Ishtar had suspected would happen. But I'd had a double dose of the desert version—first when I'd planted it, and then again in the downpour. As a result, my vitality had only increased. I didn't need to sleep anymore. I never got tired, and any nick or scratch sealed up within seconds. But I still couldn't handle more than a spoonful of the Baghdad.

I hadn't really wrapped my mind around all that. I mean, I could barely plan for next week, and here I was looking at eternal life. I suppose I'd just have to take it one day at a time, like everyone else.

As for how New York City was faring, if the Big Rain by itself wasn't enough to keep the conspiracy nuts from working overtime, we now had headlines on the front page of the *New York Post* like "The Gods Walk Among Us" and "The Miracle of Manhattan!"

Fresh theories about what had happened to the city popped up every day. Aliens were trending this week. The battle between Ishtar and Nergal on Venus Street had over ten million views on YouTube, though plenty of people were convinced it was just an online marketing campaign for the next phase of superhero movies. And there was the mystery of the seven-tiered ziggurat that had appeared overnight in the middle of Central Park. I'd tried visiting it, but it had been sealed off by the park authorities. When I'd asked about the gardener, no one had seen him.

"You been to the masjid lately?" asked Daoud as he worked his way carefully around the edge of a window. "The crowd has spread into the parking lot. Same with the local church.

I hear it's standing room only these days."

"Everyone's waiting on the next miracle," I said. "How about we—"

Daoud's phone rang. He paused his rolling and winced apologetically at me. "That could be a callback, Sik. . . ."

"Go ahead, take it."

He smiled gratefully and slid it out of his back pocket. "Hey, Claire! Sun still shining in Hollywood? What have you . . . ? Calm down! I can't understand what . . . The lead? For real? Let me get a notepad." He gave me a thumbs-up and disappeared upstairs, the painting completely forgotten. Typical Daoud.

But he wasn't the same. Like everyone else, he'd recovered from Nergal's disease. His skin glowed as brightly as ever, his hair had grown back, and his muscles rippled under his tight T-shirt. But he now had a couple of new features: a bridge of pearly-white front teeth, and also a dashing scar on his face, thanks to Idiptu. For some reason, the mark hadn't disappeared, but it *had* launched Daoud's career.

Offers were coming in day and night. When a casting agent went to sleep in Tokyo, a modeling scout was waking up in London. *Vogue* wanted Daoud in Libya next week for their "Urban Conflict" campaign.

"Hello, Sik."

Belet crossed the street.

𒀸𒊺𒂊 𒀸𒁲𒂠𒐎𒌍𒊑𒆥 𒂍𒀻𒂊 𒈾𒀸

"Salaam. Long time no see." I put down my roller and wiped my hands on a rag.

"Looking good." She blushed a little. "I mean the place."

"Yeah. We got some builders in, the sort of guys who usually do mansions in the Hamptons. They installed a brand-new, top-of-the-line kitchen. Someone paid them in advance," I said. "You wouldn't happen to know who that was, would you?"

"Someone with more money than sense." She held out a rustic-looking wooden box. "Here. I brought you a deli-warming present from Gilgamesh."

I took it. The box was long but not heavy, and there was a whiff of perfume coming from it. "He couldn't bring it himself?"

She shook her head. "He wants his privacy, Sik. You can't blame him for that."

"I guess not," I said. "And how have *you* been feeling these days?" She'd had a dose of Mo's Promise after all.

"See for yourself." She sighed and pulled up her sleeve, revealing a long scar from wrist to elbow.

"Oh. I was getting used to the idea you might be . . . you know . . ."

"You were changed by the flower itself—I wasn't. Daoud's perfume contained impurities, so the effects were never going to be the same. Just think about it," she said as she rolled her sleeve back down. "If it had been as powerful, we'd now be living in a city with eight million immortals."

Ugh. That didn't sound appealing at all. But Belet living forever was a different matter. "You disappointed?"

"Just open the box, Sik."

I obeyed and found several tall green stalks ending in white velvety petals, narrow and pointed like swords, and flecked with gold. Their scent reminded me of my favorite dreams. "Shukran."

Belet smiled. "Gilgamesh calls it Ishtar's Heart."

Something lay among the stems. Something gold. "He gave me his royal seal?" I asked, picking up the ring. The sunlight glinted off the engraved images of the king and his lion.

Belet nodded. "You never know when you might need it."

"No, I guess not." I gestured to the doorway. "You want to come inside while I get a vase? Say hi to Sargon?"

"How's he doing?" she asked.

"Settled in with Daoud. Got a cushion all to himself by the window. Come on and tickle his chin."

Belet shook her head. "I can't stay, Sik."

"Why not?"

"I'm off to rescue my mother from Kurnugi."

Of course she was. "You have any idea how you're going to get in? And then out again?"

𒀀𒈾𒌁 𒀭𒇷 𒂍𒋾 𒊏𒋛𒊑 𒂍𒈪 𒈾𒂠

"Mother has friends around the globe. One of them will know the routes into the netherworld."

"Sounds like a plan," I said. "Let me go upstairs and get my passport. I have one somewhere. . . ."

"And leave Manhattan?" she said, gasping mockingly. "How will you manage?"

"But I promised Ishtar. . . . I should come with—"

"No," Belet said firmly. "Your place is here for now. With your family."

I glanced toward the kitchen, where Mama and Baba were busy cooking. So many times I had wanted to leave, to go on exciting trips with Mo. Now I couldn't think of anywhere I'd rather be.

But as strange as it felt to admit, I would miss Belet. "You swear you'll come back?" I asked.

"Mother would never want to skip New York Fashion Week, would she?"

I breathed a huge sigh of relief. "There's just one more favor I need before you go."

She arched her eyebrow. "Yes?"

"You've got to try my new sauce. We're calling it the Manhattan. It's full of surprises."

She grinned even as she shook her head. "I'm going to regret this, I know it."

I grinned back. "Hey, where's your sense of adventure?"

* * *

The deli isn't big. You'd hardly notice it if you were in a rush, and *everyone* in Manhattan is always in a rush. It isn't going to win any awards, but it has a lot going for it.

The windows let in the morning sun, so you can spend a while sitting and watching the world. The tables are big enough for you and your friends, gathered around to share a plate of meze. Mama believes in big portions, so you won't go away hungry, and you'll leave with change from a ten. There is a steady buzz. People chat, and they crowd around the counter, but they know how to wait their turn. Patience is essential if you want good food. The flavors are fresh, and they are spicy. The pitas are warm, cooked on the grill, right at the front. The coffee is strong and the sweets sticky.

You'll want to come back, and that's the best praise any deli can receive.

Yeah, it may never appear in the Michelin Guide. But if you ask for it by name, anyone in the neighborhood will point you in the right direction.

Mo's.

Home.

𒀭𒌐𒈪 𒈠𒁲𒈗 𒊑𒈨𒀸 𒂍𒈨𒀝 𒈦𒀭

AUTHOR'S NOTE

I WROTE *CITY OF THE PLAGUE GOD* IN 2018, WHEN THE world was a very different place and the concept of a disease threatening us all was the stuff of pure fantasy.

The circumstances described in this book are, of course, radically different from our own reality, but there have been some similarities. We have been reminded that the only thing that truly matters is keeping our loved ones safe, and that our heroes are often society's underdogs.

That is Sik's story in a nutshell. He wants to save the people he cares about and is willing to fight an enemy far, far greater than him to do it.

As of this writing, all of us are living that same story.

Sik's just a kid. He wants to be better than he is, he wants the best for his loved ones, and he wants those same loved ones to be proud of him. That is his jihad, his noble struggle. He's been raised to believe in Allah as the one and only god, and yet he has breakfast with Ishtar, an ancient goddess. It was an interesting challenge to merge existing religion with what is now called mythology, to appreciate the similarities and yet keep them clearly distinct. For Sik there are super-human beings referred to historically as gods, and then there is the truly divine.

Which brings me to why it has taken me twelve years and eleven books to get around to writing a Muslim tale.

I resisted writing one because I was afraid any celebration of my heritage would be seen as something scary or sinister. Phrases like *jihad* or *Allahu Akbar* are so horribly misunder-stood nowadays. But then, everything writers do can elicit strong feelings. Simply putting our thoughts, beliefs, and hopes on paper and sending them out into the world is a provocative act.

Then came Rick Riordan. Alhamdulillah!

I've followed Rick's mythic work from the beginning, and as much as I enjoyed all the escapades, what I admired most was his stance. He, like his characters, does not hide from the fight, and while everyone else just talks about diversity, he has acted. In doing so he has given a generation of kids new heroes that are like them.

Thus being invited to be part of the Rick Riordan Presents imprint was an unbelievable honor, and a huge challenge. I hesitated, but not for long. It was time to measure up to the standard Rick has set. To bring kids the types of heroes still sorely lacking in children's fiction, and provoke a reaction. If you're reading this, you must have found something engaging enough to get you to the end. Thank you for sticking with Sik!

So, huge thanks to the one and only Rick for bringing Sik, Belet, and Daoud into the RRP family of heroes. The guy is one himself through and through. I have enjoyed getting to know Kwame Mbalia, Jennifer Cervantes, Carlos Hernandez, and the others at RRP, and I envy their talent more than they can possibly suspect. Many thanks to my editor, Stephanie Lurie, who is the power behind the throne. As ever, I am grateful to my agent, Sarah Davies, who made sure I didn't succumb to total panic. To make *Plague God* happen and to make the most of Sik's complex heritage, I could not have managed without the help of Saadia Faruqi and Moe Shalabi. It is no exaggeration to say everything I know about Mesopotamia I learned from Stephanie Dalley, Fellow of the Oriental Institute at Oxford University. Read her amazing books. The cuneiform you found throughout was kindly provided by Megan Lewis and Dr. Joshua Brown of Digital Hammurabi, taken from the original translation by Andrew George, which is given below. All that is good and splendid is due to them, any errors are down to me.

Finally, my biggest thanks goes to my family, the reason

behind every word I write. My wife and girls back me up, challenge me, and remind me of what truly matters. I love you.

* * *

The cuneiform that appears throughout this book reads: "seru i-te-si-in ni-piš šam-mu / ša-qum-meš i-lam-ma šam-mu iš-ši" and corresponds to lines 305–306, tablet 11 of the standard *Epic of Gilgamesh*. It translates as: "A snake smelled the fragrance of the plant / silently it came up and bore the plant off." (Translation by Andrew George.)

GLOSSARY

I thought a glossary might be helpful, given that the story includes a wide variety of terms that may be unfamiliar, some taken from languages that haven't been spoken for thousands of years. Each term is either Arabic (A), Islamic (I), or Mesopotamian (M). While all the Islamic terms are Arabic, not all the Arabic terms are Islamic. I hope that's clear!

Abubu	M	Supernatural weapon
Alhamdulillah	I	God be praised
Allah	A	Arabic word for God
Allahu Akbar	I	God Is Greater
Baba	A	Father
Basmu	M	Gigantic serpent with multiple mouths
Bismillah	I	In the name of God, often used before taking action, commonly said before mealtimes
Dua	I	A prayer

Inshallah	I	God willing
Jihad	I	A righteous struggle
Jummah	A	Friday. The main weekly prayers are held on Friday.
Kasusu	M	Supernatural weapon
Kurnugi	M	The netherworld, ruled by Erishkigal and Nergal
La	A	No
Lamassu	M	Winged bull or lion. Guardians against evil.
Mabrook	A	Congratulations
Mama	A	Mother
Mashallah	I	God has willed it. Often used as "well done."
Masjid	I	Islamic place of worship. Also called a mosque.
Salaamu alaikum	I	Traditional greeting
Salat	I	An obligatory prayer
Shukran	A	Thanks
Sura	I	A chapter from the Quran, the Muslim holy book
Takbir	I	The religious phrase *Allahu Akbar*. Often found on display in Muslim stores and homes.
Ugallu	M	Lion man
Ya Allah!	A	Oh God!
Ya salam!	A	Oh wow!
Yakhi	A	My brother
Yallah	A	Hurry up, get a move on